Museum of Seraphs in Torment

ISBN: 1-4811-3249-0
ISBN-13: 9781481132497

Museum of Seraphs in Torment

An Egyptological Fantasy Thriller

David Pinault

2013

Dedication

For Jody

with love always

and

in memory of

Paul George Pinault

1947-2011

friend and brother

chapter 1

Liberation Square
Cairo, Egypt

IF IT WEREN'T for the money—the hope of making lots of it, fast—Ricky Atlas would have run off hours ago.

The crowd was turning ugly. Mid-afternoon, it'd been a more or less orderly demonstration. Speakers with bullhorns; cries from the crowd—*Democracy now! Down with the tyrant!*—while the government's troops nervously stood by and did nothing. Vendors sold Pepsi and patriotic t-shirts.

But it was getting dark now, five o'clock, and the crowd had surged, getting bigger and bigger, filling the square, pressing up against the gates of the Egyptian Museum. Ricky had been told to wait—*You will get a call,* Mister Hamdi had instructed him, *and the call will tell you precisely when to enter*—but the wait was getting dicey. The crowd had become a mob.

How will I get inside? Ricky had asked. *There're soldiers and security guards all over the place.*

That, Mister Hamdi had said, *has been arranged. We will create the opportunity. You will make use of it. Mind you do your part.*

Easy for Hamdi to say. Hamdi operated at a distance—Ricky had done a dozen jobs for him but had only ever met him once—and whatever happened now, Hamdi wouldn't be implicated.

Whereas Ricky: his knapsack—slung over his back as if he were just another low-budget tourist—held a hammer and boltcutter and flashlight and gloves and length of knotted rope. Cops everywhere in this crowd; and Ricky didn't want to have to explain the bag's contents to the authorities. He'd been in an Egyptian jail once, thank you very much; he had no desire to repeat the experience.

For the millionth time he slipped a hand into his tweed jacket, checked to make sure his cellphone was on.

Wait for the call, Hamdi had said. Yeah. Again the thought: easy for him to say. Ricky was sweating, even though the late-afternoon air was turning cold and a winter breeze from the Nile blew through the square. Not much light left. *Hope I don't have to do this job in the dark*, he thought. *Damn.*

He knew what was making him sweat. Fear. The crowd was swelling now, getting louder, angrier. The soldiers looked about as if for orders, fingered the trigger guards on their rifles. Anything could happen.

This job might not go well at all.

Then:

Smoke, suddenly, lots of it, billowing in clouds from the Government Party building adjacent to the west wall of the museum. A crackling sound, and a whoosh of air. Flames shot from a dozen office windows.

Damn. Hamdi's guys don't play around.

The mob in its hundreds surged to the gate. Smoke enveloped the museum. The soldiers coughed, looked at each other, saw the crowd advance, and then abruptly ran away across the square. Vendors scurried right and left.

The cellphone rang. "Now, Doctor Atlas. The museum is all yours."

Ricky hated it when Hamdi called him that. He'd given up trying to correct him: *You shouldn't give me the title Doctor. I never finished grad school; I dropped out. (Forced out, was closer to the truth. Forced out in disgrace. "Under a cloud," as his dissertation advisor had said with disgust. Ricky didn't tell people that if he could help it.)*

But *Doctor* was what Hamdi kept calling him. From Hamdi it felt like a taunt, a nasty reminder. Richard Greyling Atlas, once an up-and-comer in Egyptology, with oh-so-shiny prospects of a prestigious PhD from the University of Chicago and a cozy spot in some tenure-track job.

And now? Elbowed by a crowd in downtown Cairo, with every chance of being trampled in a goddamned revolution, his eyes tearing with smoke, unable to see a thing, and facing the prospect of jail—or worse—if this evening's job went wrong. Which it very likely would.

Again the cellphone. "Doctor Atlas?"

"Right. Right. I'm on it."

Getting into the courtyard was a snap. The mob swelled and pressed—while the luckless demonstrators in front were pinned and crushed against the metal staves of the gate—and then a flood of demonstrators burst through, pushing the gate to the pavement. *Democracy,* roared the flood. *The tyrant: down with him!*

No need, he saw, to worry about being challenged: he was just one dusty figure trailing a mob in its thousands. He stepped over the gate and around the injured individuals who'd been thrust underfoot, and carefully—very carefully—he watched to see what would happen next.

The mob paused. Ahead: the museum's main building, with all its treasures. Problem: its massive tall doors—bronze and unyielding—were barred and bolted shut.

The mob's roar sank to a hum. Indecision. One man tried to reason with the horde. *Ahsan izza rigi'na ila'l-maydan.*

Ricky's knowledge of Arabic was good—he'd lived here long enough—and he caught the plea in the man's voice as he tried to remind his peers of the purpose of their gathering: *We should return to the square. We're here to bring down the government, aren't we?*

But the throng faced temptation. Inside the courtyard, off to the left of the museum: a gleaming new souvenir store.

A shout from someone up front. *Yalla narooh li-dukkaan al-hadaaya: Let's head for the gift shop!*

The attempted rebuttal—*Bring down the government*—was drowned by another cry from the front: *Fi dahab guwwa; fi fadda—There's gold inside, and silver!*

Ricky knew the claim was true. The shop stocked necklaces and ankh-earrings and counters offering 22-carat cartouches-with-your-name-on-it for knickknack-crazed tourists.

Gold inside, and silver. The mob took up the cry.

Slogan-painted placards—*Leave now, you tyrant! Democracy now!*—were dropped to the ground. In an instant, the throng pivoted to one thought: the prospect of loot.

A rush to the left, as the souvenir shop was swarmed; and Ricky Atlas stood alone before the museum.

Now his own moment of indecision. Eyes smarting from smoke. Arms wet with sweat. Throat dry from fear.

If I'm caught in there, it means ten years in Tura Prison. Minimum.

He tried to swallow. *Don't just stand around out here,* he urged himself. *Move.*

Instead: paralysis. Paralysis.

The cellphone again. "Doctor Atlas?"

"I'm on it."

Move, move, move.

And he did. Across the courtyard, humping his knapsack. To the right of the papyrus fountain, then at an awkward run—he prided himself on being in good shape, but this stupid burglar's bag slowed him to snail-pace—he headed around to the back, to the north face of the museum.

There, just as he remembered: an external staircase, with a neatly lettered warning: *For Use in Emergencies Only.*

Well, hell, he told himself: *Riots, looting, nationwide revolt. This constitutes an emergency. So, Ricky boy, you're entitled to use the stairs.*

His private joke made him smile, and that smile gave him nerve for the climb: up, up, three flights of rickety metal steps.

The flat roof provided a good view out over the Nile—or would have, on a normal day: cruise boats, there should have been, and lateen-sailed feluccas, full of laughing tourists.

But not today, not in this revolution. No boats on the water. Instead, government buildings in flames, their windows scorched black.

Far below, in the courtyard, he could just make out the museum's alcove of statues honoring Egyptology's Great and Good: Lepsius, Maspero, Mariette Pasha—white marble shrouded in smoke.

But now to work. The central part of the museum's roof was a sheet of glass—a fine skylight, but also a vulnerable entry point. Hence his hammer, and the knotted length of rope.

Both unnecessary: a jagged twelve-foot-square hole had already been punched in the glass. The top of a ladder protruded from the hole.

Damn. Someone's already broken in. No telling how many. He edged to the hole, peered down the ladder. Night coming on. Too dark to see. *Anything could be going on down there, and Hamdi expects me to dive down that hole?*

The cellphone again. "Doctor Atlas. Are you in?"

Ricky explained the problem.

"I see." Ricky heard his boss murmur something to someone else. A muttered exchange.

The connection wasn't good. All he caught was Something something *al-nas dol 'ayzeen nafs al-haaga: Those guys want the same thing.*

"Doctor Atlas." A brisk businesslike tone. "You will have to hurry. There may be some competition."

"Competition? What kind of competition?"

"Nothing you can't handle. We have every confidence in you."

Ricky wanted to bellow into the phone: *You mean you expect me to climb down someone else's ladder, in the dark, while looters are tearing the neighborhood apart, and while creepy-crawlers—who knows how many?—are lurking around down there, maybe ready to tear me limb from limb? You told me this would be a clean in-and-out job. Your exact words: 'A clean in-and-out job.'*

Instead, he swallowed and hesitated and before he could say a word: "Doctor Atlas. Under the circumstances, the Corporation is willing to raise your fee by twenty per cent. But we must have the wand. Excuses will not be accepted." No mistaking the threat there. "Besides, the competition employs clumsy hands. They don't

know their way around this museum. Unlike you. You're a professional." A reassuring purr over the phone; an attempt at flattery.
"We have every confidence in you."

"Twenty per cent extra?"

"Twenty per cent."

Not that the increase will do me much good, Ricky cautioned himself as he descended the ladder, *if I don't live to collect it. Damn.*

chapter 2

Interior of the Egyptian Museum
Cairo, Egypt

WOBBLY RUNGS; NOT exactly confidence-inspiring. Six steps down, and another buzz from his phone. "One afterthought, Doctor Atlas."

Great: I'm perched on a ladder, trying to execute a felony, and my freaking boss has to bug me with freaking afterthoughts? Aloud he said: "Yes, Mister Hamdi?"

"The artifact we've commissioned you to, ah, retrieve actually constitutes only one half of the wand. The decorative knob. The finial, to be precise. The other half"—he heard Hamdi clear his throat as if aware the news might not be entirely welcome—"is in a separate location."

"Separate location?" Ricky wanted to bellow the words but kept his tone to a hiss. For all he knew, the competition might be swarming below around the foot of the ladder. "Now look. You promised me I had to do only one more job for the corporation, and then I'd be free of the contract." Hell of a location to be entangled in a labor dispute.

"And so you will be. The job consists of securing *'asaayat Suleiman.* Once you've done that, you receive your commission and you're a free agent again. It just so happens that this object is in two pieces. This means that after this evening's chore, you'll need to make a brief stop at a separate location."

"What kind of separate location? How far away is it?"

"Oh, not far. Not far at all." Mister Hamdi's voice counterfeited reassurance. "Just pick up the finial downstairs and then we can discuss the remaining details."

"Well, I sure hope it's not far. You never told me—." Click. Apparently Hamdi didn't feel like further discussion.

Just as well. Ricky had enough to worry about.

Bottom rung of the ladder. His foot felt in the dark for the floor.

There. Broken glass crunched underfoot. Good thing he was wearing boots.

No need yet to switch on his flashlight. He knew where he was: the second floor of the museum, the balcony overlooking the indoor 'Great Hall' of the museum.

In the dark loomed the limestone bulk of the statues of the enthroned Amenhotep the Third and Queen Tiye, seated side by side. The statues' base was situated sixty feet below, on the pavement of the Great Hallway; the heads of Amenhotep and Tiye were at eye-level with him, up here on the second floor, right by the ladder.

Hmm: potentially useful info.

He knew where he had to go: downstairs, the Amarna gallery. An impulse to rush, get the job done, get the hell out of here.

Instead he fought the impulse, made himself stand motionless. *Wait*, he told himself. *Listen.*

Outside: faint cries of looting. Ululations of triumph and a crescendoed shout: *Allahu akbar.*

Indoors: nothing.

He held his breath, listened harder.

Good. Maybe, just maybe, the competition had already come and gone. Good.

Well, good only if they hadn't found what *he* was supposed to find: *'asaayat Suleiman.* King Solomon's wand. Or more precisely, the finial to that wand.

The artifact's other half, in the 'separate location' Hamdi had just mentioned: he'd worry about that later. Wherever in Cairo that 'separate location' proved to be, it had to be easier to rob than a museum in Liberation Square in the middle of a revolution. *Ricky boy, you sure know how to pick 'em.*

His palms were sweating. To calm himself he wiped his hands on his jacket. Worn gray tweed; reassuring—his favorite coat.

"Ratty and tattered," Harriet Kronsted complained, the first day he wore it to class. They'd taken a Coffin Texts seminar together at U Chicago's Oriental Institute. "Let me guess. You've been shopping again at Salvation Army thrift shops. How much did you pay? Ten dollars?"

"Ruck roo, lady. Five." Actually he used to like Harriet, still did, though he knew it'd mean career-death for her to so much as speak to him now. Anyway, he'd worn this ratty coat through four years of grad school in Chicago and it'd brought him luck nonstop.

Well, almost nonstop, right up until what folks at the Institute still referred to as the Ushabti Incident.

A nasty thing to remember. *Focus, idiot,* he told himself. *You've got money to make.*

He reached in his knapsack, risked a brief glow from his flashlight.

Glass all along the second-floor balcony. He'd have to be careful.

Stepping around the shattered fragments, he moved away from the balcony, toward the north staircase leading to the ground floor. As he moved he felt in his coat pocket for a talisman he always kept with him, an old Zippo lighter. Gift of a friend; another bringer of luck.

He hadn't gone more than a few paces when he saw a rounded shape at his feet. He stooped and lifted it and flicked on the light again.

Shadows jumped from eye sockets: a human skull, mummified. Bits of linen still clinging.

To the left, against the wall: a smashed vitrine. Mummy limbs on the floor. Another skull, and a third. Someone had been in a real hurry, had torn apart the mummies, looking for something.

Clumsy, was the way Hamdi had spoken of the competition. *That's for sure,* Ricky thought. *They don't know where to look. They're ready to tear the whole place apart.*

Still no sound of the competition. Maybe they were gone; maybe luck really was with him tonight. After all, he was wearing his lucky coat. He walked more quickly in the darkness, a bit less wary now.

Even in the dark he knew this corridor well. The semester he'd won a Fulbright overseas research grant—four years, and a million lifetimes, ago—he spent every day in this museum, copying inscriptions. He'd been part of Chicago's Epigraphic Survey, along with his dorm-mates, Iggy Forsythe and Francis Valerian Hammond.

In fact, right up here on the left, near the staircase, was a wooden sarcophagus he remembered. The nobleman Mesehti. Burial site Beni Hasan, Twelfth Dynasty.

The three of them had spent days studying its texts. Standard Middle Kingdom funerary formula.

"An offering that the king gives," Iggy had read aloud, "to Osiris, lord of Abydos, in order that Lord Osiris may bestow upon the deceased a thousand loaves of bread, a thousand meals of roast duck and beef, a thousand jars of unguent, a thousand jugs of beer..." Conscientious Iggy, ever studious.

"Hell"—Ricky, as usual, hadn't been able to resist irreverence—"I'll settle for a sixteen-ounce Bud Lite in the afterlife."

And Hammond, as usual, had gotten upset at his levity and started muttering a string of prayers to ward off curses from the Guardians of the Underworld Gates.

Fluent prayers, too, in four-thousand-year-old Egyptian. Like he'd grown up speaking the stuff. Crazy Hammond.

Pharaoh Frank, was what his grad-school rivals and enemies—quite a few of them, too—used to call him.

But Mesehti's repose had apparently just been disturbed. The vitrine protecting the case was smashed, the lid atop the sarcophagus wrenched away.

The competition, whoever they are, really are dummies, thought Ricky. *They're wasting time if they think Solomon's Wand is hidden in Twelfth Dynasty gear. Eighteenth Dynasty is where they should be looking. Amarna era, to be precise. Artifacts from the city of Akhetaten.*

He reached the north staircase, paused, listened. All quiet. His luck was holding. Still, best to hurry.

He descended the steps. Decorating the stairwell wall: framed papyri with vignettes from the *Book of the Dead.*

How often he'd lingered here, right here, studying these texts at his ease, back when he'd felt he owned the joint, recipient of a Fulbright, up-and-coming Chicago grad student with a bright future ahead.

But that was before Crazy Hammond's crazy stunt. The stunt that torpedoed Ricky's career, and Iggy's, and Hammond's. The stunt that the Dean's investigation had discreetly labeled '*The Ushabti Incident,*' although *Catastrophe* would've been a better choice of word.

And what an aftermath. Hammond had disappeared. No goodbyes; poof. Two months later, Harriet Kronsted claimed her friend Nora Loftgren over at Cataloguing in Regenstein Library had seen Hammond when she was driving long-distance on a car trip through the Southwest.

"Standing in the breakdown lane on I-40," was the way Nora recalled it, "all by himself. In Arizona, near Diablo Canyon. Hitch-hiking, I guess. Or praying. Or maybe scratching himself. Doing something funny. Sunset; light was bad. Hard to tell. I just glimpsed him in the rearview mirror."

Nora said she'd stopped her car. "Thought I'd give him a ride or some cash or something. Felt sorry for him. But he ran off, who-ever he was. Not even sure it was him."

Ricky guessed it'd been Hammond all right. Hitch-hiking, or praying, or scratching himself: fidgety Pharaoh Frank, to a T.

No knowing where he was now. Penny Woodridge, clerk at the Campus Bookstore, claimed she'd seen him—or a scruffy drifter looking a lot like him—at a rest stop south of Salt Lake City, rooting around in a dumpster. "Pretty sure it was him," she said. "The guy had red hair. A redhead, just like Frank."

And Savitri Patel in Accounting swore that while she was visiting friends in Colorado Springs she'd glimpsed Frank at a Starbucks, moving from table to table, eating leftover bagel-bits and drinking coffee-dregs. He'd left fast when she called out his name.

And Ignatius Forsythe? His career, too, had been ruined; but he'd salvaged something from the wreck. No more cushy tenure-track hopes for him, to be sure; still, the last Ricky'd heard, Iggy had gotten a lowly part-time position at the Institute, teaching undergrad adjunct courses for the lowest wage going. And he'd only gotten that by groveling and begging Professor Thorncraft for mercy.

As for Ricky: he wasn't the groveling type, he told himself. Unh-uh. No way. He'd had business cards printed up: *Richard Greyling Atlas, Antiquities Acquisition Consultant.*

"Acquisition Consultant?" Iggy had sounded dubious. "Acquisition, as in theft and artifact smuggling?"

"Acquisition as in independence," Ricky had boasted. "Freelance work. I'm not ever gonna ask the Institute for help again. Not after what they did to us."

Independence. Yeah. That had sounded good, when he left Chicago and Iggy and Francis and Harriet and everyone else he knew. The hell with 'em all. Independence.

Except now here he was, skulking down the stairs at the Egyptian Museum in the dark, skulking like a thief—hell, face it, he *was* a thief—where once he'd been a Fulbright king, worrying now about bumping into other thieves, worrying about mobs outside in the thick of a revolution.

Independent: except he was utterly under the thumb of Mustafa Hamdi and his Corporation, hoping to break free, hoping this'd be his last job.

He reached the bottom of the stairs, turned left towards the ground-floor Amarna gallery.

Felt in his pocket for the Zippo lighter, touched it for luck. A cast-off gift from Hammond, who'd announced one day he was giving up cigarettes. "The ancients didn't smoke, so I shouldn't, either."

Pharaoh Frank. Even after the man had ruined his career, Ricky still carried the lighter. A memory of better times.

He paused, unslung his pack, reached for the boltcutters.

Calm. Stay calm. Almost there. All you have to do is head down this corridor. Locate the Solomon artifact, get the hell out of here, and with any luck before you know it you'll be kicking back with an impious Bud Lite.

He was just in the process of cheering himself by calculating how much he'd make from this job—*let's see, thirty-five thousand bucks base rate, plus the twenty per cent extra Hamdi just promised, that's thirty-five plus seven, comes out to forty-two thousand smackers for an evening's work, plus whatever extra I can squeeze out of Hamdi's freaking Corporation for picking up the other half of the Wand at that 'separate location,' which is one hell of a lot more than the forty-five hundred pitiful bucks Iggy's getting right now for a whole semester's worth of adjunct teaching*—and he was starting to feel like he just might pull off this job without a glitch and by God tonight his lucky coat really was bringing him luck, when something in the dark lunged up at his throat.

chapter 3

Interior of the Egyptian Museum
Ground floor, near the Amarna/Akhetaten Gallery
BAM.

The Egyptian Museum is paved with marble. Ricky Atlas hit the floor hard.

Two hands at his throat. Strong, and strangling. A bulky figure crouched astride him, forcing his chin back. Ricky felt his neck ready to snap.

Hina. Ta'allu hina. Bi-sur'ah. His opponent's bellow boomed down the hall in shrilled Cairene Arabic: "Here, come here! Hurry!"

From down the hall, the smash of glass, and cries in reply. Ricky's foe rose slightly and shrilled again.

Now or never, thought Ricky: he drew his legs up, planted his feet in the other man's chest, and pumped his legs straight.

His foe flew back, struck a stone sphinx.

But up on his feet just as fast as Ricky. Still yelling for help, the man reached in a pocket. Something gleamed: the blade of a knife.

Shit, and what do I have? Ricky darted a look at the floor.

Close by: a plundered mummy, limbs strewn about.

His foe lunged. Ricky ducked, stooped, grabbed a mummified arm.

With his free hand he reached for the Zippo, flicked it open, touched the dry linen.

The ancient arm flared into a torch. A smell of resin and dried perfumes.

Impiety: Pharaoh Frank might not approve, he thought, and he thrust the flaming limb at his foe's face.

Startled, the man retreated a step, still bellowing.

Footsteps; judging from the sound, they were emerging from the Graeco-Roman Room; five galleries down.

That gave him maybe sixty seconds.

The torchlight showed something else on the floor: his boltcutters.

He dropped the torch, stooped for the tool, just as the other's knife sliced a near-miss at his face.

Ricky grabbed the cutters and launched a swift upward swing.

Connecting with the side of his opponent's head. The man fell again against the sphinx but this time didn't rise.

At least, figured Ricky, *this clown won't sound any more alarms for the next half hour. By which time I'm long gone. Assuming I stay lucky.*

At first it seemed his luck wouldn't hold.

A few quick steps brought him to the Amarna alcove, where he knew the wand-finial would be. Problem: all the display cases—every blessed one—stood shattered, their shelves empty, glass underfoot.

Mister Hamdi's competitors must've given their goons orders that were nice and simple: smash and grab; take everything you can from this corner of the museum; the loot can be sorted out later.

A shout from the other end of the museum. *Ya 'Abdoo. Inta fayn?*: "Hey 'Abdoo! Where are you?"

'Abdoo must be the gentleman, came the thought, *who nearly wrenched my head off just now. Well, I'm afraid 'Abdoo's indisposed at the moment.*

The voices down the darkened hall sounded hesitant. Ricky guessed 'Abdoo was the guy in charge of this break-in, and the others were unsure now what to do.

He had bare seconds to exploit this uncertainty.

That's when the inspiration came (Pharaoh Frank, he knew, would've called it guidance from the gods).

Guided or not, Ricky knelt and searched the man he'd downed. This 'Abdoo was wearing a peasant-style *gallabiyah* gown. Ricky turned out its capacious pockets.

Dozens of small artifacts, wrapped hastily in handkerchiefs and twists of cloth. Baboon-amulets. Faience *wadjet*-eyes. Figurines of Sekhmet and Thoth.

And there: a late eighteenth-dynasty ivory finial, its surface carved with an Amarna sun-disk and rows of minute hieroglyphic inscriptions.

Ricky recognized it at once. *'Asaayat Suleiman.* King Solomon's wand (one half of it, at least). Bingo.

Ricky stuffed the prize in his tweed jacket. This old coat was still bringing him luck.

A stab of illumination, then another and a third, interrupted his self-congratulation.

Flashlight beams.

'Abdoo's pals. Quite a few of 'em, too.

From the northwest and southeast wings of the museum. Converging on him.

Time to go. Move.

A beam caught him. Brief blinding glare. He threw up a hand to shield his eyes.

Shouts and an urgent command. Ricky caught part of it: *The ground floor is sealed. Don't let him get to the stairs. Keep him from the roof.*

But Ricky Atlas had in mind an alternate route. He ran from the lights and slipped into the unlit Entrance Hall.

Even in the dark he knew his way. Deftly he threaded a path among the profusion of objects displayed here in the grand hall: pyramid-capstones, victory stelae, canopic jars, votive boats that rowed gods through the night. Old friends, each of 'em.

His pursuers, it seemed, knew the hall less well: he heard one stumble and curse. *Bi-sur'ah*, urged another: Hurry.

A stab of flashlight-glare, a beam over his shoulder that caught an Anubis statue and threw huge shadows of a jackal's snout. *Hinaaka*, came the shout: *Over there!*

Explosive cracks of sound, just past his ear: gunshots.

A bolt of fear made his throat clench: *These bastards mean business.* Someone yelled at him to stand still or be killed.

They'll kill me anyway, or leave me as a gift for the cops. Nope. No way.

He ducked and stooped and ran at a crouch, heading for the giant seated king and queen at the back of the hall.

Ya inta! Ma feesh khurooj min hina, came another shout: *Hey you! There's no way out of here.*

That's what they think. And Ricky sprang up towards the limestone knee of Amenhotep.

Tricky, this: the smooth stone didn't offer much of a grip.

But he'd done this before, more than once, in fact, back in his Fulbright days, after hours, when the museum was closed after a long day squinting at inscriptions. A few cans of beer, and a crazed yen to cut loose, were enough to make him bet Iggy and Hammond he could jump up on Amenhotep's lap.

Frank the Pharaoh would always warn him about dishonoring the gods, and Iggy would fret about his health and safety and what if a guard were to come walking in. And then Ricky would do it anyway.

And one time—speaking of health and safety—he'd slipped and fallen and nearly broken his neck.

But this time he was luckier. He grabbed the stone knee and reached the lap and looked up for his next grip.

A bullet pinged beside him and gouged rock from Amenhotep's waist.

Move, man, move. He stepped up onto the king's bent arm, hoisted himself onto the statue's shoulder. A glance down: a fat cursing man tried the climb, slipped and fell back.

More shots. Splinters of stone burst from the king's neck, peppered Ricky's tweed coat.

Now: atop Amenhotep's crown.

From here a horizontal support beam extended ten feet to the second-floor balcony railing. Not more than six inches wide, this beam: *narrow, damned narrow.*

He used to be scared to do this part, back when he'd show off for his more-prudent colleagues in his beer-fueled blowing-off-steam moods.

A six-inch-wide beam, over a sixty-foot drop.

Iggy'd always beg him: *Ricky, come down!*

Another shot gouged the railing. *Move, man, move.*

There: the railing. A quick spring onto the balcony. Feet safely back on firm flooring.

And there was the ladder, and up overhead: the broken skylight, and the night shining through. Talk about welcome sights.

More shots from below, but wild now; those clowns didn't have a clear view.

An adrenalin-burst dash up the ladder, and once onto the roof: a fierce kick knocked the ladder with a crash back to the balcony. *That'll slow 'em up.*

Down the emergency stairs, across the courtyard—he saw in the mob a grinning boy emerge from the gift shop, holding up high a souvenir Nefertiti bust—then back out into Liberation Square. Still thousands of demonstrators here; and now he knew he was safe.

A squad of black-shirted paramilitary police was advancing across the square.

He hailed the sergeant in charge. "There are thieves inside the museum, on the ground floor."

The sergeant nodded grimly, led his men at a trot into the courtyard.

Let the competition deal with that.

But Ricky kept moving, away from the square, down Tal'aat Harb Street, then over to an old haunt: Filfila's. Even in all the chaos, the restaurant was still open.

He ordered a favorite—*shay bi-na'na,* mint tea, thick with sugar—and sank back in his seat with a sigh.

He made his breath slow down. *It's okay. You did it. You did it.*

His heart still raced. He sipped tea, let the fear ebb, lifted a mint leaf from the tea and chewed it.

It's okay. You did it.

He allowed himself a feeling of satisfaction.

Wonder what Iggy and Pharaoh Frank are doing right about now?

Iggy's probably grading a pile of undergraduate papers, slogging through the semester-grind.

Frank's probably wandering around Arizona or Utah or Colorado or God knows where, doing God knows what.

Hey, if they could see me now, I'd tell 'em: this independent freelance life isn't so bad. At least it's not boring.

He sipped more tea, savored the mint and sugar, began to relax.

Another jolt: this time the cell phone. "Success, Doctor Atlas?"

"Success."

"Ah." If a man could purr, Mustafa Hamdi was doing it now. "Ah."

Ricky knew Hamdi to be a hard man but figured his boss would be in a good mood after the great job he'd just done for him. "Hey. You don't mind if we wait till tomorrow for me to locate the other half of that wand, do you? You know, so I can take the night off, take it easy a bit?"

"I'm afraid that won't be possible, Doctor Atlas."

Ricky sat upright. *Whew.* It was just beginning to hit him: he was exhausted.

"All right, Mister Hamdi. Which part of Cairo do I have to go to for the other half of the wand?"

"Actually, it's not in Cairo."

"Wait a minute. This is getting complicated."

"In fact, the Corporation has booked transportation for you tonight on the 9pm Egypt Air flight to Sanaa."

"Tonight? Sanaa? That's in Yemen, for crying out loud. Why do I want to fly all the way to Yemen?"

"Because that's where the other half of *'asaayat Suleiman* is to be found."

"Wait. Aren't they in the middle of a civil war or something over there?"

"I'm confident that a man with your capabilities will rise to the challenge."

"Yemen. You're kidding me, right?"

Impatient silence. Then: "Doctor Atlas, the Corporation requires the other half of that wand."

"Okay, okay." *So much for relaxation.* "What time is that flight tonight?"

"9 pm."

"9 pm? That doesn't even give me time to finish my tea."

"You can order another tea during your flight."

"But Egypt Air doesn't make good mint tea the way they do at Filfila's." He knew he sounded pathetic.

"Just be on that flight, Doctor Atlas." Click.

Damn. Ricky stood and drank the last of his tea, slapped the glass onto the table.

And if Iggy and Pharaoh Frank could see me now, what would they say? Probably something like: So much for your independent freelance life.

chapter 4

Sunball Café
Cottonwood, Arizona

YAVAPAI COUNTY DEPUTY sheriff Bartholomew Kincaid shifted his considerable bulk and hitched the barstool closer to the counter.

The stool was too small for a man of his size—he'd much rather have taken one of those big cushioned booths, where a fellow could stretch out—but the counter was staffed by Doris Cunningham, and Doris was the most knowledgeable waitress at the Sunball Café. Knowledgeable in a way that was valuable to a deputy sheriff who took his job seriously and insisted on knowing all the comings and goings in Cottonwood.

"Any interesting individuals come through lately?" He stirred his coffee, eyed the dessert menu, tried to decide what kind of pie he wanted today. He was torn between blueberry and apple.

"What kind of interesting?" Doris wiped the counter.

"Goofballs. Potential troublemakers. The kinds of individuals the law ought to know about."

"You going to stare at that menu all day or you going to make up your mind?"

"Don't hurry me now." She liked to chaff him; he thought of himself as a slow-mover, and she was always zip-zip-zip. But they got along all right.

"Goofballs. Troublemakers. You sound like you got somebody in mind." She wiped the counter some more.

He closed the menu, announced his decision: apple pie.

"Go with the blueberry. It's fresher."

He said okay. "Well, actually I do have somebody in mind."

He sipped his coffee. "Tall fellow. Real tall. Skinny. I mean, bean-pole thin. Red-head. Kinda wild-looking. I seen him walking down 17, not far from the Camp Verde exit, and I gave him a lift. All scruffy and scraggly looking. A real mess."

Doris placed a plate of pie by his elbow. "He wearing a blue ID tag on his right wrist?"

"Now that's what I like about you, ma'am. You got good eyes." He spooned a big bite of pie, then realized with regret he'd been so preoccupied with Mister Scraggly he'd forgotten to order his favorite side-dish—a scoop of vanilla ice cream.

"This what you missing?" And there was his ice cream.

"You're a mind reader." He took an appreciative bite.

"I'm a waitress. Same thing. Yeah, I seen him, your bean-pole customer. Came in here two, three days ago and sat at the counter. Same place you're sitting, in fact."

"I'm thinking he's trouble."

"What kind of trouble?"

"Drifter. Dope-dealer, maybe. Meth-head."

"Not a meth-head. Methamphetamines rot out all your teeth, your gums. This kid had a nice smile, nice teeth. Kinda shy. Drifter? Probably." She refilled the sheriff's coffee. "But definitely not a dealer."

"And how are you so sure, Miss Detective?"

"Dealers come in here loaded, buy whatever they want, look around like they own the place. Mister Scraggly just asked for a drink of water but looked so hungry I felt sorry for him."

"Knowing you, that meant you probably fixed him a sandwich for free."

"As a matter of fact I did. That a crime?"

"Take it easy. Just kidding. That blue ID tag. I saw it too. Couldn't get a good look at it."

"Had a label on it. Faded, hard to read. I think at first he knew I was curious because he kept it kinda tucked out of view. But then when I gave him his sandwich he chowed it down so fast he let down his guard. I got a good look."

The deputy sheriff put down his spoon. "You make anything out of it?"

"Couldn't read all of it. But I did catch part. 'Bellevue Clinic. Psychiatric Unit.' Nice and clear."

"Psychiatric Unit." He whistled. "So we could be dealing with some sorta potential problem."

"You going to eat your ice cream or you going to let it melt?"

"I'm eating. I'm eating." He tapped the spoon thoughtfully against his lips. "A drifter, and a potential psych ward runaway."

"Well we don't actually know that, do we? In any case I don't think he's planning any kinda crime."

"And how pray tell do you know that?"

"Because he strikes me as the innocent type. I mean innocent like a little kid. Plus he told me he's looking for someone."

The deputy paused with a spoonful of pie halfway to his mouth. "Looking for who? Did he say?"

"Yeah. But it was some funny name. No way I was going to remember. And I tried to, believe me. Because I knew my favorite officer of the law would come by the Sunball sooner or later and ask me if I've seen any interesting individuals lately, the way you always do."

"Just doing my job. So you don't remember the name."

"Like I said. A funny name. Wait. Ha-Em. Prince Ha-Em. Prince Ha-Em, and then something or other after that. But I can't remember the rest."

"Well he ain't gonna find any Prince Ha-Em around here, and that's a fact. Fellow sounds like a head-case, all right. Psych ward. But harmless enough. Anyway, I got bigger fish to fry."

He took a paper napkin, wiped his mouth. "Gotta give you credit. You got more out of 'im than I did. When I gave him a lift he said hardly a word."

"Well maybe you shoulda offered him a free sandwich the way I did. That'll make a man talk."

"You're probably right," he laughed.

"I'm always right. And you probably want another slice to go with that ice cream."

"Right again."

chapter 5

MOST NIGHTS ANNIE Martinez was a sound sleeper. Not tonight.

She told herself at first it was just her dogs keeping her up. "Gabby, Micky. Can't you tone it down?"

They wagged their tails—nervously, she thought: they seemed to want reassurance tonight—then went back to yowling and sniffing at the front door. Just as if there were something on the other side of that door, trying to get in. Something that frightened her dogs.

Not good. Her trailer was in a pretty nice location—nice, that is, if one liked peace and quiet, which she did—a bit north of Cornville, close enough to Oak Creek Canyon that she could hear the water gurgle nearby.

"Off a dirt road, at the end of nowhere," is how the site was described by her work colleague Tad Foster at the Sonic Drive-In. "Why anyone would want to live there is beyond me. No wonder you never get any customers for that weird little shop you run."

"It's not a shop. It's a museum." She knew Tad talked like this just to get a rise out of her when things were slow at the Sonic; but still she felt she had to defend what Tad called her "little experiment in free enterprise."

"Besides," she added whenever they had this argument, which was often, "I get exactly as many visitors in my museum as I want.

Not too many. I don't want to be overrun, the way all those shops are up in Sedona."

Sedona, New-Age capital of the Southwest, thronged with healers and psychics and spiritual counselors and UFO-clairvoyants; she wanted no part of that scene.

Museum, she knew, was a grandiose word for what perched on her property beside the trailer: a shed containing things she'd found lying about on the ground (or sometimes just below: she always brought a trowel and sometimes did a bit of digging when no one was looking) over at Montezuma Castle National Monument and the V-Bar-V Ranch. Still, as far as she was concerned, what her museum contained was special, and more than a little strange.

Which was part of the reason she kept it open to the public—to anyone, at least, willing to follow the signs from Cornville out here to her dirt road at the end of nowhere. The things in her shed puzzled her, and she would've liked it if someone could have explained just what they were.

But since she'd taken her discoveries from government property, she couldn't exactly go too terribly public in asking for help identifying her finds. So she'd just have to go on living with the mystery.

Gabby—the braver of the two dogs—was getting more agitated now: she put her nose to the base of the front door, sneezed, and then gave a low throaty growl that made Annie sit up in bed.

Gabby did that only when she was well and truly frightened. Which succeeded in scaring Micky: he tilted back his head and howled.

Which succeeded in scaring Annie as well.

"It's all right, you dodoes. There's nothing out there this time of night."

I just wish, she thought, *someone could tell __me__ it's all right and there's nothing out there.*

That was the only problem with living alone: plenty of freedom, no one to tell her what to do once she finished her shift at the Sonic; but if trouble came up, she was on her own. That's why she kept two oversized ferocious-looking mongrel mutts (even though, once she'd brought them home from the shelter, she discovered they were a pair of sweethearts).

The sound of her voice seemed to make the dogs feel better; they lay down by her bed. She relaxed and did what she always did when she had difficulty sleeping, told herself just to listen to the water in Oak Creek.

And that's when she heard the snap of a twig.

No calming the dogs now. They howled and howled.

"I told you guys: there's no one out there." But she didn't believe it any longer herself.

She threw on clothes fast—jeans, flannel shirt, boots ("strictly no-nonsense," was how she described her wardrobe to anyone who asked)—and pulled open the door.

All quiet; just the gurgle of the creek. She stood in the door. The dogs pressed against her legs, gazed up at her.

"You're not gonna quiet down till we have a look round, right?" She stepped out from the trailer, stopped, then reached back inside the front door.

She emerged holding a twelve-gauge pump-action Remington. That gave her confidence for whatever was out there. The dogs followed, staying close by her legs.

Nothing. Wind in the pine trees. Water in the creek. Far off, a cry from a coyote. Nothing. She lowered the barrel of the Remington.

Then Gabby growled.

There. Motionless, under the pines: a figure, upright, one arm lifted. Annie felt a hammer-jolt of panic, swung the barrel back upright, pulled the pump-handle on the weapon, chambered a round.

Still motionless, that figure, whatever and whoever it was. The dogs took courage from their mistress, yowled and growled and danced about her.

She pointed the Remington at the figure. "This here's a shotgun," she called. "Can't miss at this range."

The figure stepped forward, its arm still raised. It advanced ten paces, close enough for Annie to get a look.

A man, but a tall raggedy red-haired scarecrow of a man. Gaunt. Hungry-looking. *Like he hasn't eaten in a week*, came the thought.

He wasn't looking at her. Arm still raised, index finger extended. *What's he pointing at?*

Reluctant to take her eyes off him, not knowing what he might try, she kept the Remington fixed on him but glanced where he pointed.

Her shed. Her museum. He was pointing to the sign over the shed. Neon lettering; she'd forgotten to turn it off when she went to bed.

Museum of Seraphs, announced the neon. *Gallery of Angels.*

"A big-deal name for a piss-poor setup," had been Tad Foster's verdict when he visited one night (it hadn't been exactly a date, more like an invitation for a beer and a look round her museum; but once Tad had said that, she knew they had zero in common).

"Place is closed," she said firmly. "All the signs out on the road spell it out: open weeknights 6 to 9. And it's practically midnight now. Plus I got to go to work in the morning."

The scarecrow said nothing, just stared and stared at the sign. Slowly he lowered his arm.

One thing, anyway: this guy didn't look dangerous. The dogs sensed it, too; they sat on their rumps beside her and just watched.

Up close like this, the scarecrow seemed more than hungry. *Famished* was how he looked.

He uttered two words; two questions, really. "Seraphs? Museum?"

The words came out as a croak. This guy wasn't just famished, but thirsty, too, from the sound of him.

"Seraphs, yeah." She was never sure how to explain to people what was in her shed. "That's what I call them. Fancy word for some things I found over at the V-Bar-V and Montezuma Castle."

She was pleased to see the flicker of interest that lit his face. "Montezuma," he croaked. "Yes."

She lowered the shotgun. Hard not to feel sorry for the guy. *Why not invite him in for a minute, give him some food and a beer?*

Then she saw what was fastened to his wrist. A blue plastic ID tag. *Like the kind you get in hospitals.* "Hey, have you been hurt or something?" She took a step forward.

And at that the scarecrow stared down at his wrist and at the blue plastic as if it were some hideous alien growth. He raised his face: a look of terror in his eyes, as if he'd just recalled something awful.

He glanced once more at the neon lettering and then turned and ran fast and disappeared into the pines.

The dogs howled but stayed close beside her. For a long minute she gazed out at the trees.

"Come on, you two," she said at last. "Let's get to bed."

chapter 6

Verde Valley, Arizona
Southeast of Oak Creek Canyon
Highway 17, Exit 289
THE LAMINATED BADGE announced her name and rank: *Anita Martinez, Assistant Manager.*

Working at the Sonic Drive-In wasn't Annie's dream job—as assistant manager, she had to deal nonstop with customers' demands. *How about some placemats my kids can color in, and some crayons to go with them? Can I get half-price on this refill of Coke? Can I get this next refill free, because I just spilled my last one, and by the way could you get someone to wipe up this mess before my seat gets all sticky?*

Today the demands seemed more tiring than usual, and she knew why. After last night's encounter, she hadn't been able to sleep. The dogs kept pacing by her bed, and she'd lain awake, wondering why that skinny scarecrow had been so interested in her museum.

In her museum, and in Montezuma Castle, too: after all, he'd said no more than four words, and one of them had been *Montezuma.* Which just happened to correspond to an interest of hers, as well.

Because that was why she'd sought out this job supervising burger-flippers at the Sonic: it was less than two miles from the entrance to Montezuma Castle, the site where she'd discovered her first seraphs. And this stranger, this scarecrow—Mister Gaunt, she called him in her thoughts as she recalled last night's encounter—

must have some kind of compelling interest in seraphs himself—else why would he have come tramping in the dark all the way out to her trailer? He looked as if he sure had a lot to say on the topic.

Or would have, if his voice hadn't croaked so bad and sounded so weak and he hadn't been so famished. And all day during her shift as she served customers, she imagined offering Mister Gaunt his choice of Drive-In foods: *How about a Supersonic jalapeno double cheeseburger? Or maybe a footlong quarter-pound Coney hotdog, topped with chili, cheese, onions, and mustard? That'll fill you up.*

And for a quick-energy pick-me-up, she continued in her thoughts as she wordlessly smiled her way through the workday, *how about a Sonic Blast for dessert: sweet vanilla ice cream, which you can mix with toppings of your choice—Reese's peanut butter cups, chopped-up Snickers, crumbled Oreos, or old-fashioned M &Ms, with a twirling of Dairy Whiz whipped cream on top?* She imagined how grateful he'd be to eat, and how glad.

"Man oh man, you are sleep-walking today." Tad Foster, underling, right at her elbow.

She didn't like Tad's insinuating leer and the way he stood too close, all apparently on the strength of two hours at the trailer back when and an almost-but-not-quite date.

"Didja stay up too late again with that junk in your museum?" He was an oversized guy, with a bad habit of crowding people.

The taunt helped her to an impulsive decision. (She did a lot of things on impulse, which kept getting her into jams.) "You cover the afternoon shift. I'm punching out early."

"But *I* was thinking of punching out early."

"Not today you aren't."

She disregarded the annoyance on his face as she wiped her hands on her apron and hurried out.

"Yeah. Yeah." She knew he was striving for some witticism to fling after her. "Get your beauty sleep. You need it."

Four o'clock, and still plenty hot, but she left her car and walked the two miles downhill along the winding paved road to the Montezuma Castle entrance.

A park ranger was starting a tour for a cluster of tourists, and she followed a few paces behind, staying quiet as usual, not wanting to draw attention to herself or her private interests.

The 'castle' in question was an ancient mudbrick dwelling, some five stories tall, built high up in the cliff-face of the hills surrounding this valley. Annie liked this place, liked the dusty green of the junipers and sycamores growing along the visitors' trail, liked the white-and-red striations of the cliffs, liked the loud hum of the cicadas from the creosote bushes and the sweet smell of the breeze that carried the breath of yucca and velvet mesquite.

A little boy in the crowd—all eager enthusiasm—asked who used to live up there.

"A native American people called the Sinagua," explained the ranger. Farmers, he said; agriculturists, first drawn to this site because of nearby Beaver Creek.

"The Sinagua abandoned this place many centuries ago," he continued. "Nobody knows exactly why."

The little boy seemed fascinated; others in the crowd, less so. An old woman with binoculars kept her glasses fixed on the cliff-dwelling.

Annie had heard this talk many times before. She waited for the question someone always asked, the question she herself had asked, the first time she came here.

And here it came, from the eager little boy: "How come it's called Montezuma Castle?"

The ranger chuckled. "Oh, the Anglo settlers who first started homesteading around these parts saw a big old site like this and they wanted to tag it with a big old name. They'd heard of the Aztecs, and they'd heard of the Aztec king Montezuma; so they figured maybe those folks had come up from Mexico and conquered this place or something to that effect."

"So this isn't really an Aztec castle or palace or anything?" The boy sounded disappointed.

"Sorry." The ranger chuckled again.

Annie wanted to interrupt, wanted to say *Wait, little boy. Actually I've come across some things right near here—things I call seraphs, never mind why for the moment—things that make me think there might just be something to this Aztec connection that people laugh off so quickly. Even if it's not quite Aztec the way we usually think of Aztec.*

But she knew better than to speak. She'd tried her theories out once on Tad Foster and he'd been quick to laugh, and to announce to everyone else working the counter at the Sonic: "Listen up, everybody! Boss-lady here has got a crackpot notion you're just gonna love."

She was in no hurry to trust her private visions again to the world at large. People would have to prove themselves first.

The ranger said something else about the Sinagua. The old woman with the binoculars kept her eyes fixed on the hundred-foot-high cliff-dwelling.

The little boy seemed to have recovered from his disappointment. He pointed upward. "What a neat place to live," he enthused.

The old woman moved her field glasses slowly from right to left, as if scanning for something.

"I don't suppose"—a wistful tone in the boy's voice—"anyone still lives up there."

"Absolutely not." The ranger's tone took on a note of authority. "This is a national monument. Protected by the Park Service. Anyone who tried out any funny business like that, squatting around up there, they'd be in big trouble. Big trouble. And mighty fast, too."

"In that case, young man"—this from the old woman, who was still staring through her binoculars at the cliff-dwelling—"can you tell us how come there's somebody moving around up there?"

"What? Where? Gimme that." He snatched the field glasses, then recovered his poise sufficiently to apologize. "Sorry, ma'am. But I'll need to have a look for myself here."

Annie in fact had her own glasses but had forgotten them back at the Sonic. Like everyone else in the crowd she stared up at the cliff.

Above, in the late afternoon heat, canyon wrens darted. Their cries echoed off the stone.

Squinting against the glare, Annie stared at the Sinagua castle, scanned its mud ramparts and the projecting guard tower and the apertures in its walls, scanned them for movement, a shadow, the trace of a presence.

A long minute's silence.

The ranger grunted. "Nothing." He handed back the binoculars. "Sorry, ma'am. Your glasses probably just picked up a rock squirrel. We got lots of 'em round here."

"Aww," said the little boy. "I wanted somebody to be up there."

Annie hadn't seen anyone, either.

She didn't need to.

She knew who it was.

Stay out of sight, scarecrow. She breathed the words as a prayer. *Stay hidden for me.*

chapter 7

Sonic Drive-In
Verde Valley, Arizona
Southeast of Oak Creek Canyon
Highway 17, Exit 289

FIORINA DE LA PAZ and Tomasina Guardina watched as their boss blended a super-sized smoothie. "Peanut butter and strawberry?" Fiorina cocked a penciled eyebrow. "Who you making that for? Nobody ordered anything like that."

"It's for me." Annie snapped a lid on the shake. She didn't look at either of her workers. "Just putting together a take-home dinner."

"But those things are fattening." This from Tomasina, the more assertive of the pair. "Drinks like that, lots of calories. You've been warning us all the time."

Annie acted as if she hadn't heard. She put the smoothie in a big paper bag, grabbed a bucket of fried popcorn chicken from the warmer, added that to the bag as well.

"All you been eating every day is carrot sticks and apple slices, and now all of a sudden you decide to pig out."

Annie rolled her eyes at *pig out* but said nothing. She opened a drawer, grabbed a handful of Reese's peanut butter cups, still in their bright-orange wrappers, added them to the bag. *That should do it.*

"I don't get it," said Fiorina.

"I do," said Tomasina. "Too many carrot sticks. She can't handle her diet any more. She's gone out of her mind."

"Don't you see what's going on?" A loud comment from across the diner. Tad Foster had been mopping the floor.

Still carrying the mop, he stepped closer. "Boss-lady ain't gonna eat that herself. She's on another one of her feed-the-poor kicks. Who you adopted today?"

He waved the mop. "Lemme guess. Another jobless vagrant. Another friggin' bum. Another illegal alien. You know what I call those types? Road kill. Road waste. 'Cause it's a waste of time and money, encouraging their kind to hang around hoping for handouts."

He waved the mop again for emphasis. "I'll bet I could go out back right now and find whoever it is hiding in the dumpster, just waiting for his handout."

He barked a laugh, glared at his supervisor. "Don't you get it? Every one of those bums you ever been nice to, they all took advantage of you."

This one's different, Annie wanted to say. *Different. I can tell.*

Aloud she said, "You're dripping water. Get over there and finish up."

Tomasina and Fiorina grinned. Tad frowned as if struggling to generate a snappy riposte but gave up and stalked off with his mop. "Road waste," he muttered at the floor.

"I'm punching out, girls. Make sure Bright-Boy stays hard at work."

Tomasina grinned again. "We're on it. You have a nice night, you and your Reese's."

On her way out Annie passed through the adjacent 7-Eleven, wondering if she'd packed enough food. On the counter a new novelty was on sale, a Jurassic Dinosaur Fern. "Just 99 cents—put fern in water and watch it come alive!" urged the label.

The seedling was packaged with a logo of a pterodactyl, wings flexed for flight, perched on a cliff atop a prehistoric jungle. Perched on a cliff and looking hungry, she guessed. On impulse she threw down a dollar and took the seedling.

Evening coming on, air suddenly cool. She walked fast and turned up the collar of her jacket, hoping no one would notice she was heading for Montezuma's this time of day.

The gate was locked. *Closed,* warned the sign. *Cars and Pedestrians Prohibited.* The gate wasn't much of a problem—she'd climbed it many a time, on her nighttime seraph-scavenger hunts—but it was trickier with her take-out bag.

There. She was over, and without spilling a drop of her smoothie. *Doing just fine. Just fine.*

She'd done this so many times in the dark she knew her way well. But tonight felt different. She paused, listened, on her guard.

All quiet. By now the last of the rangers would've left.

Then she realized: tonight, she knew, there was an additional presence here. She could feel it, she was sure. Hopefully a friendly presence.

After all, the reasonable side of her warned the impulsive side, *you've got exactly four words of conversation from the scarecrow to go by. You really have no idea what this Mr. Gaunt's like, whether he's harmless or harmful or road waste like big-mouth Tad was saying.*

A loud fluttering overhead in the trees. She flinched. *Owl; hawk, maybe. Get a grip. Everything's going to be fine.*

She followed the path to the visitors' center, paused at the water bubbler for a drink, wiped her mouth with her hand. *He's probably still hiding up in his castle, thinking maybe he should wait till it's darker to try coming down to scout for some food.*

A few minutes' walk brought her to the base of the cliff.

She looked up and realized: *I'm no mountain goat. Couldn't climb that in daylight, never mind at night. Don't know how he did it. Assuming of course he's really up there, or anybody's up there besides squirrels. Maybe this is a dumb idea; dumber*—her reasonable side added—*than your usual dumb ideas, Anita Martinez.*

What to do? Undecided, she headed to her favorite spot at the site—the place she'd discovered on her first after-hours expedition here, the place that, as far as she knew, hadn't yet been discovered by anyone else.

A cave, one of many pocking the base of the cliffs, its entrance obscured by thick growths of juniper and brush.

She crouched—the mouth was less than four feet high—and listened. Silence.

She felt in her pocket for a flashlight—*shoot, did I forget to bring it? Okay, there it is*—and made her way to the back of the cave. Carefully she placed the take-out bag on the ground, and then she stooped and searched the cave-floor for her cache of seraphs.

Seraphs, at least, was the word she used to describe what she'd discovered here months ago. Terracotta fragments, hundreds and hundreds of them. So many, in fact, that she'd decided to take only some home to her museum and leave the rest here.

These things had an aura—she felt it every time she handled them—and she didn't want to weaken what she knew to be the cave's power by taking away too many of the potsherds.

Different, each one of these sherds, each painted with black ink on a baked red surface.

The ink showed figures of varying kinds. Most she couldn't make much sense of.

But some of them—a couple dozen, at least—showed creatures of some kind. Creatures with multiple wings, two pairs, or even three. And some creatures had multiple eyes, as well.

Annie knew her Bible pretty well, and she knew what the Bible called creatures with three pairs of wings. *Seraphs.* The Seraphim, in Isaiah and the Apocalypse.

And when she gazed at these seraphs, and especially when she handled them, they gave her visions.

No other word for it. Visions. Breakthrough visions.

Old: these seraph-fragments felt old—who knew how many centuries ago they'd been left here?—and their age communicated itself in the smooth feel of each sherd in the hand.

But no time for handling or gazing tonight.

Because she knew the order of her seraphs, and tonight the order was disturbed.

In her own way Annie Martinez was an orderly person, and after every session with her sherds she arranged them in rows, with a seraph-sherd leading each row. She liked the feel of it, liked the look.

But tonight they were out of order.

They'd been rearranged. Not scattered by some burrowing fox or nesting rabbit. Rearranged.

And rearranged by someone with just as strong a sense of order as Annie had. Except the seraphs no longer led the rows. The sherds were in some new arrangement, juxtaposed as if someone had tried to align them to reveal some new pattern, some message. But she could make nothing of it.

Except now she knew she needn't worry about how to climb up to the castle and deliver her take-out dinner to Mister Gaunt. Because it seemed Mister Gaunt had already found a second lair, right here.

She wanted to wait for him, wanted to have the pleasure of watching him eat his popcorn chicken and drink his smoothie and unwrap his Reese's peanut butter cups. Wanted to be able to hear him say *Yes I'm full now* and *thank you so much*.

But she knew enough about wild things to guess that wouldn't work.

Instead she placed the food in front of the sherds, where he'd be sure to find it, and propped the fern-packet with its pterodactyl-logo in front of the take-out bag. *As a cliff-percher, he should appreciate another cliff-percher,* she thought, and she smiled.

She stood and wiped her hands on her jeans and was about to leave when she had an urge to leave him a message. She felt in her pockets. A pencil. She knelt and took the fern-packet and jotted a note beside the pterodactyl:

The sherds. Are you trying to connect with Montezuma's spirit?

She wanted to add more, wanted to say *Because I've been trying that, too, trying to contact Montezuma and the ghosts of all those old Aztecs I'm convinced traveled all the way up here, and somehow my seraphs help make that connection.*

But the fern-packet had only so much blank space beside the dinosaur logo and so she decided to keep the note brief. She put away the pencil and propped the pterodactyl once more in front of the food.

Enjoy your smoothie, she said aloud, and she headed back into the night.

chapter 8

TAD FOSTER DIPPED his mop in the bucket and thought: *I could do her job.*

Assistant managers made three bucks an hour more than floor help like him—he'd checked around. As far as he could see, they didn't do much more than he did.

And now he saw an opening.

There she was, bagging up take-out chicken for herself, punching out an hour early, for the third night in a row. Why not send Regional Management a little email, short and sweet: *Your employee Anita Martinez isn't performing her duties.*

Something like that should stir things up, create a vacancy.

Or maybe—he watched as she said a hurried Good night to Tomasina and Fiorina and rushed out the door—maybe he should wait. Whatever she was up to—and she was up to something, of that he was sure—she was about to get into real trouble.

He could feel it. Trouble a lot worse than skipping from work an hour early. Trouble that would terminate her job but good—as long as someone as sharp as Tad Foster was on hand to document the mess.

In that case, he told himself, watching her through the glass as she strode across the parking lot, *just wait. Just give it time.*

No answer last night.

Annie had rushed to her cave—their cave, she called it now, hers and Mister Gaunt the Scarecrow's—hoping he'd found the food, hoping he'd eaten so he'd keep up his strength and not get caught by park rangers and get expelled from the castle, hoping, above all, that he'd leave her a message, a reply to her question: *The sherds. Are you trying to connect with Montezuma's spirit?*

Well, two out of three.

When she'd reached the cave last night, she found evidence that he was still holed up in the vicinity. The food had all been eaten, and not by coyotes: the leftover paper napkins and trash had all been stowed—even the empty Reese's peanut butter cup wrappers, which had been neatly folded into squares—inside the take-out bag.

The seedling packet with the pterodactyl was gone. Maybe that meant he liked it. No way to know. But there was no written note, no answer to the question she'd left, no communication.

Unless one wanted to count her seraph-sherds. A glance told her they were in a new order, different from the preceding night, arranged in unfamiliar columns. She sat and studied them—*is he making some attempt to tell me something?*—but concluded if there was any message, it was only to himself.

So last night, with a feeling of mounting loneliness that surprised her—she prided herself on her self-sufficiency—she'd left a fresh smoothie-chicken-Reese's dinner for him, and had written on the take-out bag a new note: *I'm trying to connect with Montezuma. Are you trying to reach him, too?*

All day today, distracted and sleepless and going through the motions of her job, she'd jeered at herself for writing such a dopey note: *Trying to connect with Montezuma.* How stupid that sounded, even to her.

Putting into writing such a hope, such a longing, and then expecting someone else to share her same sense of loopy visionary quest: *what would the scarecrow make of that?* She was glad no one at the Sonic could read her thoughts.

Just imagine what Tad Foster would do if he found a note like that: he'd laugh and laugh.

No wonder Mister Gaunt hadn't bothered to reply last night as he ate his popcorn chicken; he'd probably just laughed, too, as he slurped down his drink.

In the end, maybe her scarecrow was just that: a scarecrow— no heart, no feelings, no capacity to respond, greedy for a handout and ready to move on, like the other bums she'd helped in the past.

Maybe he hadn't left a note because he was planning to leave today. Maybe he'd cleared out this morning.

Maybe Tad was right: guys like that are road kill. Road waste. A waste of her time.

And yet:

This evening, with the light dimming, with night coming on as she climbed the gate—take-out bag balanced in one hand— and as she hurried along the visitors' path, a path she knew well by now, as birds in the pines overhead settled in for their sleep with by-now familiar cries, as cliff-side swallows darted overhead and shrilled her a welcome, and as the bulk of the castle loomed up in the dark, a hospitable and friendly shape, the thought came to her: This is where I belong. I'm home, and this is his home, too.

And then with joy she knew tonight there'd be a note.

Except:

She'd forgotten to leave him a pencil.

Maybe that's why he hadn't replied! How many scarecrows— famished, their straw-stuffed minds focused on food—go around with writing implements? How could she expect an answer when she hadn't left him something to write with?

Stupid, stupid.

She ran all the way, almost dropping the dinner, not knowing what to think, what feeling to trust.

The cave. There.

She rushed in, bumped her head on the rock, fumbled for the flashlight, clicked it on.

Last night's bag, food all eaten, trash tucked away, positioned carefully in front of the seraph-sherds. And there was the note she'd penned on the bag: *I'm trying to connect with Montezuma. Are you trying to reach him, too?*

She stooped. Had he written a reply underneath her penned lines?

Nope. Nothing. Nothing but bare white.

She clapped her hands to her eyes, felt ready to cry, called herself names for letting all this mean something to her.

You are a stupid shit. You are a stupid shit.

She slumped to the dirt, tasted the bitter weight of crushed hopes.

Stupid shit. Stupid shit.

Slowly the hurt ebbed. *Calm down. Just calm down.*

She'd feel better, she told herself, when she got back to her trailer and gave her dogs a hug.

This is what you get for getting your hopes up.

And then, blinking away tears, she saw it, saw the writing.

Not on the bag, but beside her, in the dirt of the cave floor, scrawled with a stick (so he really did lack a pencil!), in answer to her question.

She shone her flashlight over the reply:

Yes, I'm trying to reach him. Also trying to reach Prince Khaemwaset.

Khaemwaset: a riddle to her. Not a name she knew.

She didn't care. Only one thing mattered: she had a reply.

She sat by her seraph-sherds, scooped up a smooth handful, pressed them to her lips and breathed a quick prayer.

Thank you. Thank you. Thank you.

chapter 9

Yavapai County, Arizona
Unincorporated land between Sedona and Cornville
Near Oak Creek Canyon

THE SEARCH ONLINE hadn't been too helpful.

She'd googled *Khaemwaset*. If the name meant so much to Mister Gaunt, then it was worth researching. After all, it was almost the only clue she had so far as to what made her scarecrow tick.

Now she sat in her trailer, pondering the display on her computer screen. Lots of information, more than she knew what to do with.

Khaemwaset: ancient Egyptian, lived in the thirteenth century BC. Son of Ramses the Great. Crown prince. A scholar, and some kind of priest.

"The problem, my friends"—she had a habit of addressing Gabby and Micky as she sat with her laptop—"is knowing what to make of all this info."

She tried googling *Khaemwaset + Montezuma*.

Nothing. Or at least nothing that made any sense to her, that suggested any possible reason why a scarecrow and drifter would be interested in both names.

One on each side of her, the dogs watched as her fingers tapped away at the keyboard. "And what makes it harder," she yawned, "is that I'm dead, dead, dead tired." She leaned over and rubbed Gabby's flank, which made Micky press closer for his share of attention.

"But I'll let you guys in on a secret, as long as you promise not to tell anyone." They gave her their full attention. "I left our friend Mister Gaunt another note in the cave tonight. And you know what it said?" Both dogs wagged their tails.

"It said, 'How about we meet here in the cave?' What do you make of that, hmm?" The dogs cocked their ears.

"I know. My feeling exactly: it may have been a stupid thing to do. I may have frightened him off altogether. I should've known better."

More tail-wagging.

"You're right, guys." She closed the lid on the laptop. "I'll find out tomorrow night. No sense getting obsessed about it. Let's go to bed."

***

Next day at work she filled her lunch hour by sitting at an empty booth and jotting on a Sonic Drive-In placemat an itemized list.

What I know about Mister Gaunt:

One—He's got some kind of interest in angels. He walked all the way to Cornville & out to Oak Creek Canyon to see my seraph collection—-even though he ran away before he got to see a thing. Plus he keeps rearranging the terracotta pieces in the cave.

Two—He's been in a hospital or some sort of clinic lately. Still wearing an ID tag on his wrist.

Three—Sloppy about his appearance. What type of person walks around still wearing a plastic tag after they get out of the hospital? Or maybe he's some kind of mental patient, maybe it's a tag from a mental health clinic, & he's so far out of it he doesn't even realize he's wearing it. Hope that's not the case!

Four—Speaking of appearance. Famished looking. Hungry, hungry, hungry!

Five—Interest in Montezuma. No question. He said the word the night I met him. He's living somewhere around the castle. Confirmed he's interested when I wrote him that question.

Six—Problem: no idea how an Aztec emperor links up with an Egyptian pharaoh's son. Montezuma + Khaemwaset = ????

Seven—Lots of ancient Egyptians; what makes Mr. G so interested in this Khaemwaset?

Eight—Most interesting thing I found out about Khaemwaset when I googled the name again this morning: he loved wandering the desert by himself, studying ancient things, things that were already old even 3,000+ years ago.

Nine—So: Khaemwaset=A spiritual quester, a kindred spirit, like Mr. G, like me?

Ten—

"Howdy. What'cha scribbling?" Tad Foster, right at her elbow.

"Nothing." Hastily she folded the placemat.

"You been scribbling seems like forever."

"Meaning you've been watching me like forever?" She stuffed the paper in her apron-pouch.

"Nah. I wouldn't do that." He gestured at the placemat. "Must be something important."

"Nothing important."

He made an attempt at a smile. "Hey. I'm driving down to Phoenix tonight. Gonna catch the stock-car tournament at the Raceway. Thought you might wanna come." As he spoke he stared at her apron.

"I'm beat. Planning on turning in early tonight. Soon as I punch out." She stood up, moved away from him. "Thanks anyway."

"Hey. No problem." He watched as she strode back to the counter.

⌐╫¬

Five-thirty. This time Annie made up two smoothies, grabbed two buckets of chicken, an extra handful of Reese's. She was in such a hurry she spilled a bit of the first smoothie on her apron. Impatiently she pulled off the bib, tossed it on the counter.

"Gotta go." She saw Tomasina and Fiorina watching her with looks of quiet surprise.

She stuffed the food in two bags while keeping an eye on Tad, who seemed to be preoccupied with mopping the floor.

Good. Maybe she could get out of here without any more questions about her activities.

Out the door. Whew. She was afraid she'd have to talk her way all over again out of going to the Phoenix Raceway.

Big question now: would her scarecrow be there, waiting in the seraph-cave?

He'd better be. Otherwise I know a pair of dogs that'll be dining on popcorn chicken tonight.

"Hey. I thought she ate only carrot sticks. Shit like that." Mop in hand, Tad stood beside Tomasina and Fiorina as the three watched their boss hurry across the lot.

Fiorina shook her head. "Did you see how much take-out she had in those bags?"

Tomasina shrugged. "Dinner for two. Probably lined herself up a hot date."

"She wanted a hot date, she could'a gone with me to the Raceway." Tad turned to the counter, noticed the discarded apron.

"Maybe she didn't want to go to the Raceway." Tomasina scowled at the floor. "You're dripping water again. You better clean that up."

"Yeah. Yeah." Tad lifted the apron, removed the placemat, tossed the apron back onto the counter. "I'll clean it up."

Tomasina saw him carefully fold the placemat and place it in his shirt pocket. "What's that?"

"Nothing. Piece of paper."

"Well, finish mopping the floor."

"Yeah. Yeah." He shambled over to the booths, pushed the mop back and forth.

Fiorina turned to Tomasina. "What's he grinning about?"

"I got no idea."

chapter 10

'ADNAN ABU UMAIR al-Harithi—fifty-two years old, aged, even elderly for this line of work—gave no more than half his attention to his subordinate's complaints.

"This is a place of impiety," hissed Hasan Zubayr.

"This is the most comfortable hotel in the city," his commander reminded him, "and where we're sitting now offers the most beautiful views in Sanaa."

'Adnan knew the views were wasted on Hasan. Here they were, ten floors up, enjoying the Burj al-Salam's open-air rooftop terrace, and a vista that included the Old City's minarets and crumbling gateways and labyrinth of alleys, and, on the distant horizon, the mountains of the central highlands.

None of that, 'Adnan knew, mattered to Hasan. All the young man could focus on was a picture decorating the terrace wall.

"Impiety," repeated Hasan. He jabbed a finger angrily at the picture.

A waiter thought the gesture signaled a request for refills. Quickly he brought a fresh pot of coffee.

And this, thought 'Adnan, was coffee the way he liked it. Strong, black, and bitter. It went well with the food on their table—apricots, olives, bread, cheese. Through thirty-five years of jihad, he'd developed simple dining habits, and he kept those habits even in moments such as this, where he could have indulged himself if he wished.

"Why do we have to meet our guests," complained Hasan again, "in a place that offers distractions and impieties?"

The distraction in question—the object of Hasan's fascinated glower—was a cheap picture on the terrace wall, a copy of an old Orientalist painting showing two harem girls lounging on a divan.

'Adnan sipped his coffee in silence.

"I cannot fathom," resumed Hasan, apparently unsatisfied with his superior's lack of response, "why hotel owners who call themselves Muslim would hang a picture of women, half-naked women, at that, where decent men have to look at them."

"Look at something else, then," suggested 'Adnan equably. "Look at this fine city view."

His subordinate, 'Adnan knew, was disappointed. Hasan wanted to impress him—'Adnan al-Harithi, after all, was the deputy-commander of *Ansar al-din fi'l jazeerah al-'arabiyah*, 'Those who help bring about the victory of the faith in the Arabian Peninsula,' one of the most high-profile Islamist groups in Yemen.

Hasan wanted permission to come back and bomb this hotel or at least shoot the manager. Hasan wanted clarity. Hasan wanted purity.

"The problem with you young people"—'Adnan couldn't resist the temptation to lecture his subordinate while they awaited their guests—"is that you let yourselves be angered by minor irritants, when you need to focus on your primary target."

Hasan started to say something—'Adnan knew the youngster probably wanted to cite a pertinent fatwa or the like that he'd memorized while studying at one of Sanaa's Wahhabi-funded Koran schools—but stopped himself.

The young man glared once more at the harem girls, then at the waiters, and finally settled into his chair with a pout.

"Ah. Our guests." 'Adnan stood and offered a hand in welcome.

The guests—two of them, there were—hesitated at the table. The older of the two spoke, assessing 'Adnan and Hasan in the exchange of handshakes. "I'm supposed to meet someone named al-Afghani."

'Adnan gave a slight bow. "I'm known as al-Afghani."

"You don't look like an Afghan to me." The objection came from the younger of the two newcomers.

"Afghani is an honorific title." Hasan Zubayr hastened to his commander's defense. "A title he won on jihad. Four years in Afghanistan fighting the Soviets." Hasan's frown showed he was ready to dislike the strangers just as much as he did the harem girls.

The younger stranger frowned back. "That still doesn't mean we can trust you."

"Come." This from the older guest. "No need to quarrel." The four sat at the table. A server brought coffee.

The older man introduced himself: Waheed Shafeeq. His younger colleague was named Obaid Tantaawi.

Egyptians, both of them, guessed 'Adnan, to judge from the dialect of Arabic they spoke. Waheed Shafeeq dressed like many well-to-do businessmen, smooth-shaven in an Armani suit and pressed trousers and a tie by Christian Dior.

Obaid Tantaawi favored very different attire. Long robe, skull-cap, full beard, upper lip shaven clean—enough to identify him with one of the Salafist forms of Islam.

But what 'Adnan noticed most was that his subordinate Hasan was staring at the *zabeeba* on the young Egyptian's forehead: the callus that displayed one's piety.

It came from rubbing one's face hard on the mat every time one prostrated oneself in prayer. It took years to develop a *zabeeba* as big and conspicuous as Obaid's. Hasan was dressed piously, too; but he lacked such a mark of piety. He frowned again and looked away.

Coffee; platters of sweets; another refilling of the cups. Waheed Shafeeq voiced pleasantries about the fine view.

"But too cold," said the younger Egyptian, "up here in the mountains. The altitude must be at least three thousand meters." He shivered.

"If you want to engage in jihad in Yemen," boasted Hasan, "you learn to endure cold weather. Unless all you value is comfort."

'Adnan laid a restraining hand on his wrist, as if to warn *No need to taunt.* The last thing he wanted was a quarrel between these youngsters when work was at hand.

"Well," smiled Waheed Shafeeq, "Obaid in fact will have a chance to learn to endure this weather, since he'll be accompanying you on this task."

"Oh?" 'Adnan disliked having untried newcomers on his hands. This wasn't how he'd survived four years in Afghanistan. "We don't need extra personnel."

"My employers insist that their interests be represented on this mission."

"Perhaps you'd better explain the mission you have in mind."

"Certainly." The organization he represented, began Waheed—no need to identify the employer by name—had been frustrated in acquiring a certain ancient artifact in Cairo. *'Asaayat Suleiman*, it was called: King Solomon's wand. Or, more precisely, the wand's finial, one half of the artifact in question.

Attempts were being made even now, explained Waheed, to retrieve the finial within Egypt. But, according to ancient Egyptian legend, Solomon's wand had been broken in two many centuries ago, and the wand's other half—the staff atop which the finial once rested—had been spirited from Egypt in some bygone age and hidden in a certain locale in Yemen.

"Where precisely in Yemen?"

"That information is encoded in the Cairene portion of the artifact; and unfortunately we haven't yet retrieved that piece."

"Then how"—hostility and impatience in Hasan's voice—"are we supposed to hunt about for it?"

Obaid, equally quick-mouthed, shot back, "Perhaps you should pray to God for guidance." The hostility between the two youngsters was clearly mutual.

'Adnan admired how Waheed retained his equanimity. "You won't have to hunt about. All you have to do is follow a certain foreigner, who arrived here last night on an Egypt Air flight. Keep him in sight. He'll lead you to it."

Hasan Zubayr turned abruptly to his commander. "We're mujahideen. We're here to wage jihad and create an Islamic state. Why should we run about fetching dusty old objects for strangers?"

"Because"—'Adnan reminded himself to lecture his subordinate later about disagreements in front of outsiders—"these gentlemen are going to pay us generously for our time. And that payment will fund us as we pursue our goal of creating the Islamic state we all want."

The commander turned to his guests. "Describe this artifact for us." 'Adnan took detailed notes as Waheed spoke.

"And the name of this foreigner who's looking for your artifact?"

Waheed reached into the inner pocket of his suit, extracted an i-phone, tapped at the screen. "Richard Greyling Atlas."

'Adnan kept writing. "Nationality?"

"American."

"Ah." 'Adnan laid down his pen. "And how should we deal with this American?"

"Do nothing until he leads you to the artifact. Retrieve the artifact. Be sure it is intact, and undamaged. At that point"—he gave a dismissive shrug—"you may do with him as you wish."

"Is this American a believer?" Eagerness, now, in Hasan's voice.

"No, he's not Muslim."

"An American," mused Hasan, "plus a *kafir*." Now, thought 'Adnan, he's suddenly interested in the job.

"I've never had a chance to kill an American," announced his subordinate.

"Neither have I," responded Obaid Tantaawi. The two youngsters glared again at each other.

"Well," declared Waheed expansively, "now you'll both have an opportunity to earn merit. But just remember: we want the wand undamaged."

The young men glared some more and said nothing.

"Don't worry," 'Adnan assured him as they shook hands in farewell. "There'll be no damage. No damage, at least"—*time for a bit of a joke,* he decided—"to the wand."

And at that they all shared a laugh.

chapter 11

Arabia Felix Hotel
Sanaa, Old City
Yemen

THE HARD PART was having to sit around and wait.

What Ricky Atlas preferred—and this had always been his style—was a quick in-and-out. *Target the loot; snatch it; scoot.* Mad dash for the border, and don't wait around for cops or questions.

"You mean you prefer being a tomb-robber," Iggy Forsythe had accused him, the day Ricky announced he was quitting grad school, after that messy Ushabti Incident, "instead of slogging it out to finish your Ph.D."

"You got that right," had been his reply. "I lack the patience for all the crap associated with the academic life."

Except here he was, cooped up in a cheap hotel in Sanaa's Old City quarter, forbidden to step outside until Mustafa Hamdi and his stupid Corporation gave Ricky the O.K.

He'd been here almost two weeks, surviving on the grub served here by the Arabia Felix: orange Fanta, greasy fries, gristly chicken, ghastly goat. *And I thought I'd had it hard in Chicago. Talk about needing patience. Jeez.*

One consolation: over the past two weeks, he'd made good progress with the inscription on the finial he'd heisted from the Egyptian Museum. Not that Hamdi had let him keep the artifact. "After all," said his boss, when he'd met Ricky at the Cairo airport to see him off, "if something unfortunate were to befall you in Yemen, we wouldn't want harm to befall this precious piece as well, would we? Safety first."

Yeah, safety first, Ricky had wanted to reply, but he'd stood there in silence as two of Hamdi's hired goons plucked the finial from his bag and then frisked him to see if he'd acquired anything else of interest in his little trip to the museum.

"I'm clean. I'm clean," Ricky had protested.

"Of course you are," agreed Hamdi. "I assume you've already taken photos of the inscription?"

"I've got 'em stashed in my cellphone."

"Good, good. I approve of your initiative. You'll need to translate the inscription before we can pinpoint precisely where the other half of Solomon's wand is to be found." He said that so far the Corporation's worldwide contacts had succeeded only in hearing rumors and legends to the effect that the missing object was to be found in Yemen.

"And Yemen is a rather large haystack in which to search for a single but valuable needle," he added. "We're counting on your ability to translate this text to provide us with more clues as to the location." Otherwise—and Hamdi said this with a sigh—he'd never have the pleasure of reuniting the sundered halves of this treasure.

"We'll let you keep these," he said, as one of his men opened Ricky's knapsack to reveal the books he always carried: Faulkner's *Concise Dictionary of Middle Egyptian* and Hannig's *Grosses Handwörterbuch Ägyptisch-Deutsch.*

Ricky would've much preferred to work on the translation in Cairo, where he could have made use of the many philological reference works to be found in the city's Egyptological libraries. But Hamdi had insisted he leave that same night: "We want you out of the country before the competition can trace you to Yemen. Safety first, Doctor Atlas: we want nothing bad to befall you."

"And if the competition does find me?"

"We have confidence in your ability to improvise. But be careful. We don't want to have to find a replacement."

Thank you very much, had been Ricky's thought as his boss waved him a cheery goodbye in the departure lounge. *Dear Mister Hamdi,* Ricky had longed to tell him, *every time you look at me I always sense a two-word assessment: expendable; disposable.*

But today, seated in the inner courtyard of the Arabia Felix, he was feeling pretty good, feeling he was about to prove to Hamdi that in fact he was valuable and not at all expendable. Because he'd just finished translating the most important part of the finial's inscription.

Actually the artifact bore two inscriptions, dating to two different historical periods. The older inscription seemed fairly standard fare dating to the late eighteenth dynasty, the reign of Akhenaten. It listed within cartouches the honorific titles of the king, his wife Nefertiti, and the Aten—the sacred sun-disk worshipped by the pharaoh and the queen.

Much of the lettering seemed to have been deliberately excised—unsurprising, given how later pharaohs had condemned Akhenaten's notorious religious innovations as heresy. Still visible, however, were the final words of the formulaic conclusion: *di 'ankh djet er neheh*—*...given life enduringly, through all the cycles of eternity.*

Accompanying this inscription was the usual Aten iconography: solar rays—each terminating in a caressing human hand—emanating from a sun-disk. At the base of the disk reared a cobra, its hood flared, its neck encircled by an ankh.

Nothing unusual there, at least at first glance. More interesting was the inscription that had apparently been added at a later date, carved in minuscule lettering around the base of the sun-disk. Too small to read unaided; and his first day at the Felix, Ricky had asked one of the waiters, a friendly plumpish young man named Khuwaylid, if he could somehow locate a magnifying glass mounted on a stand. Khuwaylid had struck him as energetic and attentive, always ready to offer him a fresh Pepsi; so it seemed worth a try.

Ricky hadn't really expected results, yet the next day there was Khuwaylid, all smiles, at the American's table in the courtyard, with a jumbo-sized lens fitted to a brass gooseneck lampstand.

"Where'd you find that?" marveled Ricky as he rewarded the young man with a handful of cash.

"Sanaa University, graduate research library," explained Khuwaylid. "Everything's shut down over there, with all the fighting in that part of the city."

Thereafter Ricky had puzzled over the hieroglyphs for days, seated at a table in the courtyard, in a corner shaded by palm trees. What few guests there were at the Felix—a French film crew, a team of BBC reporters—had left him to himself; they were too busy rushing about covering anti-government riots and street clashes.

Every few hours Khuwaylid brought him another Pepsi: "for strength," explained the server with a smile.

"Very thoughtful of you," Ricky would say absent-mindedly.

Da'iman tahta amrik, would come the reply—"Always at your service."

At last, with the aid of the lens and the dictionaries in his bag, Ricky had teased out the translation.

This text, too, was fragmentary, missing its initial words; he guessed the rest had been carved on the missing portion of the artifact:

...other part of the wand is to be deposited in the Cave of the Sunburst, in the Nile under the stone, atop Crow Mountain, in the northern hills of the Deshret beyond the Sea of the Land of Punt. May the pieces remain sundered until we are ready once more to revere the sekhemu.

So there it was, the clue to the missing portion of the wand. He pushed his chair back from the table, settled the scrawled notes on his lap, and pondered the translation.

The Sea of the Land of Punt: during Egypt's New Kingdom, a common designation for the Red Sea.

Deshret: literally 'red land,' desert, lands beyond the Nile Valley; also a term used for any foreign realm. In this context, *Deshret beyond the Sea of the Land of Punt* must refer to the Arabian peninsula. Obvious enough.

So far, so good. Ricky rubbed his hands together, suddenly realized he was hungry. As if on cue, Khuwaylid was at his table. *Talk about attentive servers,* thought Ricky. This guy's a mind-reader.

"How about some food?"

"Always at your service." Khuwaylid trotted off to the kitchen.

Northern hills of the Deshret: the terrain around Sanaa was mountainous. *Northern hills* probably referred to the central highlands somewhere north of the capital. But from this point on, he knew he was just guessing.

The Nile under the stone: ancient Egyptians sometimes used the word *iteru* or 'Nile' to refer to any flowing water or stream, even rivers in distant lands, and not just in Egypt's Nile valley. So: the site must be associated with water in some way.

Crow Mountain, Cave of the Sunburst: these places must be somewhere in the highlands north of Sanaa. But he simply didn't know Yemen well enough to decrypt these last clues.

This was as much as his text would tell him.

He punched in a number on his cellphone. "Mister Hamdi? I think I've got something for you."

"Excellent, Doctor Atlas. My man will be there in thirty minutes. Be ready to check out of your room."

"I'd like a bite to eat first."

"I don't pay you to eat." Mustafa Hamdi, normally so cool-and-in-control, was clearly excited. "The Corporation wants the wand."

"Give a guy a break. I've been busting my butt for you."

"Thirty minutes, Doctor Atlas. Eat fast."

And stop calling me Doctor, Ricky wanted to add, but he channeled his feelings of defiance into ordering a big lunch. *Let 'em wait. They can't find their wand without me.*

While he ate he thought about the rest of the text. *May the pieces remain sundered until we are ready once more to revere the sekhemu.*

That word *sekhemu:* he thumbed through his dictionaries. Many possible meanings: *powers, divine beings, holy places, sites of worship.* Not enough context to clarify what was meant.

And who were the 'we' in this sentence? Akhenaten and Nefertiti? Unlikely. This fragmentary second inscription seemed somewhat later in date—nineteenth dynasty, he guessed—than the eighteenth-dynasty cartouches of Akhenaten's reign.

But there was a third text to the finial Ricky had stolen from the Egyptian Museum—a text completely unknown to Mister Hamdi. Ricky had found it as he sat in the Filfila teahouse while waiting for Hamdi's crew to show.

As he'd relaxed with his mint-tea, stealthily turning the object about in his hands, he'd glanced at the carved cobra-and-ankh motif at the base of the sun-disk. A hole no more than a quarter-inch wide had been drilled into the cobra's mouth.

The cobra-and-ankh were common enough; not so the hole. Ricky had peered more closely.

In the snake's mouth, barely visible: a tightly-rolled bit of material. A scroll? A message on a papyrus?

Nothing so ancient. A small sheet of paper, barely a hundred years old, with writing inked on the surface. He'd had barely enough time to slip the sheet into one of his dictionaries before Hamdi and his goons had come charging in.

Now as he sat in the courtyard of the Arabia Felix he felt an urge to eye the sheet again. Cautiously he slipped it from the book.

"Sorry, sir." Khuwaylid laid a platter before him. "The chicken seems to be greasy again."

"Isn't it always?" Ricky was still on his hieroglyph-high. *Hey,* he wanted to shout, *It's no problem, bro. Greasy chicken is always trumped by translation-triumphs.* But that sentiment could only be appreciated by the likes of Iggy Forsythe and Pharaoh Frank. He wished they were here now.

Aloud he said, "The chicken will be fine."

"Always at your service."

He smoothed the sheet on his knee, furtively read it again while he ate.

Hotel stationery, apparently. Yellowed with age, it offered a letterhead that read *Winter Palace, Luxor.* Below it was penned:

29 Nov 22/ with help of Gardiner and Winlock have just deciphered the inscription but have misled them as to provenance. Carnarvon has agreed to finance an expedition to Yemen to retrieve the other half of this artifact. But must keep this secret for now. H.C.

November 1922. Every archaeologist in the world knew what had happened then. The greatest discovery in the history of Egyptology: the unearthing of the tomb of Tutankhamun.

Lord Carnarvon, of course, had been the sponsor of the excavation.

Given these clues, there was no question as to the author of this note. What Ricky held in his hands had to have been penned by the finder of Tut, a frequent guest at the Winter Palace.

H.C.: Howard Carter.

But how had this finial come into Carter's hands? And why had Carnarvon agreed to finance an expedition to Yemen, just after finding the Egyptian burial-site the two of them had quested after for so long?

King Tut's tomb: surely the treasures Carter had found ought to have been enough to keep him busy for the rest of his life. What was so special about this so-called Solomon's wand that would have made Carter and Carnarvon interrupt their work in Egypt's Valley of the Kings and go dashing off to Yemen?

All questions, no answers. Frustrating.

But one thing's for sure, Ricky told himself: *this wand is worth a good deal more than Hamdi's letting on. If nothing else, I should squeeze him and his Corporation for another cash bonus when I wrap up this job.*

"Excuse me." A discreet cough at his side. Khuwaylid pointed to the lobby. "Someone's waiting for you."

"Have him wait." Ricky hastily folded the sheet, tucked it back in his dictionary, pushed his plate away. "Still gotta pack."

"Certainly, sir."

As the American hurried upstairs to his room, Khuwaylid pulled a cellphone from his pocket. "The foreigner will be leaving in a few minutes. No, I didn't get a good look."

An angry voice at the other end of the conversation lectured him at length, pointed out that al-Afghani expected better results.

In the midst of this lecture the American descended the stairs, knapsack over one shoulder, and waved a goodbye as he crossed the courtyard. Khuwaylid beamed him a big smile and waved goodbye in return. "Always at your service," he shouted cheerily, and smiled again.

Then back to his phone conversation. "He's leaving now," snapped Khuwaylid. "Be ready."

chapter 12

"MISTER RICKY? TAHA Shu'ayb." Hamdi's man introduced himself. "Your guide. Your servant."

Ricky's first impression: *was this the best the Corporation could do?*

For one thing, the guy seemed to be a *qat*-fiend. Ricky knew many Yemeni men were hooked on this and chewed the narcotic leaves through much of the night. *But here it is, barely midday, and this individual shows up for guide-duty—damned important guide-duty, too, with a lotta cash and maybe my life riding on the outcome—with one side of his mouth bulging so much with the stuff it's like he's got a tennis ball tucked in his cheek.*

Plus the guy struck him as too young. Hamdi had promised Ricky an experienced guide, someone who knew the region well. "Better than anyone else does," Hamdi had promised. So Ricky had expected a wizened and knowledgeable old man.

But Taha Shu'ayb looked like a teen. Early twenties, tops. Short and skinny. Dressed in tight jeans, pointy black shoes, a tattered black-and-white pinstripe sport jacket. Kept under his arm a plastic trash bag filled with something.

A friendly grin—Ricky gave him points for that—even if the guy drooled green *qat*-leaf slime when he smiled. *Well, gotta work with what I have.*

Ricky summarized his hunch. "Somewhere in the central highlands. North of Sanaa." All they had to go on, he explained, were a few clues: Crow Mountain. Cave of the Sunburst. Nile beneath the stone.

Taha nodded, said nothing, chewed. He untied his plastic trash bag.

Contents: several branches from a *qat*-shrub. He offered one to the American. Ricky declined.

Taha plucked a leaf, added it to the wad in his cheek, and resumed his chew.

Ricky didn't like standing around in front of the Felix. Much too conspicuous. He was on assignment, and he wanted to stick to his rule. *Target the loot; snatch it; scoot.* But the next move was up to Chewy Qat-Man here.

Taha plucked another leaf, chewed some more. Ricky looked about the street in front of the Felix. A throng of people bustling by; from a nearby loudspeaker, the call to midday prayer. The cry resounded in a cascade-echo along the stone-wall labyrinths of the Old City. Nothing out of the ordinary.

Except: across the street, two men, a pair of idlers. One of them caught his attention: skull cap, shaven upper lip, long bushy beard. Plus a conspicuous prayer callus on his forehead. *Funny; kind of thing I'd expect to see in Cairo; not so much here.*

At that moment Bush Beard stared at him and then looked quickly away. The other idler said something and it looked for a second as if the two were quarreling.

Another stare in the American's direction. Then the two strode away down an alley.

Now Taha was talking to him. Except, what with the unfamiliarity of the Yemeni dialect, and Taha's mouthful of *qat*, Ricky couldn't understand a word.

Ricky apologized and asked him to repeat himself.

Taha obliged with a smile.

Ricky still had no clue. *Man, this is frustrating.* He smiled back and asked him to say it once more.

This time—with a look of real regret—Taha spat out his chaw. *Jibal al-shamal, jebel al-ghurab, kahf shu'a'at al-shams: ana a'raf hadhihi'l amakin.* Now his Arabic was perfectly clear: "The northern hills, Crow Mountain, the Cave of the Sunburst: I know these places." He was one hundred per cent sure he could find them with ease.

"One hundred per cent? Are you positive?"

"Okay, Mister Ricky. Ninety-eight per cent. But we'll find what you want."

"Well, let's not stand around. You've got a car?"

"A motorcycle."

"A motorcycle? Is that the best you can do?"

"A motorcycle," explained Taha with another smile, "will be better for the roads we must travel. Come."

Down an alley, to where they came upon an old Kawasaki, scuffed red in color, with a dented gas tank. "This thing'll run?"

"Oh yes." Taha opened his bag again, fussed about among the branches, selected several leaves, and began another chaw.

Ricky used this interval to make one more phone call. He was worried: Bush Beard, and the way the two idlers had stared and then hurried away: that didn't feel right. "Excuse me one moment."

Taha smiled and chewed. "*Tafaddal*": *please, help yourself.*
Hope the guy I'm trying to reach is on duty.

Someone picked up on the fourth ring. "Yeah."

"I'm trying to reach Colonel Charles Gordon."

"You got 'im."

Charles Gordon, he knew, was never a man of many words; and Ricky didn't have much time. He got straight to the point.

"Colonel, you remember that favor you said you owe me?"

"Sure do. Still grateful."

"I may have to call in that favor."

"Ah, roger that."

"Is that UAV still positioned over Sanaa?"

"Half a sec."

Ricky waited, looked about to see if anyone else on the street was staring. All clear. Taha stood by the bike and placidly chewed.

"Ah, that's affirmative."

"Fantastic. Can you have that thing keep an eye on me this afternoon? I'll be on a motorcycle. A red Kawasaki. Heading north out of Sanaa."

"Roger that." Click.

Ricky turned to his guide. "Ready to go."

Taha stuffed one more leaf in his mouth. "Now I'm ready, too."

chapter 13

COLONEL CHARLES GORDON was a man of fixed habits. He didn't like interruptions during his sack time, and the phone call he'd received had broken his sleep after he'd just finished eight hours' duty on the night shift in the camp's UAV ground control station. But he owed the caller a favor—a big favor, he had to admit—and Charles Gordon was meticulous about paying his debts.

He emerged from his quarters into daylight. The usual headache glare of the sun, and the usual weather. Hot, damnably hot, and humid, with a lifeless drift of scorched salt air from the Gulf of Tadjoura.

Get it done, get it over with, then get some more sleep. He strode purposefully across the camp, the crunch of gravel under his boots.

He passed rows of neatly arrayed tents, protected by sandbags and wire and, in the distance, a series of watchtowers. All of this was manned by the Third Marine Expeditionary Force.

They provided the security for the hush-hush part of the base, a five-thousand-foot runway and a ground control station for the CIA's Unmanned Aerial Vehicle program. Colonel Gordon was one of six US Air Force officers seconded to the CIA's Djibouti program in this one-time French Foreign Legion outpost.

A real hell-hole, this spot, and the funny thing was that he'd volunteered for the posting. He'd flown F-16s for over fifte years—Kosovo, Iraq, Afghanistan—but what with getting married and eventually having two kids, he'd accepted training as a drone pilot so he could be based Stateside, be a family man.

Hester had appreciated that. "This way we get to see more of you." She'd loved the setup. "You commute to work every day. We don't have to worry about you getting killed. And you still get to fly."

Sort of. For three years he'd served at Creech Air Force Base in Nevada, jockeying a chair on the ground, operating the controls on a drone that did its business six thousand miles away. He'd step off the base after work, drive home past all the Burger Kings and Wal-Marts and people who had no clue what he did.

So when the opening came for a posting in Djibouti, he'd talked Hester into letting him go. "Ninety days, that's all. Still just as safe as Stateside. But this way I can feel closer to the action."

Six weeks into the posting, and he sure understood why the assignments were limited to ninety days. Killer heat, nothing to see, nothing to do. He was ready to be home with Hester and the kids again. Ready for suburbia and Stateside. No more complaints from him ever again.

Funny thing about family: if it weren't for family he'd never have owed this caller a favor, which meant he'd still be asleep instead of hurrying across the camp in this midday furnace-blast heat.

It was on account of family—he relived the memory as he made his way to the UAV ground control hut—that he'd accepted Lieutenant Hickman's invitation four weeks ago to join him on a forty-eight-hour sightseeing leave in Cairo.

A flat *no* had been his initial response.

"Sir, don't you want some excitement? See Egypt in the middle of a revolution?" Hickman thought of himself as a daredevil.

Again a curt *no*. Then he'd remembered: Hester had made him promise to bring home souvenirs for the girls. Djibouti offered little in that line. So he'd changed his mind.

Being a man of fixed purpose, Colonel Gordon had told the cabbie at Cairo's airport to take him straight to wherever was the city's best emporium for souvenirs.

Which had landed him in the middle of Khan el-Khaleeli: a blaring tourist-souk of crowded alleys filled with vendors thrusting junk in his face. He'd stumbled around in there, disoriented, not speaking a word of the language, and within five minutes a knot of teens had spotted him as a mark.

The ringleader—some punk in pimples and sunglasses—had stepped in his way. A sudden collision—Gordon was knocked off balance—a profusion of apologies, and they hurried away up some alley.

Not ten seconds later he'd felt for his wallet—cash, credit cards, military ID, photos of Hester and the girls: gone.

"Hey." Too late.

Or would have been, if not for some guy who showed up just then at the other end of the alley. Skinny fellow, not very tall, not the type you'd expect to step into a crisis.

But as the punks ran past him, this skinny fellow stuck out a foot, gave a well-timed shove, and sent the pimply ringleader into a table of trinkets. Then he stooped over the kid, extended his hand—for a second Gordon thought the stranger was helping the kid to his feet—and then suddenly caught the punk's wrist and twisted his arm until the kid yelped. The stranger said something—Gordon couldn't catch what—and the punk sullenly reached into a pocket.

"Keep this somewhere safe." The stranger handed Gordon back his wallet.

Gordon responded with something he did seldom. He smiled, made himself be sociable. "Can I buy you a drink or something?"

In fact the stranger had given him a day-long tour of the city. Souvenir shopping ("Not here. Just touristy stuff here. Let's head over to Bab Zuweila"). The Pyramids and Sphinx. The Citadel and the Muqattam Hills.

Over drinks at the Ramses Hilton the stranger had handed him his card. *Richard Greyling Atlas. Antiquities Acquisition Consultant.*

"Antiquities acquisition. That must get dicey in this part of the world, with revolutions and so on."

"It does get ticklish." This Atlas had stories. Snaking through tombs a hundred feet underground. Stowing away on a Nile camel-transport ferry to smuggle stolen treasures out of the country. Side-stepping guards at the Egyptian-Sudanese border.

Charles Gordon, not usually given to words, had shaken his head in admiration. "You get into some crazy things."

"Crazy life. Gets addictive. Gotta stop sometime."

Gordon had listened, had remembered his own crazy days, F-16 days, back when he'd flown—really flown, none of this ground-based remote-control stuff—with a rack of Maverick air-to-ground missiles under his wings, launching strike after strike, blowing Iraqi radar sites and gun emplacements to hell. Good flying. Good memories.

"Tell you what." Gordon had been feeling grateful. "You ever get into trouble in this part of the world and you need an eye in the sky, you give me a call."

Then he'd done something he shouldn't have; he mentioned his UAV work and gave this Atlas fellow his card.

Shouldn't have, obviously; breach of security. But he'd liked the guy and had a strong hunch this fellow might be needing help in the near future.

And apparently that near future was now.

He reached the ground control hut. Lance Corporal Hewitt was the duty clerk. "Sir?" He knew Gordon wasn't due on deck until tonight.

"Carry on, Corporal."

"Yes, sir."

The hut's dark air-conditioned interior was a relief after the hot sun-glare outside. Dim green light glowed from a row of computer screens. Gordon slid into the familiar cushioned pilot's seat and nodded to Lieutenant Hickman, who as sensor operator was responsible for camera work on all UAVs aloft.

"Lieutenant, if memory serves we have a MQ-1B stationed currently over Sanaa."

"Yes, sir."

"Call up the view for me, and let's see what we have."

"Yes, sir."

Lieutenant Hickman typed in the coordinates. He was the chatty sort. "Sir, maybe you can help me resolve a little dispute I've been having with the lance corporal."

"Possibly."

Hickman said he'd been complaining to Lance Corporal Hewitt about there being no sites worth seeing in Djibouti and how everything looked all the same—"wasteland, like the surface of the moon, sir"—but Hewitt claimed they should grab a Humvee and drive out to some place called Lac Abbé. "Big volcanic vents, with steam coming out of the ground."

"Lieutenant, are we going to get a visual on Sanaa?"

"Coming right up, sir." He assured his superior it would take just one second.

"Anyway, sir, Lance Corporal Hewitt claims this Lac Abbé is where they filmed *Planet of the Apes*. You know, with Charlton Heston. I told him, no way they got Charlton Heston to come out to this God-forsaken place. I told him, 'Man, you are shitting me.'"

"Lieutenant, he is not shitting you. They really did film *Planet of the Apes* out there."

"Hey, that's great, sir. Maybe I should go see it."

"Maybe you should. Now let's focus on Sanaa."

"Yes, sir."

chapter 14

Shibam highway, northwest of Sanaa
Central Highlands, Yemen

'Highway' was how Taha Shu'ayb had described the road from Sanaa. Heading to a little town called Thilla, he'd said. Thilla would be the starting point of their search. No more than fifty or sixty kilometers from the capital. An easy drive.

Ricky Atlas guessed *easy* would be an over-optimistic assessment. He was right.

The first few miles out of Sanaa, the road was paved, but after that, the highway became a gravelly track, with gouges in the earth and scorched hulks of vehicles upended in the dirt.

"Fighting," shouted Taha over his shoulder. Steering a bucking, jolting motorbike didn't keep the man from chatter. "Improvised explosive devices. Mines. We must be careful."

"By all means," Ricky shouted back through his helmet.

The other thing slowing their drive: occasional checkpoints.

The first ones were manned by green-uniformed government troops. An hour north of the capital, the dress was more ragtag. Rebels, explained Taha. Zaydi separatists, hoping to form their own emirate up by the Saudi border.

Best to say nothing, he suggested, as he slowed the motorbike for another makeshift barrier of oil drums blocking the road.

Ricky needed no urging. He kept the visor of his helmet down and was glad the visor was of smoke-opaque plastic.

But none of the guards looked closely. Taha offered each a fistful of riyals and a packet of Marlboros—"all billable to the Corporation," he laughed after each stop—and then they were waved through.

Again and again as they drove, Ricky twisted about in his seat to see if they were being followed. No sign of pursuit.

I thought sure that Bush Beard character in front of the Felix was a spotter. This feels too easy. I've never done a job yet that's gone smooth.

He told himself to relax, save his strength, concentrate on not getting jounced off the bike on the next bump in the road.

The road climbed steeply, high into the bare rocky hills of the central highlands. Three hours brought them to a stony outcropping of houses. Atop a ridge crouched what looked to be the weathered granite remains of a fort.

"Thilla." Taha switched off the engine. "We walk from here."

Worn stone stairs climbed the ridge. Flanking the steep path was a wall of piled boulders. Behind the wall rose tall houses with barred doors and closed wooden shutters. No sound, save a stuttered tinkling of bells from above. No human voices save their own.

"The war has come," explained Taha. "Everyone has fled."

"Or almost everyone," he laughed, pointing up the stairs. Descending the steps came a dozen goats, the bells around their necks explaining the sound Ricky had heard. The goats hesitated and then rushed in a bleating mass down the hill.

"We, too, should hurry," suggested Taha. "I don't think it's safe here."

Ricky breathed hard—the ten-thousand-foot altitude was demanding, and Taha was taking the stairs two at a time—but he gasped out the question that he'd been pondering on the back of the bike. "Are you sure this is the best place to start looking for the missing half of the wand?"

Quite sure, Taha assured him, because of a story told him by his grandfather. "When he was a boy, many years ago—this would have been soon after the first European war—my grandfather saw a group of foreigners arrive. English, they were. They had come from Egypt. They, too, said they sought something."

Ricky gasped another question as he climbed the stairs beside Taha. "Did they say what they wanted?"

"Oh yes. A wand. Just as you seek."

The English spent weeks, he said, searching the whole vicinity. Jebel Haraz. The towns of Kawkaban, Taweela, and Mahweet. Wadi Dahr, Hababah, and Shibam.

"Until, eventually, they reached the foot of Thilla, and the stairs that you and I are climbing right now. But they weren't allowed to ascend."

"Why not?"

A civil war raged then, explained Taha, just as one raged now. "Villagers shot at them and accused them of being foreign spies, agents of the Imam, agents of the government."

The English tried to explain they weren't spies, just explorers, hoping to discover something that had been lost for ages. Something for which they would pay, and pay well, should they ever find it.

Something that might possibly be atop the summit of Thilla. A summit known to the local population as *Jebel al-ghurab*: Crow Mountain.

But the villagers refused. And then a messenger arrived from Sanaa with word for the English. This word was enough to make the English depart at once and never return.

"Did your grandfather ever learn what had been in that message?" They were almost at the summit now.

"Yes. The patron of the English, a very wealthy man, had suddenly died. In Cairo. Rumors attended the news: Allah had struck this wealthy man as punishment for trying to steal treasure from our highlands."

Ricky paused on the stairs. *Lord Carnarvon, dead of an insect bite in April 1923. Or slain by Tut's curse. Or punished by Allah for seeking the missing half of the wand. Take your pick.*

Howard Carter must've talked his old friend into financing the Yemeni venture. But with Carnarvon's death the financial backing dried up and all bets were off.

And Carter became so busy, cataloguing the finds from Tut's tomb, he would never have had time to come search in Yemen again.

But one thing is sure, Ricky told himself as he gathered his strength for the last part of the climb: *if Carnarvon and Carter, in the middle of excavating Tutankhamen's tomb, had been willing to spend time and money on a scouting expedition out here, then there's more to Solomon's wand than Mustafa Hamdi and his Corporation let on. This thing might not be just some antique collector's trinket. The question is: what is it then?*

"Come." Taha had sprinted ahead up the steps. "We are almost there."

From the summit, Ricky could see how this hill had acquired its name. Crows everywhere. Wheeling overhead. Stooping to peck weeds from the ground. Cawing croaked warnings to each other at sight of the two humans. Perching on the shattered walls of the fort.

Min ayyam al-atrak, explained Taha with a nod at the fort. "From the time of the Turks."

"Crow Mountain," enthused Ricky. "I can see why the hieroglyphic text called it that. But what about the next part, the 'Cave of the Sunburst'?"

"Come," invited Taha, taking him by the arm. "I think I know what's meant by that name."

So fixed were the two on their goal that it occurred to neither to step back to the stairs and look down. If they had, they might have noticed three vehicles approaching along the dirt track leading to Thilla. Three vehicles driving as if the occupants were in a great hurry. Three vehicles that charged in a whirl of dust and gravel and then thudded to a stop at the base of the stairs.

chapter 15

Thilla, Central Highlands
Northwest of Sanaa, Yemen

IN PARADISE, ACCORDING to the Holy Book, there is to be no quarreling among the Blessed as they recline on silk couches.

In that case, mused 'Adnan al-Harithi as he recalled these Koran verses, today he was clearly still a long way from heaven.

Obaid Tantaawi and Hasan Zubayr were at it again. The Egyptian claimed his tactics should take precedence because he was the deputy of Waheed Shafeeq, who in turn represented powerful interests in Cairo—"far more powerful than you've ever encountered here in your wasteland."

Hasan pointed out he was the deputy of 'Adnan the Afghan, seated right here beside them in the cab of this truck. "And he is the assistant leader of Ansar al-Din, which has sworn allegiance to al-Qaeda in the Arabian Peninsula. And al-Qaeda is the real power here, not some outsiders from Cairo we've never heard of before."

"May I have a bit of peace in here?" 'Adnan's scowl silenced them, or almost.

Hasan muttered he still thought the best thing was to storm up the stairs now and kill the American before he could get away. Obaid fumed they should wait till the foreigner descended and then kill him right here.

"I said I wanted silence." Another scowl. "Now. This is what we'll do."

The three vehicles were to park a quarter-mile away in an inconspicuous spot. "Hasan, you will stay here and keep watch over that thing." He pointed to the red Kawasaki, propped upright by the wall.

Hasan swelled with pride at being chosen for the task.

"You will stay out of sight," 'Adnan instructed him, "until the two of them return, the American and his helper. Do not confront them, do you understand? No violence."

Hasan didn't like this but he nodded agreement.

"Watch to see if they're carrying the object they're seeking. Then phone us, and we'll come and seize them. At that point we'll confiscate the treasure, whatever it is, and then we'll dispose of the prisoners."

"And how will that be done?" Eagerness shone in Hasan's voice.

"If you and brother Obaid here refrain from squabbling, you may both shoot the American."

"Both?" The rivals muttered their disappointment. They each wanted exclusive bragging rights.

"But if I hear any more of your feuding," he added severely, "then I'll shoot him myself."

At that they subsided.

"Besides," he concluded, "this Richard Greyling Atlas may not be so easy to kill. I've heard him described as wily and cunning."

"I too am wily and cunning," declared Obaid with pride.

"As am I," countered Hasan.

Another frown silenced them again. "Now," announced 'Adnan, "let's get these vehicles out of sight."

chapter 16

Above Thilla
Central Highlands, Yemen

THE MQ-1B PREDATOR circled at an altitude of fifteen thousand feet. Modest in length—twenty-seven feet from nose to tail—its propeller-driven frame made only a slight buzzing, no more than the noise of a small Beechcraft or Cessna. Thus it was hard to detect from the ground.

Had humans been aboard, they would have had no view; the drone lacked a glassed-in cockpit.

Windowless and eyeless, this Predator—but not unseeing. Its cameras and rangefinder swept the earth below.

chapter 17

Camp Lemonier, Djibouti
Horn of Africa
"I THINK WE'VE got something, sir." Lieutenant Hickman tapped his screen.

"All right, son. Let's have a look." At Colonel Gordon's nod, Hickman enlarged a frame on the display.

"Three technicals, sir. Toyota Hilux. Usual armament. Tripod-mounted fifty-cal in the back."

The young officer studied the frame. "I'm counting twenty-one, make that twenty-two potential unfriendlies, not counting whoever's still sitting inside the trucks. Should we request permission to engage?"

"Ah, let's not be hasty, Lieutenant." Gordon stood beside him and stooped over the display. "We need a bit more information. Do you think you can get that camera of yours to zoom in on the license plates of those Toyotas?"

"Not a problem, sir."

As Hickman toggled the instrumentation, Gordon called to the duty clerk. "Would you ask Mister Wilcox to step in here?"

"Yes, sir." Lance Corporal Hewitt picked up a phone.

"What do you have today, Colonel?" Alastair Wilcox was the Agency's representative and chief intelligence analyst in Djibouti.

Gordon sketched the situation, omitting any reference to Richard Greyling Atlas. *No need to tell the CIA I'm using government property to do some civilian a personal favor.* "We've got an MQ-1B over the Central Highlands that's just picked up the license plates on three technicals with heavy weaponry. Thought you might like a look."

"That I would." The analyst scanned the read-out.

"This one." Wilcox picked one of the three. "Registered to a high-value target. 'Adnan al-Harithi. Also called Afghani. Member of a local al-Qaeda affiliate. He's got a long history."

Implicated in the Nairobi embassy bombing in '98. Involved in the attack on the USS Cole, October 2000, while it was docked in the port of Aden. More recently identified as a colleague of the late Anwar al-Awlaki and a plotter in the attempted aircraft terror attack over Detroit in December '09.

"Permission to light 'im up?"

"Hold on." The CIA analyst scratched his chin. "The missiles on that Predator cost our taxpayers sixty-eight thousand dollars apiece. We want to make sure we get maximum yield from each one." He smiled grimly. "More to the point, Langley's going to want positive ID on our target before we engage."

He turned to Hickman. "Think you could get me facial close-ups on that crew down there? I'll recognize our friend if we see him."

"Yes, sir." Hickman adjusted the camera's instrumentation again.

Ten minutes' patient scanning yielded a grunt from the analyst. "Nope. Twenty-two faces in that crowd. Harithi's not one of 'em."

"Sir, he could be one of the men seated inside the trucks. The video feed will give us a good look if they step outside."

"No problem. We can wait. We've got plenty of time." Wilcox pulled up a chair and sat.

The only problem, worried Gordon, *is that Richard Atlas may not have plenty of time.* Aloud he said, "We've got a confirmation on the license plate. Isn't that enough for authorization to engage?"

"Wish it were, my friend." The analyst grimaced. "Nowadays the Agency gets so much flak for our drone attacks that all field operatives are required to supply absolute ID confirmation wherever possible."

He pointed to the screen. "Let's give it a few minutes. They don't look like they're going anywhere." He stretched, yawned. "Hell, we've got all day."

Yes, Gordon wanted to say, *but Richard Atlas doesn't have all day.* He excused himself and said he had to step outside for a quick phone call.

He stood outdoors in the heat and tapped in a number. *Hope Atlas picks this up.*

chapter 18

Summit of Crow Mountain, Thilla
Central Highlands, Yemen

"THIS," ANNOUNCED TAHA Shu'ayb, "must be the place."

He and Ricky Atlas stood before a massive outcropping of rock, some fifteen feet high, atop Crow Mountain.

"But I'm looking for a cave, remember?" Ricky cast a skeptical gaze on the rock. "The Cave of the Sunburst, it's called in the text."

"Come over here. Come." Taha pointed to the far side of the formation. He clambered onto the rock, scrambled up. "Look."

Atop the pinnacle was a hole some twelve inches in diameter. Ricky crouched over it. "Say." He bent closer. "This is a carving. The work looks ancient."

He recognized the pattern: rays emanating from a disk. The Aten, the insignia of the heretic Akhenaten and his young son Tutankhamen.

"*Shu'a'at al-shams,*" grinned Taha, looking pleased: *the Sunburst.*

"You're right." Ricky grinned back.

Still crouched atop the rock, he gazed eagerly about. "But does that mean we're sitting on a cave? Is there an entrance?"

"Yes, but a secret one. Few people know of it." Taha said he'd found the entrance when playing on the summit as a child. "Here."

"I don't see anything."

"You must look more closely." Taha gestured at what seemed to be no more than a projecting overhang in the formation, some six feet below the pinnacle.

"I still don't see anything."

Taha told him to run his hand along the underside of the projection. "There."

Then Ricky felt it: an opening, obscured by the shadow cast by the overhang. He lowered his face to the opening, felt along the rim. The dark mouth exhaled a draft of cool moist air. "I think I can just squeeze in."

"Good that you're not large," laughed his guide. "Come. We can both fit. I've done this many times."

Ricky eased himself through the opening, found himself standing on a stone step. Dim light from the aperture overhead showed him stairs that descended into the mountain.

"Follow me," Taha invited him. "But be careful. The steps are steep, and very worn."

Down, down, the stairs spiraled. Ricky counted thirty-six steps. Sunlight from the Aten-aperture above them followed them all the way.

"What's that noise?" Ricky paused on the stairs.

"Listen."

A gurgle and the sound of a rushing flow: water.

At the base of the stairs was a carved lip of rock and beyond it a pool. Sunlight from the Aten above them danced on the water's surface.

"The Cave of the Sunburst," breathed Ricky. "Just as described in the text. This has got to be the place."

Crouching, he thrust his hand into the pool. The water, intensely cold, pulsed in a flow against his fingers. "I can feel a current of some kind."

"There's a river or a stream somewhere in Crow Mountain," said Taha. "My grandfather says the Turks used this place as a cistern when they held this country centuries ago. But they didn't build these stairs. The carvings feel much older."

"To judge from the sun-disk up there, I'd guess all this is pharaonic work," murmured Ricky, more to himself than to Taha. "I wasn't aware the ancient Egyptians ever ventured to Yemen. But then there's a whole lot we still don't know about Egypt."

He looked about the cave—the hewn walls, the stairs, the pool. No sign of any wand.

This has got to be the place, he thought. *'Northern hills of the Deshret, atop Crow Mountain, in the Cave of the Sunburst,' just as described in the hieroglyphic text on the finial I heisted from the Egyptian Museum.*

He stood, paced about the cave, ran his hands along the walls. "Nothing."

"I'm afraid the place is empty," sympathized Taha. "I'd know if the Turks or anyone else had ever left treasure here. I was here often enough when I was small."

Ricky's cellphone rang in his pocket. *Damn.* He was in no mood for distractions.

Charles Gordon's voice. But faint; what came through was mostly static: "…Urgent…out…hurry…"

"Sorry, Colonel. I'm sort of in the heart of a mountain at the moment. Guess it's not the best place for cellphone reception."

He wanted Gordon to hang up, wanted to get back to his problem, wanted the wand. But Gordon kept saying something.

"Sorry, Colonel. Can't hear you. Transmission's breaking up. Can I call you back?" Click.

There. Now he could think. He stared absently down at the cistern, then suddenly clapped a hand to his head.

"Taha, I'm an idiot. I'd forgotten the rest of the inscription: *in the Nile under the stone!*"

He threw himself flat on his belly, rolled up a sleeve, thrust his arm shoulder-deep into the water. His fingers probed the pool's submerged rim.

Nothing.

"It's got to be in there. Got to be." He sprang up, tossed his knapsack aside, stripped off his jacket and shirt and shoes.

"That's mountain water," protested his guide. "Too cold to swim in. I know. I tried as a child."

The American ignored him, gulped in several deep breaths, jumped in feet-first.

Whew. Taha's right about one thing. Water's plenty cold. Too cold for swimming.

Deeper than he'd thought, this cistern. He sank a dozen feet before his feet touched bottom. His toes felt stone. He crouched and kicked upward.

He treaded water, keeping his head beneath the surface, rotating and scanning the pool's subsurface circumference.

Even here, he saw, radiance penetrated from the sun-disk aperture far overhead. By its light he saw the closely fitted stones that made up the rim of the pool. But no sign of any artifact, of any wand.

Uh-oh: running out of breath.

He kicked to the surface, gulped air. Taha, an anxious look on his face, cried "*Kullu tamaam*—Everything okay?"

Well yeah, he wanted to say, *aside from freezing and half-drowning and not being able to find the freaking wand and finish this freaking job, everything's great.* But he just nodded, spat water, gulped more air.

Too cold to stay in here much longer.

One more try. He ducked his head, let himself sink six feet, swam to the rim and touched the inner part of the perimeter wall.

His fingers felt their way along the worn stone, hoping for a gap, a hiding place, an unseen place of concealment.

Nope. Nothing. Nothing. Nothing.

Fingers numb. Head hurting from the lack of air. *Gotta quit. Wait.*

He backed up, felt again for the spot his fingers had brushed.

An opening of some kind in the stone. Plenty big.

Heedless of what might be within, he thrust in his arm.

Touched something, something deep within the crevice.

He tugged, and it came free.

He withdrew his arm, clutched the thing, kicked hard for the surface.

He gasped, spat water. *God, that air feels good.* Taha pulled him clear of the pool.

"What did you find?"

"This!" Dripping wet, cold, and shivering: none of that kept the triumph out of Ricky Atlas's voice.

What he thrust forth for Taha's inspection was a hollow tube, some three feet long.

Made of some kind of precious metal, this tube. But translucent. The length of it glowed in the sunlight from the Aten overhead. The light picked out what was carved along the length of the tube: hieroglyphs, cartouches, each etched in gold.

'Asaayat Suleiman, breathed Taha: King Solomon's Wand.

Then he saw how the American shivered. "Come, my friend. Let's get you out of here." He scooped up Ricky's knapsack and clothes and led the dripping explorer up the stairs at a run.

Back out into daylight. Ricky grabbed a towel from his bag and dried himself as best he could. "Oof, that sun feels good."

Hair still wet, he paused to admire the wand again. Towel draped over one shoulder, he stooped to pluck a dictionary. *Maybe I could start by deciphering the names in the cartouches...*

"Mister Ricky"—a worried tug on his arm from Taha. "Maybe we should get away from here first."

"Yeah, yeah. Just a minute."

The phone again. This time the signal came through loud and clear.

"Yes, Colonel?"

"I've been trying to reach you, Mister Atlas. You've got three truckloads of angry militants down below. All waiting for you. I suggest you haul ass."

"Oh."

Taha plucked the dictionary from his hands. "Time to go, Mister Ricky."

chapter 19

Village of Thilla, Base of Crow Mountain
Central Highlands, Yemen

WILY AND CUNNING, was how 'Adnan had described the American. Yet here he came, he and his Yemeni stooge, trotting down the village steps as if they owned the whole town.

Granted, the Yemeni at least turned his head from side to side as if expecting trouble. But Hasan Zubayr had to marvel at the foreigner. He jabbered loudly and excitedly, clearly unaware that even now one of the Ansar al-Din, elite mujahideen in the struggle to bring shari'ah to the nation, lay concealed behind a rock, barely ten yards from the red motorbike.

In one hand the American held a tattered tweed coat; in the other, a cylinder that sparkled in the sun. Still jabbering, the fool, as if engaged in celebration.

Wily and cunning, this Atlas? Say rather: *wonderfully clueless.* He wished 'Adnan were here now, to see how artfully Hasan had concealed himself, how well positioned he was to triumph over the kafir.

He knew his superior had told him to do no more than spy and give word. But how tempting was this target!

He felt the butt of the Kalashnikov slung across his back and recalled the words of an ancient sermon, a famous warning delivered by al-Hajjaj ibn Yusuf, emir of Kufa, to a surly and insubordinate mob: *I see heads before me ripe for the harvest, ready for slaughter.*

Something like that; not the exact words, but certainly inspirational. And here before him—before Hasan Zubayr, warrior of God—were likewise heads ripe for plucking: a kafir and a kafir's puppet.

Nonetheless 'Adnan had strictly adjured him: no violence. Watch and give word; nothing more. Hasan was supposed to share the killing with that Egyptian Obaid, the show-off with the prayer callus on his forehead.

But suppose the infidels got away? Already they were almost at the red motorcycle. Their escape would bring shame to the Ansar al-Din. 'Adnan wouldn't want that.

That's it. He'd tell 'Adnan he'd been forced to shoot, that the kafirs had seen him and rushed him and made him defend himself.

Yes. Carefully he unslung his weapon, lifted himself up. *Must be careful not to hit the cylinder, whatever it is. 'Adnan wants it unharmed.*

He raised the assault rifle, sighted it on Atlas's chest. *That stupid Egyptian will be jealous.* The thought made him smile.

chapter 20

Village of Thilla, Base of Crow Mountain
Central Highlands, Yemen

"THERE," MURMURED TAHA, as they descended the stairs. "Just beyond my bike, behind those rocks. Did you see something move?"

"Yes," replied Ricky Atlas in an equally low voice. "I think we've got company."

"The best thing," suggested his guide, "is to pretend we see nothing. Keep up that loud noise of yours."

Ricky nattered on. "Hey. Nobody here," he boomed. "Coast is clear, and I'm ready to party."

"A Kalashnikov," whispered Taha.

Ricky knew that weapon's magazine held thirty rounds. At this range, a burst couldn't miss.

One advantage they held, and one only: whoever was hiding behind those rocks must want the wand intact and wouldn't want to risk damaging the thing with gunfire.

Casually he stepped in front of Taha, screening the guide's body with his own; at the same time he waved the three-foot artifact in front of himself as if he were toying with a baton.

Best I can do, he thought, and he felt his heart race and his throat go tight. This is gonna be close.

There: they'd reached the foot of the village stairs. Still no gunfire.

Ten yards away, those concealing rocks; must find a way to cover that distance.

Only one chance. Casually, turning to chatter at Taha as he sauntered, he advanced towards the rocks. He still waved the wand, held the tweed coat in his other hand.

My old jacket, he thought; *it's always brought me luck.* He swallowed hard and prayed it'd bring luck again.

"*Qif inta*: You. Stop right there!" A figure reared up before him. Young, from the look of him, close-cropped beard, long curling black hair. Wearing a green army vest, cast-off military issue, over a flowing white robe.

Nervous, too. *Qif*, he shouted again. He shifted his Kalashnikov from Ricky to Taha, who'd stepped out slightly from behind the American.

All the distraction I'm gonna get, decided Ricky.

He hurled his coat at the gunman's face.

Briefly blinded, the man yelped and stepped back. Ricky and Taha dived low; the *mujahid* staggered and shot high.

Beside Ricky where he crouched: a stone the size of his fist.

The gunman tore the tweed coat from his face just as the American flung the stone.

Right between the eyes. The gunman hit the ground hard.

"Lights out," announced Ricky.

He let out a great sigh, began to feel trembly and wobbly, wanted to sit down, but knew this wasn't the time to let down his guard.

Weakly he scooped his jacket from the ground. *Still my lucky coat.*

"Do you mind," inquired Taha politely, "if I keep the rifle? Russian. For my collection."

"Be my guest."

"And now"—Taha slung the weapon over his shoulder—"we should go, before he awakes or anyone else arrives."

"Which way should we head?"

Taha studied the ground. "See these tracks? Three vehicles. Trucks. They came from Sanaa."

He announced they'd best head north. "In fact"—he lifted his head—"I hear motors now. I fear someone's coming."

He sprang to the bike. "Come, Mister Ricky."

Feeling more wobbly than ever, and thirsty, too. Man I'd love to sit down.

"Mister Ricky?"

"I'm with you, friend." He swung a leg over the back of the Kawasaki, positioned his feet on the foot-pegs, clutched the wand to his chest. A tap to Taha's shoulder—"All set"—and his guide gunned the bike into life.

chapter 21

Wadi Sirhan
South of Thilla
Central Highlands, Yemen

THE TROUBLE WITH these Yemenis, decided Obaid Tantaawi, was that they were insufficiently pious.

Case in point: their music. From a cassette player propped atop the dashboard blared some lascivious pop number. The music was loud enough to be heard by the occupants of all three trucks, which idled in a sun-scorched wadi not far from their target village.

Didn't they know that the Prophet himself had frowned on displays of frivolity? And if this hip-writhing melody didn't qualify as frivolous, then everything in this world was permissible.

The driver chewed *qat* and pounded his steering wheel in time to the rhythm. Obaid frowned disapproval but, wedged in as he was between the driver and 'Adnan the Afghan, he felt it wise to say nothing.

'Adnan had apparently caught his frown. "Don't you like Husain Muhibb?"

"Who?"

"The singer. The music you've been listening to."

Obaid wanted to protest. *I've been doing my best <u>not</u> to listen*, he almost said. But prudence prevailed. *Remember*, his Egyptian boss had warned him, *you are a guest. Do not argue with your Yemeni superiors.*

'Adnan seemed in a happy mood. Obaid guessed it was because they were about to recover the artifact and kill some kafirs and then have a nice dinner back in Sanaa's Old City.

'Adnan and the driver were both singing along with this Husain Muhibb, something about lovely gazelles, lovely to behold, with lovely limbs. Or nonsense to that effect.

The ring of a phone in 'Adnan's pocket. The leader smiled as he responded. "Yes?" Clearly he was expecting good news.

"What? You did what?" 'Adnan snapped the phone shut, bellowed to his driver, stuck his head out the window and shouted at the idlers in the other trucks. *Yalla! Ta'allu! Bi-sur'ah!* The trucks roared out of the wadi, their tires spinning gusts of dirt as each vehicle lurched onto the road.

Another command from 'Adnan, and the gunners behind the cab hastily spat out their *qat* chaws and fed an ammunition belt into the heavy machine-gun mounted on the flatbed.

Suddenly Obaid glimpsed 'Adnan as he must have been in his old Afghan days: not dreaming over gazelles, but yelling in holy rage as he led warriors against ungodly Soviets.

Within minutes they were back at Thilla. No sign of the kafirs; nor of the red motorcycle, for that matter. Nothing but that arrogant fool Hasan Zubayr, who stood by the side of the road rubbing his head and looking humbled.

The lead truck slowed. 'Adnan opened the door and jumped to the ground.

Hasan kept rubbing his head as if hoping for sympathy.

His superior scanned the ground, stooped and gathered a fistful of brass casings. From the cab Obaid heard him say to Hasan, "You shot at them, didn't you? You wanted the credit all to yourself."

Hasan tried to explain that wasn't really how it'd happened. His explanation was cut short by a slap to the mouth.

"And where's your rifle?"

Miserably Hasan conceded it must have been taken by the American kafir.

Obaid enjoyed the spectacle. *Allah, thank you for humiliating my rival.*

Swiftly 'Adnan turned and scanned the dirt road.

"There," called Obaid from the truck. "Tire marks. A motorcycle. They must've headed north."

'Adnan nodded curtly, sprang back into the cab with the grace of a much younger man. *Ta'alla,* he urged the driver.

"Wait for me!" A plaintive cry from Hasan, who stepped unsteadily forward.

"Men ride," proclaimed 'Adnan from the cab. "Boys walk. Follow our dust."

Obaid turned in his seat to enjoy an additional pleasure: the sight of his rival limping up the road behind them. *Thank you, God. Thank you.*

chapter 22

"SIR." THE EXCITEMENT in Lieutenant Hickman's voice was audible. "I've got motion again on those three vehicles."

"Confirmation yet on our high-value target?" Charles Gordon peered at the screen.

"Not yet, sir. All I can confirm is that they're resuming their trajectory north. Back towards coordinates Victor Tango seven-three-one-five."

"Ah, stay on it, son."

"Yes, sir."

Gordon glanced over at Alastair Wilcox. Legs stretched out, the CIA liaison man reclined at ease in his chair, gazing at the screen as if relaxing over Sunday afternoon football.

Of course he doesn't know the life of Richard Greyling Atlas is riding on this. Gordon turned back to Hickman, started to say something, told himself to be patient.

"Sir. The technicals have come to a stop. Sir, the passenger-side door on the lead Hilux is opening."

Alastair Wilcox sprang from his chair so fast he bumped shoulders with Charles Gordon. The two men laughed and flanked the young lieutenant. All three bent their heads over the screen.

"There." The CIA man nodded. "The individual who's getting out. Can you get me a close-up on his face?"

"Yes, sir." Hickman adjusted the camera.

The individual who'd emerged from the lead Toyota Hilux stood about for a full two minutes, apparently discussing something with a young man. Then he startled the three observers by slapping the youngster.

"Why's he doing that?" wondered Gordon aloud.

"Not sure. But what's more important is that I recognize him." The analyst's face took on a thoughtful cast. "Bingo. 'Adnan al-Harithi. Wondered when we'd catch up with him again."

"Positive ID?" Gordon didn't want to waste another second.

"Oh, yes. I know his face well. Just missed him in Aden, October 2000. Almost nailed him when we took out Anwar al-Awlaki in 2011. It's him all right."

"Use of lethal force is authorized?" Gordon had already hurried into his pilot's chair and fitted earphones over his head.

"Lethal force is authorized." The CIA man sat back to watch the show.

chapter 23

"CAN THIS THING go any faster?" Ricky Atlas had said this five times in the last five minutes, ever since he'd spotted the Toyota Hiluxes churning up dust clouds behind them.

"Not really." Taha shouted something else over his shoulder. Couldn't make out what he said: plenty of distractions on the back seat, as Ricky tried to grip the wand and keep from being thrown from the bike as it jounced over rut after rut.

Ricky apologized and yelled he'd missed the last part of what Taha had said.

"I said you could pray God for a miracle."

No miracle yet. Instead, from behind them, a sharp punch to the air: *taa-ta-ta-ta-tat. Taa-ta-ta-la-tat.*

He leaned forward and shouted. "They're shooting at us."

Taha nodded, apparently unsurprised. "Fifty-caliber, five-round bursts. For the moment, they're just trying to get our attention."

Just trying to get our attention: Ricky understood. Those goons wanted the wand intact, wanted them to stop and meekly hand over their treasure. But he had a pretty good idea of what would happen to them both once their pursuers had grabbed what they wanted.

Pray for a miracle: good suggestion. Time for heavenly intervention.

Speaking of which. This was a good moment to call in a favor.

The cellphone was in his lucky tweed jacket. Not easy to reach, what with clutching the wand with his right hand and holding on for dear life with his left.

He'd have to risk it. First he'd need to remove the helmet; it was too small for him to fit a phone near his ear.

He wrenched the helmet free and for a second let it dangle.

Taa-ta-ta-ta-tat.

The five-round cluster shot the thing from his hand, burst the helmet like a kick to an overripe orange.

Damn.

There. He fished the phone from his coat.

"Colonel Gordon?"

"Ah, yeah. I was trying to reach you again."

"We could really, really use some help down here." Nicky twisted again in his seat. The lead Hilux was gaining fast.

"Son, get off the road fast."

"Get off the road?"

"Do it now! You're all about to have company."

Taa-ta-ta-ta-tat. Another five-round burst.

Ricky leaned forward, shouted the orders from Gordon.

Taha nodded and told Ricky to hang on. "I'll try to spin us onto the shoulder."

The shoulder in question was an eight-foot-deep ditch by the side of the road.

The last thing Ricky heard was Taha screeching *Pray for a miracle.*

Good advice, he thought, as both wheels left the road.

chapter 24

TRULY A HIGH moment in his life, exulted Obaid Tantaawi.

Accompanying a distinguished holy warrior as he struck a blow for the faith. A warrior who'd doubtless provide him a recommendation for further advancement in the path of jihad.

'Adnan the Afghan had smiled at him in approval, and not five minutes ago had left that stupid Hasan to hoof it on foot and eat their dust. Jihadi life was good.

The only hindrance to his full enjoyment of this moment: the jack-hammering noise level.

He didn't mind the fifty-caliber machine-gun being fired just behind them on the flatbed of the Hilux, the crack of fire and the *chink-chink* of spent casings as they spewed to the floor.

That was part of the pleasure of war, that, and the sight of what happened when a bullet tore the helmet from the hand of the kafir on the bike. He only wished it'd been the American's head. He cared not a fig for seizing worldly treasures intact.

No, the only noise he minded was the pop music still blaring away here inside the cab.

He dared not complain. The driver sang and chewed *qat* and tapped the steering wheel in time while he fought to keep the truck on the road. Even 'Adnan hummed along and moved his right index finger to follow the rhythm.

Hip-writhing. Impiety.

Kafir music. Fifty-caliber bursts. But there was a third sound, too. No one else seemed to notice.

A light buzzing sound. Faint, but getting louder.

A whine like a mosquito, or like a small aircraft, far, far away.

chapter 25

Above Amran Township
Altitude: twelve thousand feet
Central Highlands, Yemen

THE MQ-1B PREDATOR is not a high-velocity aircraft. Its cruising speed averages only some 80 to 90 miles per hour. The Toyota Hilux trucks on the ground were racing along at 75 and if they'd been aware of the drone could have gone much faster.

But each Predator carries a rack of AGM-114 Hellfire missiles. Each missile has a thirteen-inch wingspan and is sixty-four inches in length. The payload consists of a seventeen-kilogram high-explosive anti-tank warhead.

And the Hellfire's speed—supported by a laser-guided homing system—is a brisk Mach 1.3: nine hundred and fifty miles per hour.

The first missile targeted the heavy machine-gun in the lead Hilux. It detonated upon impact with the gun, obliterating armament, metal, and flesh. A tire flew high into the air, bounced, and spun down the road.

The second Toyota slammed to a halt, fishtailing sideways and receiving the force of the third Hilux, which drove straight into the cab on the driver's side. The second Hellfire struck the center of the tangle and blew both trucks apart.

The only survivor: a limping mujahid on foot, his face still stinging from a slap, who cringed from afar as he saw death rain from the sky.

chapter 26

3 kilometers south of Amran Township
Central Highlands, Yemen

"I'M VERY SORRY about your bike, Taha." The motorcycle sprawled in twisted ruin at the bottom of the ditch.

"Don't be, Mister Ricky." The two men—bruised and shaken, but otherwise unhurt—had just helped each other scramble back up onto the road. "I can buy another. The important thing, thank God, is we're still alive. And"—he announced with a smile—"this at least didn't get hurt." He opened his bag of *qat* and plucked a fresh leaf.

Ricky, too, felt grateful. The two of them had been flung clear of the Kawasaki and landed face-down in the ditch.

A good location—seconds later they'd heard a concussive *boom* and a storm of shrapnel from the Hellfire-Hilux blast. Metal bits from the hit had shredded the leaves on an acacia tree just above where Ricky lay.

For a long minute, stunned, he'd lain there. Slowly, slowly, he'd raised his head, spat dirt from his mouth, realized with astonishment he was still alive.

Then came the thought: *the wand. Where is it?*

But it, too, was intact. It lay only inches from his hand, at the foot of the tree.

Not a scratch on it: I don't know what kind of metal this thing is made of, but it's got to be pretty tough stuff.

Now the American and the Yemeni stood by the side of the road. Taha tapped a number on his cellphone. "My cousin, in Amran, lives only a few minutes from here. He'll provide us a ride."

"Super. Then I can get back to Sanaa and give Hamdi and his precious Corporation the wand." His bruises didn't keep Ricky from feeling exultant. "Then I can get paid off and terminate my contract."

"That may not be the only thing to be terminated."

"What do you mean?"

Silence.

Fear suddenly clouded Taha's normally cheerful face.

For a moment the young Yemeni remained silent, eyes downcast, as if struggling with a decision.

Then he looked directly at his companion.

"I like you, Mister Ricky, and I don't want to see you come to harm."

"Thanks, Taha, but I don't understand what…"

The guide raised a hand to prevent further interruption. "Listen. When I received my instructions from your Mustafa Hamdi, I heard him tell someone that once you've turned over the missing piece and he has both halves of Solomon's wand, your usefulness will be concluded."

Taha frowned, shook his head. "Hamdi said he didn't like to leave loose ends. He said he'd give you what he called a 'big, big bonus' by way of goodbye. He laughed when he said it, and his friends in the room laughed along too."

"But the man owes me money! Besides, he wouldn't really go around killing off his own employees, would he?"

"How well do you know this Hamdi? And, what's more important, how much do you know about this Corporation for which he works?"

"Not a lot."

"Then take this advice. If you have some alternative way of exiting Yemen—and I don't mean through Sanaa airport, they'll be watching for you there—you'd better use it."

The whine of an engine approached along the high-desert road from the north. "That will be my cousin. If you want, you can come with us. I'm going to hide for a while in the mountains by the Saudi frontier. With the war going on, no one will be able to find us."

"Give me a second. Let me see first if I can find an alternative exit." He pulled the cellphone from his coat. "Colonel Gordon? Yes, yes, I'm fine. No need to apologize for the close shave. Now, I know I'm asking a lot, but could I possibly request just one more favor?"

The Air Force officer's chuckle came through loud and clear. "Ah, I anticipated you might have a request like that. So I arranged to have a Seahawk from the USS *Stennis* pick you up."

"You did? That's fantastic! How'd you manage that?"

Another chuckle. Gordon sounded pleased with himself. "I just told the good folks on the carrier that a US national was in trouble and in need of an emergency evac. The chopper should be over your coordinates in just about, ah, a minute and a half." Click.

"And here's my cousin now." Taha climbed onto the back of his kinsman's motorbike. "Sure you don't want a lift? We can squeeze another passenger on the back here."

"I'm good. In fact, I think that's my ride now." From overhead came the heavy whir of a combat helicopter.

Ricky thanked Taha and pumped his hand. "But what about this?" He still held the wand.

"Keep it. When you get someplace safe—I mean really safe—give Hamdi a call and say you're ready to negotiate. The wand, in exchange for the money he owes you."

"Speaking of money." Ricky handed his guide a fat wad of crumpled riyals. "To cover the cost of your next bag of *qat*."

Taha turned and grinned a goodbye as the motorcycle sped up the road.

chapter 27

"WILCOX, THANK YOU." Charles Gordon pocketed the phone and pushed his chair away from the UAV display screen. "If you hadn't made that call to Washington, I'd never have been able to persuade Admiral Turner to divert the *Stennis*. It's not every day an aircraft carrier sails two hours away from its predesignated station to launch a chopper in the Gulf of Aden."

"Glad to help. Not every day we get to rescue an American from Yemen." Alastair Wilcox tilted his chair back and stretched his arms at full length. "Especially when it's an American like this Richard Greyling Atlas."

"Wait a minute. You mean you know this individual?"

"It's the Agency's business to track individuals whose activities impinge on the national security of the United States."

"Hang on. I know this Atlas. He collects things. Antiquities. A bit on the shady side, some of his deals, but you can't tell me he's a national security threat."

"I didn't say he is. I said his activities impinge on our national security."

"How so?"

Wilcox rolled his eyes in the direction of Lieutenant Hickman, who still sat nearby, adjusting camera settings on his Predator.

Gordon understood: *this next bit of info will be confidential.* "Ah, Lieutenant."

"Yes, sir?"

"Could you find the lance corporal and ask him to bring us some Cokes?"

"Yes, sir."

A blast of desert-furnace air as the door opened and closed, and then the hut was empty save for the two older men.

"Did this Atlas ever mention to you," began the CIA analyst, "that he was working for someone named Mustafa Hamdi?"

Gordon frowned in thought. "No. No, I don't think so."

"We'd never have heard of Atlas if not for that connection. Mustafa Hamdi is a senior executive for a group called EHC. The Egyptian Heritage Corporation."

"Sounds harmless enough."

"The operative word in that sentence is 'sounds.' The reality may be quite different. They claim they're buying up artifacts to keep Egypt's legacy on Egyptian soil. Well and good. But let me show you something."

Wilcox reached into an attaché case on the floor beside him, extracted a laptop, and opened the computer screen. "This list indicates one of the two major sources of EHC's funding. See these names here? All fifteen of them are prominent members of the Salafist wing of Egypt's Muslim Brotherhood. And now that the Arab Spring and the Lotus Revolution have toppled Hosni Mubarak's government and brought the Brotherhood to power in Egypt, the Salafists have poured even more cash into EHC."

"I don't understand," interrupted Gordon. "Since when have militant Muslim fundamentalists taken a benevolent interest in pagan relics from pharaonic Egypt? Militants usually want to cover up such things, or smash them, the way the Taliban did to those Buddha statues in Afghanistan back in 2001."

"Exactly. It's a puzzle."

"You mentioned that EHC has another source of funding."

"Yes, and that's even more of a puzzle." Wilcox called up another screen on his computer. "The other big contributor to EHC's work—forty-five million dollars in 2013 alone—is the R & D division of Firthland Oil Ventures."

"I don't get it." The Air Force colonel leaned forward to study the screen. "Why would the Research and Development division of a major oil company be so interested in ancient Egyptian artifacts?"

"So far we have no idea. But we do have one small clue." The analyst displayed yet another screen, this one showing a text in Arabic beside the photo of a stern-faced bearded man in robes and prayer-cap.

"This is Hamza Baydawi," explained Wilcox, "a prominent shari'ah scholar and a big backer of the Brotherhood's Salafist wing. Hot-tempered gentleman, given to intemperate comments in public. Lately he's been boasting in his Friday sermons at al-Azhar that soon Egypt will control a new source of energy, a source that will shift the balance of power in the Middle East and throughout the world."

"Energy source? What's he talking about?"

"Not sure. Somebody in Egypt's new revolutionary government must've told him to clam up, because since then Baydawi's gone mum and claimed he'd been misquoted and that he'd only been talking about the power of prayer and so on."

"Yeah. Right. But in that case," and here Gordon watched Wilcox's face closely for his reaction, "are you thinking what I'm thinking?"

"That somehow there's a connection between ancient Egyptian artifacts and possible new energy sources? Pretty far-fetched, if you ask me. But at least the Agency wants to be open to the notion. Especially if Firthland Oil Ventures and the Salafists are suddenly paying attention to EHC."

"Which is why you don't mind asking the Navy to ferry a small-time gypsy-joker tomb thief out of Yemen?"

"When he's carrying an artifact that just might give us a clue to emergent situations affecting the national interests and energy security of the US, I don't mind at all."

"Do you plan to confiscate the piece when Atlas lands on the *Stennis?*"

The CIA man rubbed his chin thoughtfully. "No. No, we're not going to do that. The Agency still doesn't know what we're dealing with yet, whether there's anything substantial to this concern or not. The whole business may prove to be somebody's crackpot fantasy.

"For now, we'll take a hands-off approach. Atlas can go wherever he likes. But," he added firmly, "we plan to track very closely this Solomon's wand, or whatever name it goes by."

The hut door opened again, bringing another wave of oven-hot air. "Sir? A pair of Cokes, for you and Mister Wilcox."

"Thank you, Lieutenant. Just set them right there. Mister Wilcox and I are just finishing up here."

chapter 28

Airborne over the Central Highlands
Yemen

YET AGAIN—FOR the fourth time on today's sortie, by Travis Jordan's reckoning—crew chief Ernest Burkhalter complained he didn't get it.

"So our carrier suddenly gets diverted, two frigging hours' sailing time from our normal station, and then we get sent on a solo flight just to pick up this one civilian? He don't look like no hot shot."

He jerked a thumb at the passenger huddled in the jumpseat at the rear of the craft.

"Maybe he is," came Captain Travis Jordan's philosophical reply, "and maybe he isn't. Either way, we got the same orders. Pick him up, deliver him safely to the *Stennis.*"

"I still don't get it. I mean, you do realize, sir, we're pushing our operational capacity on this mission?"

"Yes, Ernie," came the patient reply, "I most certainly do." The Sikorsky SH-60 Seahawk has a maximum range of some 525 miles. Even after the *Stennis* had been diverted from its normal station in the Gulf of Aden, the chopper still had some 250 miles to fly from the carrier's deck to Yemen's central highlands in search of their evac individual—a distance that left dangerously little margin for error.

"I still say he don't look like much of a prize." Burkhalter craned his neck for another gawk.

Their passenger wasn't gazing out the open door at the barren brown hills that sped by below. Instead he stared at something he cradled on his lap, a tube of some kind. Propped awkwardly on his lap was also a pad of paper on which he seemed to struggle to make notes in the streaming rush of air.

"Hey, Marty." This to Martin Lopez on the M-60. The crew chief bellowed into his headphones over the closed-circuit cockpit channel so their guest couldn't pick up what they said—*as if we need to worry*, Burkhalter said to himself; *this civilian looks to be in a world of his own.* "Don't he look to you like the skinny runty sort? You know, a friggin' bookworm."

Lopez grinned but kept his eyes earthward. As door gunner his job was to stay alert for groundfire.

"I don't know," came the mild objection from Captain Jordan. "This guy's been kicking around Yemen on his own for a while. Looks to me like the sort that can take care of himself. Even if he is a bookworm."

Burkhalter grunted, unimpressed. "And what did he tell you he's doing back there right now?"

"Decrypting an inscription." The pilot couldn't help grin at the confusion that spread across the crew chief's face.

"What's that supposed to mean?"

"You could ask him."

Captain Jordan watched as the crew chief swiveled his head again, perplexity on his face as he studied their guest.

"Nah. Ain't worth the bother. They never are, those runty types."

chapter 29

Over the Gulf of Aden
Territorial waters of the Republic of Yemen
PROBABLY A FIRST in the history of Egyptology, Ricky Atlas told himself with pride: a successful bit of epigraphic translation while airborne in a Navy helicopter somewhere off the coast of Yemen.

He rested his eyes a moment, gazing down at the deep blue waters of the Gulf of Aden. Then he re-read what he'd scribbled on his notepad, a first-draft translation of the hieroglyphs on the metal cylinder he'd found in the 'Nile under the stone':

Khaemwaset, prince no longer, sem-priest no longer, beloved no longer of his father Ramses, says the following:

My father has renamed me 'Hateful and Ill-Omened in Thebes.' So be it.

He has stripped me of all princely titles. So be it.

He has cursed me and ordered me to depart from Upper and Lower Egypt. So be it.

For I do not repent. I do not repent. I do not repent.

I have broken the wand; I have separated the pieces; and I have done this to protect the sekhemu.

Let only the worthy know: this crest is to be replaced in the tomb of the son of the nameless king. The...

This text flowed smoothly into the second half of the inscription, the part on the Egyptian Museum's finial that he'd stolen only two weeks previously (but how long ago that seemed now, in the rush of events in Yemen!):

...other part of the wand is to be deposited in the Cave of the Sun-burst, in the Nile under the stone, atop Crow Mountain, in the northern hills of the Deshret beyond the Sea of the Land of Punt. May the pieces re-main sundered until we are ready once more to revere the sekhemu.

⊰⊱

So, Ricky Atlas, he challenged himself: *what to make of all this?*

He'd solved the riddle as to the location of the missing half of Solomon's wand—only to encounter now a perplexing series of fresh and even more puzzling riddles.

First: the word *sekhemu.* It occurred twice, once on the finial, again on the staff. Clearly important.

Ricky knew *sekhemu*'s literal meaning was "powers" or even "gods/divine powers." "*Revere the gods*"; "*protect the gods*"? But how could humans protect gods?

He felt unsure. Ricky had to acknowledge that the larger meaning eluded him. He'd always been more comfortable with fieldwork than textual studies in research libraries; philology wasn't his strong point.

Second: According to this inscription, the wand had deliberately been broken in two—and not by some latter-day tomb robber, but in pharaonic antiquity. What had been so important—or so dangerous—about this thing that it had been deemed necessary to break it and then bury the pieces in two separate and far-distant hiding places?

Third: The finial—the wand's "crest," as it was called in the inscription—was to be "replaced in the tomb of the son of the nameless king." But who had been the "nameless king" in question, and who had been his son? Another mystery.

Fourth: the reference to Khaemwaset as source of the statement inscribed on the artifacts. This was more cryptic than any other of the wand's puzzles.

Of course, Ricky—like every other Egyptologist in the world—was acquainted with the name. Khaemwaset. Lived in the thirteenth century BC, during the New Kingdom's nineteenth dynasty. Fourth son of Ramses II. A scholarly individual, with a reputation as someone who preferred solitary studies over politics and war. Crown prince of Egypt. Which meant that he in his turn would have become pharaoh, except that he'd predeceased his father.

That much every Egyptologist knew. But Ricky Atlas felt a churning of long-buried feelings—anger, sorrow, loss—as he contemplated the name, feelings that surprised him with their intensity.

Because Khaemwaset had ruined Ricky Atlas's career and pretty much—when Ricky allowed himself to admit it—his whole life, too. And not just Ricky's—Iggy Forsythe's career, and that of Francis Valerian Hammond.

Or to be more precise, the ruination had come at the hands of Francis Hammond—crazy Pharaoh Frank—who'd let himself become so obsessed with Khaemwaset that he'd engineered a notorious caper—not just a caper, but a criminal undertaking—that folks back in Chicago still referred to as the 'Ushabti Incident.'

Ricky winced at the memory. For Pharaoh Frank had somehow talked both Ricky and Iggy into joining him in this crime. Painful even now to remember the details, to think about these people. Especially Pharaoh Frank.

But Frank the Pharaoh was precisely the person Ricky needed to think about. The more he contemplated his find, the more Ricky realized how badly he missed being an accepted member of his profession, how fed up he was with telling himself he didn't mind being an 'outlaw Egyptologist' (as he sometimes said when he tried making a joke of his fate), how much he'd like to go back to grad school and finish his Ph.D dissertation and get a quiet job at a university instead of dealing with men who tried to strangle or shoot or stab him.

Four years of living hand to mouth, of looking for cash from the likes of Mustafa Hamdi.

In short, Ricky Atlas was tired.

And what he held in his hands now was a find. A major discovery. This Solomon's wand could be Ricky's ticket for readmission to the world of academia.

But for that he'd need help. Too many riddles to this find, and all of them seemed to be tied up with Khaemwaset.

But little was known of Khaemwaset beyond the bare outlines of his life. No one knew precisely why this prince had turned away from court-politics and become a solitary scholar. No one knew precisely when Khaemwaset had died, or how, or even where he was buried.

This text Ricky had found offered clues, suggested that conflict had broken out between Ramses and his son.

It must have been a pretty bad spat. "*Cursed me and ordered me to depart*": had Khaemwaset been forced into the life of a fugitive?

Puzzles, riddles. But there was no Egyptologist Ricky could turn to, no one in the field who specialized in the life of Ramses's son. Khaemwaset was a mystery to pretty much everyone.

Everyone, that is, except Francis Valerian Hammond.

Hammond, who'd destroyed his own life, and Iggy's, and Ricky's, for Khaemwaset's sake. Hammond, who'd deluded himself—and had briefly deluded Iggy and Ricky, too—into believing Khaemwaset's immortal soul would benefit from Frank's Ushabti caper.

Ricky shook his head. How could Frank ever have been so nutty? For that matter, how had Ricky ever let himself be so nutty? Painful to contemplate.

Painful, yes. And now Ricky realized he'd have to face up to yet more pain.

Because he knew what he needed to do was track down Pharaoh Frank and show him this text and the broken wand.

Frank would be able to solve the wand's riddles and maybe—just maybe—be able to achieve a healing that would allow all three of them—Frank, Ricky, and Iggy—to regain their former status in academia.

Ricky knew Iggy was the guy to start with on this quest. Pharaoh Frank had last been sighted somewhere in the Southwest—

Arizona, New Mexico, somewhere like that—and who knew where he was now?

Iggy might. The three of them had been friends once; and if anyone might have been contacted by Crazy Frank, it'd be Iggy.

Ricky knew where he could find Iggy: still in place, still slaving away as an adjunct in Chicago.

Chicago. Could Ricky really face going back there, face the jeers that awaited him as a washout and loser?

Professor Thorncraft, for starters: his one-time advisor, who'd publicly denounced Ricky as a 'disgrace.'

Harriet Kronsted: former friend but now someone who seemed to shun him even in email.

Greg Holman, Cindy Lynch, Robert Thwarter: classmates and rivals who'd rejoiced at the mess he'd made of everything.

Even Ignatius Forsythe. Iggy had found some way to stay on in Chicago and accept his reduced status. Would he really be glad to see Ricky again, re-open old wounds, relive the pain? Or would Iggy turn away too?

Can I face all that? Or should I just stay on the run, keep surviving on hand-to-mouth jobs?

"Sir?" The door gunner prodded his shoulder. "Landing in five minutes." The chopper began to descend.

Ricky nodded.

A buzz from his jacket. The cellphone. He could guess who was calling.

"Doctor Atlas?" Mustafa Hamdi's smarmy voice again, needling Ricky with a title both men knew he hadn't earned.

"Doctor Atlas, I trust you've secured the other half of the wand? If so, I have a cash bonus waiting for you. A very big bonus. Enough to make you comfortable for the rest of your life."

Should I trust him? The words *cash bonus* were tempting; four years of life as a fugitive will do that to anyone.

But he remembered Taha's warning: Hamdi might just be planning to terminate Ricky's life.

Undecided, he cleared his throat, started to speak. "Mister Hamdi."

Unsure what to do: risk meeting Hamdi, turn over the wand, grab the big bucks? Or risk a return to Chicago, with its certainty of fresh taunts and fresh humiliations?

"Doctor Atlas, I have the finial, as you know, and I want the pleasure of rejoining the two halves."

Rejoin the two halves. *And what will happen,* Ricky wondered, *once the two halves are rejoined?* Once upon a time, he'd been so influenced by Pharaoh Frank he'd actually believed that ancient Egyptian artifacts possessed mystic powers of some kind.

Believed it enough that he'd put his career on the line back in Chicago, followed Frank and Iggy's lead in making a fool of himself and engaging in criminal behavior and ruining his own career. He'd long since given up believing in mystic powers of any kind.

Or thought he had. Listening to Mustafa Hamdi, he realized he was uncomfortable with the thought of the likes of Hamdi joining together something that Prince Khaemwaset himself had broken and torn asunder.

In these circumstances, what would Pharaoh Frank do?

"Doctor Atlas, your cash bonus. It's waiting for you."

What would Pharaoh Frank do?

More words from Hamdi. "...a large bonus."

What would his old friend do, his certifiably crazy friend?

"Doctor Atlas?"

The hell with it.

Briskly, into the phone. "Sorry, Mister Hamdi. Can't hear you. Transmission's breaking up."

A darker and more menacing tone now in his employer's voice. "Doctor Atlas, don't play games with the Corporation."

"Can't hear you. You're breaking up."

Just as he snapped his phone shut: "We aren't done with you yet. You'll hear from us ag…" Click.

A sudden jolt as the craft hit the deck. Big smile from the pilot. "Welcome to the *Stennis.*"

chapter 30

3 kilometers south of Amran Township
Central Highlands, Yemen

DEAD. ALL OF them dead.

Hasan Zubayr staggered among the wreckage.

A bent machine-gun tripod. A tire from a Hilux. A bit of blue cloth from a turban. A severed human hand.

Dead, all dead. 'Adnan the Afghan, all his comrades from Ansar al-Din, all slain by the drone from the sky.

He'd be with them now in paradise if he hadn't tried to kill the American himself, been slapped in the face, been made to walk instead of ride. He felt very, very alone.

His face still stung from the slap. It would always sting, from the slap, from 'Adnan's rebuke.

Always sting, for the rest of his life.

If only he hadn't disobeyed orders, hadn't tried to kill the American himself. He'd be in paradise now with his friends.

The American. Any trace of him?

There, in the ditch. The red motorbike. Wrecked.

But no corpse. No trace of the kafir.

The helicopter he'd heard. A rescue: the kafir must've somehow escaped.

And now Hasan realized how he could make amends, undo the shame, ease the sting.

Aloud he said, "I promise, O 'Adnan, I will find this American and kill him."

There. His face still stung. But already he felt a bit better. He turned and limped down the road back to Sanaa.

chapter 31

Sonic Drive-In
Verde Valley, Arizona
Southeast of Oak Creek Canyon
Highway 17, Exit 289

STEALING A SMOOTHIE: that might not be enough to get someone fired.

The 'someone' Tad Foster had in mind was Anita Martinez. He mopped the floor and watched as she hurried across the parking lot.

She was doing the same thing she'd done previous nights. Instead of getting into her car to drive straight home, she walked away fast from the Sonic, heading down the paved road to Montezuma Castle.

Which was strange. The Park Service locked up at 5 this time of year. Which meant she had no business doing whatever she was planning on doing.

What did he have on her so far? He mopped some more, ran a tab in his mind.

Pilfering popcorn chicken. Also Reese's peanut butter cups. Plus those smoothies.

He could try phoning Regional Management. But a supervisor from Regional HQ had dropped by only last month and praised Martinez for her work as assistant manager. Tad wasn't sure a stray Reese's would be enough.

But criminal trespass: that was something else. If he could prove she was up to no good after hours inside a national monument: *hell, that might even get a news headline.*

Furtively he watched Tomasina and Fiorina—he hated those two almost as bad as Martinez; they were always thinking up more work for him—until he was certain they weren't facing his way. Then quickly he pulled from his shirt the placemat he'd found in Martinez's discarded apron.

Couldn't read most of it—the writing was scrawled—but he could make out something about a guy named Gaunt, wearing a hospital tag, maybe a mental patient (now *that* could be damaging info!), probably homeless.

Something also about his interest in Montezuma Castle.

Which meant this Gaunt guy must be camping out there. *Illegal.*

And his boss must be bringing him food and hanging out at the Castle with him after hours. *Also illegal.*

"I'm punching out." He propped his mop against the wall.

Hands on her hips, Tomasina blocked the door. "Annie told you to finish the floor."

"I'll do it tomorrow." He pushed past her. *After tonight that bitch won't be telling me to finish anything.*

Once out the door, he ran. She had a head start on him of five, maybe six minutes. But she was carrying those smoothies and bags of take-out, so she couldn't go that fast.

He wanted to be one-hundred-per-cent sure she was actually inside the site after hours before he set in motion the plan that had just come to him.

Not much light left; he might miss her in the dark if he weren't careful. He ran faster, his breath coming hard.

Making too much noise, he warned himself. *The bitch'll hear me.* But he had to make sure she was actually in the park.

He increased his pace, unused to the effort. *Shit.*

Up ahead: the entrance gate. Closed and padlocked for the night. And he was in luck.

Anita Martinez was in the process, right before his eyes, of climbing the gate. Doing it pretty fast, too, considering she had bags of take-out cradled under one arm.

Proof. Proof would be useful. A photo.

He fumbled in a pocket for his cellphone. She hadn't seen him. Fantastic.

Gotta take the photo while she's in the act.

In his haste the phone fell from his hand. *Shit.*

And now she was over the fence, hurrying off into the dark.

Too late for a shot. *Shit.*

Well, she hadn't turned, hadn't seen him. And he knew the best way to nail her. He picked up his phone, tapped in the number for the Yavapai County Sheriff's Office.

I gotta fix it so the cops show up, she gets arrested, along with that mental-case drifter friend of hers, and the cops put the cuffs on her and take her in to book her. So I gotta make this good.

"Yeah, I'd like to report a break-in on public property. Montezuma Castle. Exit 289, right off 17," he added helpfully. "In progress? Yeah, yeah, in progress. Goin' on right now."

A question from the sheriff's desk.

"Uh, not sure," he answered. "Vandalism, I think. Yeah. Two individuals. Male and female. One of 'em looks like some kind of mental patient, like maybe he busted out'a someplace."

Inspiration came as he remembered a detail from Martinez's scrawled notes. "He's got some kind'a ID tag around his wrist. From a mental hospital, maybe. Dangerous? Dunno. Yeah, maybe. Yeah, I think he might be armed."

That should do it.

chapter 32

Montezuma Castle National Monument
Near Camp Verde, Arizona

IF THERE WAS one thing Annie Martinez didn't appreciate, it was getting grease stains all over her coat.

Must've happened when I hopped the fence. She'd had to scrunch the bag of chicken between her elbow and chest to keep her hands more or less free. The amount of oil the broiler-cooks put in that popcorn-batter: unbelievable.

She pulled a paper napkin from the bag, wiped her jacket. *Not that it'll do much good.*

Worse—she inspected herself—her coat also sported a squirt of strawberry smoothie. Great: the lid on one of her drinks had come loose.

Well, aren't I all set for a date?

She wiped some more, gave it up as hopeless, hurried away from the entrance gate and made her way along the visitors' path towards what she used to call her cave, her Seraph Grotto.

Except these past few days, she'd relabeled it in her mind: now it was *their* cave, *Annie and Gaunt's* Grotto.

Didn't matter that she didn't even know the man's name. *Gaunt* was good enough for now.

Brace yourself. He might not be there. He might be too scared to show. He might be hiding up there—she glanced above, to where the Sinagua mudbrick castle loomed in the night—*or he might have cleared out. He might just be gone.*

No, not gone. She'd know if he had. She'd have felt it. At least that's what she told herself.

The cave. She took a deep breath. The grease had seeped from her coat to her shirt, which clung messily to her skin. *Yuck.*

Do it, lady. She took another breath and stooped into the mouth of the dark.

Couldn't see a thing, couldn't tell if anyone else was in there.

Blackness. Quiet. Somewhere outside, a bird called from a tree.

No one in here.

Her shoulders sagged. She felt tired. *I guess the doggies get to eat take-out tonight.* She sighed, turned to leave.

Then: a sound from within.

A cough; the scrape of a shoe against dirt.

He's been sitting here all this time, just staring at me.

For the first time in thinking of him she felt afraid.

I'm alone in a cave with this strange guy I don't know.

That ID thing on his wrist. Maybe he is some psycho-house runaway.

Maybe he's a meth-head. Maybe he's making up his mind whether he's going to spring at me right now.

No move from him yet.

You know, came the temptation, *maybe you can still get away, still stay safe.*

Just back out real slow, duck out of the cave, head back to the Sonic like all this Gaunt business never happened.

Go get in your car, and in thirty minutes you can be back home in the trailer with Micky and Gabby.

That was the temptation.

And in her mind she said: *No.*

Instead she reached in her coat, flicked on her flashlight.

And there he was.

The beam caught his face.

A long bony visage. Unshaven. Red hair, wild and uncombed. Deep staring eyes.

A childhood picture came to her mind: *Like a saint on a holy card.*

He sat, huddled near her—*near their*—seraph sherds. He raised a hand to shield his eyes from her light.

"Sorry. Sorry." Hastily she placed the light on the ground.

"Here," she offered by way of apology. "Are you hungry?"

Seemed he was; in need of some liquids, too. Thirstily he gulped half the smoothie.

"Hope you like strawberry. Hey, guess you do."

She offered him one of the take-out bags. "Try this."

Wordlessly he snatched the bag, scrabbled back in the dirt away from the light. She saw his bared teeth as he bit off big bites of chicken.

Maybe he'll feel more at ease if I provide the conversation. "You know what's funny? I'd been worried about looking presentable for our get-together. Been working all day, getting sweaty and gritty. Then on the way over here"—she said this between bites on her own hunk of chicken; she was pretty hungry herself—"I go and spill grease and milkshake all over myself. Pretty gross." Nervous laugh.

"But it didn't occur to me we'd be dining by flashlight. So I guess I'm good."

Not a word from him. *I must sound like a jerk. Shut up, Annie, shut up. You're just gonna spook him.*

Not that he was altogether silent now. In between slurps of his smoothie he muttered—but not to her, she thought. His voice was too low, too indistinct.

Sudden insight: *he's been on his own too long, on the run too long. He talks only to himself. Forgotten how to speak to other people.*

"Hey." This muttering of his was hard to take. Maybe she could get him to engage in conversation. "Hey. I've been thinking of you as Mister Gaunt. I know. It's stupid. But I don't know what to call you. Do you mind if I ask you your name?"

The muttering ceased. Then in a croak, like a crow practicing how to talk like a human: "The sign."

"Sign?"

He swallowed, ducked his chin to his chest, as if summoning a great effort. "The sign on your place."

"You mean the advertisement? My Museum of Seraphs? Oh, yeah. You wanted to see that, didn't you?"

"Should say"—his head sagged on his chin, and he spoke with his eyes closed—"Sign should say *Museum*"—a pause, then he finished in a rush—"*Museum of Seraphs in Torment.*"

"In torment?" This startled her. "Why in torment?"

"Because all these seraphs"—and now, words suddenly unleashed, he stared straight at her—"all the seraphim that've ever come to this earth of ours, have all suffered." He gulped the last of his smoothie.

"How do you know that?"

Silence. He studied his empty cup.

"Here. Do you like mocha vanilla? You can have half of mine." She poured a dollop into his cup.

He opened the grease-stained bag, discovered the Reese's. "I like these," he croaked, and he surprised her with an upward twitch of his lips. It was, she realized, an attempt at a smile.

She watched him eat the chocolate in silence.

Finally he answered her question. "I know about their suffering"—the words came now with increased assurance; *the crow's getting more confident in human speech!*—"because I've experienced their suffering."

He must have sensed her confusion. "These." From the dirt he gently lifted a handful of terracotta fragments. "These shards were once the earthly vessels of seraphs."

Carefully he folded the orange candy wrapper, put it back in the bag. "The seraphs housed in such vessels suffered terribly. They gave freely of their love. They were willing to sacrifice for others."

Questions rushed to her lips: *Suffering? Sacrifice? How can you know this?* Aloud she said only: "I don't understand."

He added to her confusion by asking, "Have you found the Portal yet?"

"Portal? Here? What're you talking about?" *Maybe he really is nuts.* She lifted the flashlight, shone it on his wrist. He still wore the blue plastic tag.

The light let her read the lettering: *Bellevue Clinic/Psychiatric Unit/Francis Valerian Hammond.*

Hoo-boy: so he is a head-case.

He saw her study the tag. "They say I'm insane. They say I might harm myself. Harm others."

Voice barely a whisper, he watched her closely as he spoke. "Do you want to leave now?" He lifted his tagged wrist, pointed to the cave-mouth.

Last chance, she warned herself, *to back out.*

"No." Her reply emerged as a hesitant syllable. Then, more firmly: "No."

She said it again: "No." *Harm myself, harm others; I won't let it happen, not to him, not to me, not to anyone.* Aloud she said, "Tell me about your portal."

"Before I do that," he announced, "I have to show you the hieroglyphs."

"Hieroglyphs? Like Egyptian hieroglyphs?"

"Some call them petroglyphs. But at least some of them are Egyptian. Pharaonic."

"Where? Around here? There aren't any Egyptian hieroglyphs here. Can't be. Not for a thousand miles around here."

"Not here. But nearby. I'll show you, then we can come back and you'll be ready to see the Portal."

Abrupt interruption from the world outside:

A wail of sirens, a screech of tires by the visitors' center.

"Police," hissed Annie in alarm. "They catch us trespassing in here, they'll arrest us for sure."

"Come then." He extended his hand to her.

"By the way," she whispered as they slipped from the cave, "I'm Annie Martinez. Assistant manager over at the Sonic."

Red police-car lights lit the man-crow's unshaven face. "Francis Hammond," he croaked, and his lips twitched again. This time he actually managed a smile. "Nuthouse escapee."

"This way then, Mister Escapee." She tugged his sleeve. "First job is to outrun the cops."

They ducked among the junipers, out into the night.

chapter 33

James Henry Breasted Memorial Egyptology Wing
Oriental Institute Museum, University of Chicago

FOR IGNATIUS LOYOLA Forsythe, existence most days was more or less bearable.

But on days he recalled the past, it descended into grey misery.

And on days he was forced to relive it, he dipped into black despair.

Today fit that latter category. The festive banner draped across the Oriental Institute's Egyptian Hall told why: *Welcome to ARCE's Annual Convention! A Special Welcome to Our Alumnae and Alumni!*

ARCE: once upon a time he'd treasured his membership in that organization, the American Research Center in Egypt, the primary professional organization in the US for Egyptologists. He used to look forward to the conferences every year, giving papers, getting feedback, enjoying the scholarly give-and-take.

Hubert Thorncraft, his dissertation advisor, had mentored him, introducing him to department chairs at other universities, talking up Iggy's work, reminding them "how promising young Forsythe looks," how he'd be finishing his thesis soon and how lucky they'd be to hire this bright-and-talented Ph.D.

Well, he'd finished his degree all right, but no university ever hired him. Not after the Ushabti Incident. Not after he'd become notorious as one of the 'Midnight Trio'—a name coined by the ever-inventive demon-cloaked-as-grad-school-colleague Robert Thwarter, who'd made all too sure the name stuck to Iggy and his partners in crime, Francis Hammond and Richard Atlas.

In a way, Ignatius Forsythe knew he'd been lucky. At least— after Iggy had engaged in what Robert Thwarter sneeringly referred to as 'maximal mea culpas' (to wit, groveling in the form of I'm-so-sorry-please-forgive-me emails)—Professor Thorncraft had condescended to the extent of allowing Iggy to stay on and finish his degree.

And now: now he was Thorncraft's personal slave. He'd never be able to get a job elsewhere—not after that ushabti business— but he couldn't bear to give up Egyptology.

Thorncraft knew this, took advantage of it, granted him the title of Adjunct Lecturer but allowed him to teach only one course per year.

That of course didn't generate enough income to live on, which meant Iggy also had to do forty-plus hours a week of facto-tum work at minimum wage to pay for his crummy studio apart-ment in Hyde Park.

His workday consisted mostly of step-and-fetch-it, xeroxing and scanning books for Thorncraft, running to Starbucks for cof-fee (cream, two sugars) and croissants to satisfy his onetime men-tor's cravings, being available on continuous standby for anything the Institute might need.

Such as today: staffing the welcome table for this year's ARCE gathering. How he wished himself elsewhere!

Any minute now the first arrivals would show, and he'd have to be ingratiating and smile while handing them their ID badges and program booklets. And since every member of ARCE knew about the Ushabti debacle—Egyptology is a small-fish-globe world, and gossip swirls fast in a bowl—Iggy would have to endure various grades of smirks and guffaws.

Even from the younger generation he'd get it.

Every year since the Ushabti Incident, a fresh crop of fledg-ling Egyptological grad students came up through the ranks. At first acquaintance, the fledglings would defer to him, impressed by his Ph.D; but soon—very soon—they'd learn of his disgrace, of the Incident, and then they'd join the procession of those who Scorned or Ignored.

Worst of all was the thought of seeing old grad-school chums— if chum could ever be applied to the ilk of Robert Thwarter and Cynthia Lynch and Greg Holman. When he thought of them he almost envied the fate of Francis Hammond and Richard Atlas.

After that night in the museum—when the Midnight Trio had been arrested, handcuffed and exposed as fools—Francis had simply had a meltdown. No more academic career for him; he'd been in and out of psychiatric facilities.

Word had it that when he wasn't being treated at one of these facilities, Francis would wander off to the Southwest. It'd become an obsession with him. Since losing his grant funding and dropping out of grad school, Pharaoh Frank had become more or less penniless. So he'd hitchhike to New Mexico and points west, following some dream, some private fantasy.

Not much to envy there, Iggy sternly reminded himself.

And Richard Atlas? If there was anything worse than being force-fed anti-psychotic drugs by white-coated interns, it had to be what Ricky had turned into: a black-market dealer who robbed ancient gravesites and thereby deprived professionals of access to data.

The last time he'd seen Ricky—Iggy squirmed at the memory—he'd had harsh words for his old friend. He knew now it was because he thought so poorly of himself in his capacity as departmental groveler and thrall.

"Tomb thief" and "money-grubbing opportunist" had been the words he'd flung at Ricky's back as his old friend stormed out the door.

"Doormat in perpetuity" had been Ricky's over-the-shoulder farewell. Words that had stung, because Iggy knew them to be true.

And now—Iggy couldn't believe his bad luck—he'd just last night received an email from Ricky Tomb-Thief Atlas.

Iggy hadn't replied—the note had stirred up such a storm of emotion he hadn't even tried—but he'd printed out Ricky's note and brought it today to the Oriental Institute Museum.

After getting a note like that, Iggy would've preferred to spend the day lying in bed feeling blue—something he'd done too much of, since the Incident—but a call from Harriet Kronsted had rousted him.

"No excuses," she'd admonished him. "I know how you feel about these ARCE conventions. I'm not thrilled about them myself any more."

She, too, had suffered—even if not as badly as the Trio—from the Incident; and her voice on the phone was sympathetic. "But I need you to work the welcome desk."

It's more than this hateful ARCE business, he wanted to say. *It's also this email I just got from my dead past.*

But he didn't know how to talk about it, knew the news would stir up painful feelings for Harriet, too—Ricky had meant something to her as well.

"I'll be there," he'd mumbled into the phone.

Now he sat at the conference welcome desk, wearing a staff badge with a printed label that read "Hi I'm_____."

He'd deliberately left the blank space blank, but Professor Thorncraft had stopped by and made him write *Ignatius L. Forsythe.* Thorncraft had stood over him as he glumly filled in his name.

As if the world needs reminding, he thought. *I could just have easily penned in Hi I'm Iggy Object-of-Scorn. Ushabti Iggy. Iggy, Trio Member Number 3. Remember me? Of course you do.*

He sighed. *Hi I'm Blank* would've suited him fine.

Carefully he darted a glance about the hall. No arrivals yet. He unfolded the email note and read it again:

Iggy!

Been a long time, hasn't it? Too long.

I'm back. I'm in Chicago.

I know those five simple words will be a bit of a shock.

But I'm here for a reason. I've got things to show you, things I've discovered. They'll make you think of old times.

And once you see what I've brought, I know you'll be willing to help me.

Because I need your help in finding Frank Hammond.

⚜

Talk about a knack for poor timing. On any possible day, a note like this, with all its reminders, would be enough to tip Iggy's existence from just-bearable to miserable.

But to arrive during an ARCE convention—when triumphant old colleagues would be swarming the campus, ready to re-open old wounds—this was simply too much.

He should've instantly emailed back: *NO DON'T COME.* Nice and simple.

Why hadn't he?

Because Ricky Atlas had been a good friend. Because Iggy, like Ricky, often thought about Francis Hammond. And because, like Ricky, Iggy, too, would like to know what had become of Frank the Pharaoh.

Except: if Ricky, with his reputation as a smuggler, thief, and black-market dealer, were to show up at ARCE, the knives would come out.

Foolish though it was, Iggy still nourished a hope that somehow, someday, he'd be forgiven, be allowed back into the academy, be granted a tenure-track job at some university somewhere.

Little chance of that, he knew. But little would dwindle to zero if he ever let himself be seen again in the company of Tomb-Thief Richard Greyling Atlas.

"Well, you're off in your own little world today." Harriet Kronsted, taking her seat beside him at the table.

"Hattie! Hi, hi. Sorry." Hastily he crumpled the note, stuffed it in a pocket. "Just dreaming."

"Save the dream for later. We've got customers, and look what just walked in the door."

She grimaced, then smoothed her expression into a smile. An elbowed nudge to Iggy. "Remember, we're the welcoming committee."

chapter 34

James Henry Breasted Memorial Egyptology Wing
Oriental Institute Museum, University of Chicago

"WELL, WELL. IF it isn't Piggy Iggy, slouched down small and hoping not to be noticed."

Just my luck, thought Ignatius Forsythe. *The first attendee to get here has to be Robert Thwarter.*

"Piggy Iggy," continued Thwarter, laughing at his own joke, "although variant readings in other manuscripts also yield the no-menclature *Igg the Pig.*"

A grad-school witticism, this, and a comment on his phy-sique. Whenever Iggy glimpsed himself in the mirror—which he did seldom: too depressing—he had to acknowledge he was on the dumpy plumpish side.

"Hi, Bob. Welcome back." Iggy all but groaned as he said this.

Looking as fit as ever, Robert Thwarter. A well-muscled speci-men and an exercise fiend, Thwarter hit the gym every day—el-lipticals, cycling, treadmill, weights—and he was the type who as-sumed you wanted to hear about each sweaty high-virtue detail when he was done.

Barks of laughter hailed Thwarter's verbal play. The barks came from another familiar figure—Gregory Holman, at 32 a slighter, younger version of Professor Thorncraft: stoop-shoul-dered, balding, face creased from too much frowning. Like many of his peers, Holman seemed always a bit in awe of the overbearing Thwarter.

As he'd often done in the past, Holman followed Thwarter's lead in enjoying a little fun at the factotum's expense. "If the piggish reference is too wounding to the feelings of our Ignatius, perhaps an alternative designation for him? Bob, what was the other name you devised the last time we met?"

"Budge the Pudge," came the prompt reply.

Both men laughed. A cluster of grad-school students, eager to align themselves with what they sensed to be the winning side, the tenure-track side, laughed along too.

Budge. Budge the Pudge: a historical reference.

Clever, this, Iggy inwardly acknowledged, even as he flushed red from the taunts. Like Ignatius Forsythe, E. A. Wallis Budge had been an amply-girthed Egyptologist; but there was another, and more ominous, comparison as well that was implicit in Bob Thwarter's barb.

Wallis Budge, the celebrated and successful Victorian-era antiquities curator at the British Museum, had illegally smuggled the famous *Papyrus of Ani* from Luxor to London. Britain was full of ancient things stolen by Budge.

A bit of a criminal, in other words, like Iggy; but whereas Budge had been fat and fortunate, Iggy was just a fat guy who'd fallen flat.

"Your ID badges. Program booklets." Harriet intervened briskly. "Drinks are over there. The reception won't start for ten minutes, but you can help yourselves." She knew Thwarter's weakness for alcohol.

Hot-faced with shame, Iggy wordlessly blessed her.

"Drinks. All right then." Thwarter moved off, leading Holman to the refreshments.

"Thanks," whispered Iggy to his table-mate.

"Thing to remember about this job," replied Harriet, "is to find a way to hang onto your dignity. Don't let them get under your skin."

She offered a tight-lipped professional smile to each group as it arrived. Students from Toronto and NYU. Overseas scholars from Leiden and Berlin. A dozen Egyptians, most of them from Cairo's Supreme Council of Antiquities.

"The SCA has a lot of new faces," she commented as they took their badges and entered the hall. "The government has cleaned house since the revolution."

"Harriet Kronsted," purred the next attendee, "you're still dressed like a bartender. A cocktail server."

This from Cynthia Lynch, another member of Thwarter's old grad-school set.

True, thought Iggy, what Harriet wore resembled a bit of a uniform: black shoes, black vest, creased black trousers, and a crisp white shirt buttoned up to the top. On trim-figured Hattie, it looked good.

A bit different from Cynthia Lynch's style. A wide-hipped big-boned woman, Cindy favored ankle-length peasant dresses topped up with plenty of jewelry. Dangly gold earrings and heavy gold neck-chains from which dangled heavy gold pendants.

Every year, to celebrate some new academic achievement, she bought another bauble. From where he sat, Iggy counted seven necklaces—make that eight. She could afford the show; she'd just been awarded tenure and promoted to associate professor at Yale.

"Poor Hattie," announced Lynch, pausing as if to decide where to insert the next thrust, "your get-up's the same as ever."

Now a show of solicitude. "You might want to think about varying your wardrobe just a tad. You know, dress for success." Cynthia laid just enough lingering emphasis on *success* to flag Harriet's evident lack thereof.

Iggy blushed for her but Hattie stayed cool. "I keep things simple," she said, calmly returning her old colleague's gaze. "It leaves me free to think about other things."

"On *your* budget," sniffed Lynch, "how much choice do you have?" With that she hailed Thwarter and moved off.

Harriet tilted her head to Iggy, pursed her lips, arched an eyebrow: Hattie's version, he knew, of a full-throated distress scream.

"Why don't you two go enjoy the reception?" suggested Hubert Thorncraft. "All the guests have arrived."

Iggy eyed the crowd dubiously. "If you don't mind, I think I'll head home."

"Nonsense." Thorncraft propelled him towards the hall with a none-too-gentle shove. "Circulate. Network. Let people know who you are."

They already know who I am, thank you very much. But there was no arguing with Thorncraft.

The first few minutes didn't go too badly. People ignored him, of course, turned their backs when he appeared; but all that was normal. A grey-misery day; bearable.

Harriet seemed made of sterner stuff, projecting a steely smile wherever she turned; but Iggy knew this was hard for her too. *Stay half an hour; act like you're fine; then go home and go to bed.*

Usually at these receptions he'd retreat as fast as he could from the thronging Egyptian wing and withdraw to the deserted Assyrian gallery, where he'd gaze up at the human-faced Nineveh bulls and take comfort from their stony blank gaze. *Blank, the way I'd like my ID tag, my memory, to be. Blank: just a bit of relief.*

But not tonight. A muscled grip on his arm locked him in place. "We were just doing a bit of reminiscing," boomed Robert Thwarter. "Remember this piece?"

Of course I do, he almost bawled. *That's the artifact that wrecked my life.* He wanted to weep, to flee, to disappear.

"Hmm? Gone mum? Can't hear you." Still with a lock-grip on Iggy, Thwarter waved a wine-glass at one of the vitrines. *He's had a bit much,* guessed Iggy; *he gets like this every year after his fifth or sixth glass.*

"Gather round, everyone," invited Bob Thwarter. "It's a fine artifact, and it's got a fine story. Take a look. Take a look."

Iggy knew the piece all too well without needing to look.

A limestone ushabti, an eighteen-inch-tall funerary statuette, on long-term loan from the Louvre. Nineteenth dynasty, bearing the likeness of Prince Khaemwaset, son of Ramses. The figure's crossed arms held a *djed*-pillar and *was*-scepter, signs of stability and strength.

Things he needed now, as he languished in Thwarter's grip and was forced to listen. "Very fine, isn't it, everybody? A very rare piece. Note the exquisite modeling of the facial features."

Some onlookers, new to this story, seemed puzzled. The initiates, cognoscenti like Holman and Lynch, giggled encouragement.

"And to think that this artifact was the object of an attempted theft."

That got the attention of the Egyptians. Several of them, Iggy knew, were SCA staff, government flunkies, always prickly about insults to their nation's patrimony.

"Of course, when this incident happened, we were asked to take into account the emotional state of the ringleader of the Midnight Trio that attempted the theft. I'm talking of course about Francis Valerian Hammond, a man who deserves our sympathy."

That's rich, thought Iggy, as he twisted helplessly in Thwarter's grip. *Frank Hammond was your rival, the only student better and smarter than you in every seminar and class you ever took. You laughed louder than anyone at Hammond's downfall.*

"I happened to be present when the police caught the Trio and took them away. My heart went out to all of them, but especially to Francis. So much talent, all gone to waste." He gulped wine, tightened his grip as Iggy tried once more to pull away.

"And what was it poor Francis said, when the police found the Trio here in the Egyptian wing in the middle of the night? What word did he use to justify himself? Budge, you remember, don't you?"

Thwarter shook Iggy's arm. "Come on. You were there. You were one of the Trio. Don't be shy. What word did he use?"

Grey misery. Black despair. Iggy mumbled inaudibly.

"Louder, Budge. They can't hear you. What word did he use?"

"Psychometry."

"Did you hear that, everyone? Psychometry. Not scholarship, not scientific research. Just good ol' mystic hocus-pocus. Or maybe just plain lunacy from someone on the tipping-point of a breakdown."

Onlookers laughed, though some seemed a bit nervous, as if the fun had gone too far.

Not hocus-pocus, Iggy longed to say. *Not lunacy. Just a method— or at least a wish, a hope—of breaking through the barriers of time, of bursting through the limitations of mainstream scholarship and making contact with like-minded, great-hearted souls of forty centuries past.*

There I go, he thought, *sounding just like Pharaoh Frank.*

But what a grand hope it had been, before everything had gone bad.

Once more he tried to twist free, but Bob Thwarter was having too good a time to let go. "Psychometry." He slurred the word.

Definitely at least six drinks, thought Iggy; *Thwarter's usually not this far gone so early in the evening.*

Boy, I'm exhausted. No escaping the grip.

"Thwarter," called a voice from behind them. "How about you let my friend go?"

"Oh. My. God." This in a gasp from Hattie.

Iggy gasped too.

For there, facing the whole crowd, confronting Professor Thorncraft, eyeing former rivals who were now securely tenured at Harvard and Princeton and Yale, wearing scuffed jeans and the same ratty tweed coat Iggy always remembered, was Tomb-Thief Richard Greyling Atlas.

chapter 35

James Henry Breasted Memorial Egyptology Wing
Oriental Institute Museum, University of Chicago

IF HARRIET KRONSTED were to compose a list that offered little boxes to check (something she enjoyed doing for many life-categories) of terms to describe herself, then 'emotionally self-sufficient' would be at the top. A good trait in a field like Egyptology, which—like most branches of academia—rewards scholarly self-absorption, maniacally unsociable seclusion, and long solo hours amid stacked reference books in late-night library niches.

Item two—another box to check on that self-descriptive list: 'orderly, neat and tidy.'

Which explained why she'd been vexed with herself, several years ago, when she realized she'd developed some liking for the messiest male biped on the University of Chicago's campus—one Richard Greyling Atlas.

Neatness counted with her, and it pained her even now to recall his sense of couture that winter semester—several years ago now!—when they'd both enrolled in an 8am section of Introduction to New Kingdom Epigraphy.

Those dark Chicago January mornings, she'd invariably arrive at 7.45, equipped with a small coffee (cream, no sugar) plus an indulgent mini-package of Drake's Coffee Cakes containing four bite-sized crumbled-sugar pastry bits. The package logo showed a cheerful duck in a baker's hat. Cheerfulness was good, a commodity in short supply among eternally sleep-deprived students.

She'd eat in the empty classroom, carefully dunk each cake in the brew, holding the cup to her chin so nothing would drip while she looked out the window at the snow on the trees. Come 8am, she'd be caffeinated enough to face even the knottiest Egyptian inscription.

A somewhat different approach than that favored by Richard Greyling Atlas.

Without fail, he'd be the last student to show, fifteen minutes into the period, yawning as he scratched his uncombed hair and apologized to the professor, tucking in his shirttail, wearing the same dirt-grey tweed jacket, rain or shine, come snow or hail.

"Lucky," he'd said of the coat, during an early spring thaw, when she asked if he wasn't a bit warm wearing that thing. "It always brings me luck."

Then one morning, near the semester's end, her alarm clock failed her and she overslept and had to sprint to class. No time to stop at the corner store. Which meant she'd have to face the inscriptions without benefit of either caffeine or sugar.

Punishment for oversleeping, she told herself. *That's what you get.*

And then in walked scruffy Atlas—with whom she'd exchanged maybe twelve words so far that year—holding a paper bag.

"Small coffee," he said, as he handed her a lidded cup, "cream, no sugar."

He reached in the pocket of his scruffy jacket and extracted a package of Drake's Coffee Cakes. "See what happened to be in my lucky coat," he said as he handed her the Drake's.

That was the first time she'd noticed: he had blue eyes. He had a nice smile.

So that was the start. Some days they had lunch off-campus in Hyde Park's Florian Café. When the weather warmed they sat in the quad by the pond and studied the gargoyles on Cobb Gate. He still wore that tweed jacket; but sometimes he thought to comb his hair.

They were by no stretch of the imagination an item, a couple. (Cindy Lynch saw them one night on the street and declared loudly she'd rather date a pigeon.)

In any case Ricky could never be pinned down—some days he'd show, some not—and Harriet for her part valued her box-checked label as self-sufficient.

And yet. And yet.

One day he brightened a drizzly cold morning by reaching in his pocket and handing her a small faience figurine. Ibis-headed Thoth.

"God of wisdom," he said as they sat on a quad bench and he put his hands back in his pockets. "God of scribes. To help you study."

So she stood it on her desk in the Oriental Institute (even in grad school she'd had a part-time position at the Institute).

And it was Thoth who'd crippled her hopes of advancement.

One day Robert Thwarter had stopped by her desk and without asking snatched the figurine for inspection.

"Do you realize," he said, "what this is?"

"Sure," she replied, keeping her eyes on her work (even back then she hadn't liked giving Thwarter any more eye contact than she had to). "The god Thoth."

"I didn't ask you to identify the deity," he snapped, in that you're-an-idiot tone in which he specialized. "I mean: did you know this is authentic. It's not a reproduction."

"Oh." Cautious as ever, she feared to say more. Ricky was always grabbing cheap flights to Cairo, making bucks in wheeler-dealer deals he never discussed. She'd just assumed the piece he'd given her was a throwaway, a cheap gift-shop trinket.

"Engaging in a bit of antiquities trafficking, are we?" He smirked as he said it. Harriet Kronsted as artifact smuggler: the notion was silly, and he knew it.

She stared at him, said nothing.

"Or maybe you want to flaunt your girlfriend status with young Atlas."

She didn't bother correcting him, didn't say *I'm not his girl-friend; he's not my boyfriend.* "What's your point, Robert?"

"My point is: watch out. Young Richard Atlas is heading for trouble. Heading for a fall. Make sure he doesn't pull you down with him. Stay clear."

Defiantly she'd maintained Thoth on her desk.

Thwarter saw that she'd kept the piece but he didn't mention it again.

It was the very least she could do, she told herself. A way of showing Thwarter he couldn't have his way in everything, even though he did manage to impress and over-awe almost everyone in the department, students and faculty alike. She knew he despised Ricky, almost as much as he despised Francis Hammond and Iggy Forsythe.

Besides, if Ricky had been dabbling in trouble, he would've told her, or at least she would've sensed it.

Wrong on both counts. Two weeks later came the Ushabti Incident. Police; arrests; scandal.

Iggy stayed on but sank into despair. Pharaoh Frank vanished. And Ricky—*her Ricky*, she almost said, which was silly—skipped the country. Not a word to her. No explanation.

Quietly she'd put away her Thoth, went back to solo coffee and solo Drake's. The duck on the logo didn't seem so cheerful anymore.

But that hadn't been the end of it. She'd managed to keep her part-time clerking job at the Institute, but every time she'd tried for a tenure-track teaching job, she'd been rejected. Never even got invited to an interview.

Nothing but form-letter rejections: *Thank you for your application. We have already filled the position.* No explanation as to her deficiency.

One day, as she'd sat at her Institute desk opening her ump-teenth rejection, Thwarter had passed by. "Heading for a fall. Didn't I say so? Well, at least I tried to warn you." He'd said it with a big smile.

So that had been the last of Thoth and Richard Greyling At-las.

chapter 36

James Henry Breasted Memorial Egyptology Wing
Oriental Institute Museum, University of Chicago
EXCEPT NOW HERE he was, unannounced, scruffy coat and all, in the midst of an ARCE convention. And from the look on his face, he was ready to resume his old feud with Robert Thwarter.

"How about you let my friend go?" Richard Atlas demanded again, this time more loudly—loudly enough to snag the attention of half the people in the crowded hall.

Time hasn't been kind to him, was Harriet's first thought. Lips cracked, skin blotched with bad sunburn, cheekbones and chin bruised as if he'd tumbled down a flight of concrete stairs.

Blue eyes, yes, but bloodshot, sleepless. Hands and face: pitted and weathered. *What's he been doing, relaxing somewhere with a blowtorch held to his face?*

Slung over his back was a knapsack from which bulged some shrouded tubular object. *Bet there's a story to that. Must ask him. That is, if he's willing to talk to me—and if I can find the courage to talk to him.*

But that thought was swept away as she saw Ricky advance a pace towards Thwarter, who still held Iggy Forsythe in a vise-lock grip.

Thwarter retreated a few steps, until his back was to the vitrine containing the Khaemwaset ushabti and a display of canopic jars and mummy masks.

The two men faced each other.

Thwarter stiffened, drawing himself to his full height, a hand-some muscled six-foot-two.

Starting to get a bit fleshy, judged Harriet—too much caloric intake from all that alcohol, despite his compulsive exercise work-outs. But he was a big guy and he could afford the weight.

His bulk made Ricky, five-foot-seven and definitely scrawny from whatever sandblaster life he'd been living, look small. Small, and vulnerable. *He's going to get himself hurt*, came the worried thought.

"Look what just crawled in," sneered Thwarter, "lurking on our threshold."

"I said, let Iggy go." Ricky rocked slightly on his feet, blind to every other presence, apparently ready to throw himself at his foe.

A sudden quiet in the hall.

Thwarter glanced about, decided on a joke. "Iggy? You mean Budge the Pudge?" Appreciative snickers from Cindy and Greg and the grad-student claque. "Budge and I were just having fun. But here, you can have him." He pushed Ignatius Forsythe into Ricky's arms.

Ricky staggered and caught his friend. Iggy rubbed his arm where he'd been vise-gripped.

Everyone's eyes were on the confrontation. But Harriet noticed something else in the crowded hall.

Something that had dropped from Thwarter's suitcoat pocket when he shoved Iggy. It lay unnoticed on the floor.

"Mister Atlas. Mister Atlas," continued Thwarter, regaining the initiative. "You know, you have less common sense than dearly departed Pharaoh Frank. At least *he* knows enough to stay far, far away. *He* knows where he's not wanted."

Hubert Thorncraft stepped forward to play peacemaker. "Richard. What a surprise. But you really shouldn't be here. You're not registered for the conference."

Both men ignored him. Harriet began to edge her way across the room towards Thwarter.

"If Frank's not wanted here," replied Ricky in a cold level tone, "it's because of what you did to him, Bob Thwarter. You set him up. You used that faux-friendly manner you always turned on whenever you wanted something, until he trusted you enough to think you were a real colleague, someone he could trust with his visions. You set him up."

"I didn't need to set him up." Thwarter gulped more wine. "Hammond was ripe for a fall. All his talk of experiential Egyptology. Epiphanies. Theophanies. Psychometry. More like psychosis."

Commandingly he looked about the room for confirmation. The claque gratified him with titters.

"You set him up," persisted Ricky. "You were the one who told him about the Khaemwaset ushabti that had just been loaned from the Louvre. You were the one who kept telling him to test his psychometric theories."

Indignant at the accusations, Thwarter stepped forward so he towered over Ricky.

The thing that had fallen lay neglected on the floor. Harriet edged through the cluster of SCA Egyptians who stood heedlessly between her and her goal.

"You were the one"—*no stopping Ricky once he got going*—"who suggested that if he could just creep in here after hours and lay his hands on that statue, he'd be able to commune with Khaemwaset's ghost."

"Don't blame me," came the harsh rejoinder. "I wasn't part of the Midnight Trio. That's your dubious criminal distinction." More supportive grins from his crew.

There. Right before her on the floor. It looked like a CD, in a clear plastic case.

"Yes, I was part of that trio. I don't deny it. But you were the one who egged him on until he confided in you and let you know what night we were going to do our break-in and have our nutty séance." Ricky shook his head. "Yeah. Nutty, all right. He even invited you to join us so you could be on hand for the psychometric breakthrough."

Again Ricky shook his head. "You were the one to tell him no, you couldn't join him. You weren't feeling well or something. But you'd be there in spirit, you said. Frank told me all about it later. And Frank also realized later you were the one who phoned the police and timed it so they'd swarm all over us before we even opened the vitrine. You set Frank up. You set us all up."

"You can't prove that." Gone was Thwarter's pretense of masterful disdain. Now he simply sounded angry.

"I don't have to. You know it's true."

Thwarter thrust his wine-glass at a grad-student flunkie, as if readying himself to punch Ricky through a wall.

That was when Iggy Forsythe roused himself. "Come on, Ricky." He grabbed his friend's coat-sleeve.

"I'm not going anywhere." Ricky glared defiance at Thwarter.

"Yes you are." Firmness now in Iggy's tone. "We're going on a tour of the library. For old times' sake." Still glaring defiance over his shoulder, Ricky was escorted from the room.

Yes. A CD. Harriet stooped and palmed the disk while all eyes were still on the Thwarter-Atlas drama.

"I don't think we've met." A man stood in her way.

Harriet knew all the regulars at ARCE conventions—Egyptology is a small field, after all—and he wasn't one of those.

No ID badge. A heavily built individual in his late fifties or so. Florid red face; broken veins in his nose. His big callused hands led to her first guess: *a field archaeologist, newly arrived back in the States from some dig; just arrived, and hasn't had time yet to register for the conference.*

"May I help you?" She managed a smile even as she slipped the CD into her pocket.

He smiled then, and that changed her impression. A pleasant smile, but behind it she sensed a sharp assessor's mind, a man good at skilled judgments.

A psychologist, she thought. *No, that's not quite the job description either.* She remembered a blackjack dealer she'd seen once in Atlantic City: the same watchful vigilance, the same quickness to respond to any turn of the cards.

"Actually, I wanted to speak to Richard Atlas, but it seems he's had to leave in a hurry." Again the smile, the watchful assessor's gaze. *Did he see me grab Thwarter's CD?*

"And since Mister Atlas had to leave, I wondered if I might ask you about him. I had the impression you two might be friends."

"Yes." This was uncomfortable. "That is...we used to be." This stranger roused her protective instincts. "Why are you interested in Richard Atlas?"

"That's a long story." Again the smile. "I'm in the consulting business. I do a bit of work for the government."

"The government?" she interrupted. "And your name is...?"

"Alastair Wilcox," and he offered his big hand. "Anything you can tell me about Mister Atlas will be helpful."

She was in no mood to be quizzed. *What I can tell you,* she might have replied, *is that Ricky's someone who used to offer me Drake's coffee cakes. Someone I want to talk to very much, before he slips away again right out of my life.*

"Would you excuse me?" She turned and rushed from the hall.

"Of course," he smiled at her retreating back. The CIA analyst asked a server for something to drink. Calmly he stood and watched Robert Thwarter.

Thwarter was being fawned over by Professor Thorncraft, who was busily telling bystanders how outstandingly brilliant his protégé was, how he'd always known Robert would excel, how proud he was that Robert had recently been tenured and promoted to the rank of associate professor at Brown University's department of Egyptology. Thwarter listened to all this patiently until he saw someone else he wanted to greet.

Wilcox watched as Thwarter hailed the new face. An Egyptian. A stout balding man in a nicely tailored suit. The two shook hands and embraced as if they knew each other well.

The analyst sipped his wine. The Egyptian. He knew him. Knew him well, at least from the file photos he'd studied while stationed in Djibouti.

A senior executive with EHC, the Egyptian Heritage Corporation. EHC's liaison with the R & D division of Firthland Oil Ventures. Someone who used to be the supervisor and gadfly of one

Richard Greyling Atlas. A gadfly who'd buzzed all the way from Cairo to Chicago.

A gadfly named Mustafa Hamdi.

chapter 37

Reading Room, Oriental Institute Library
University of Chicago
OH, YES. *I remember this place.* Richard Atlas paused in the doorway.
I should, he thought. *I spent enough time in here.*
The Oriental Institute's library stood deserted right now; everyone
was at the reception in the other end of the building. Ricky felt
grateful to Iggy for dragging him here.

After the adrenalin-surge of his confrontation with Thwarter,
after everything he'd been through these past few weeks—and it
all hit him now, exhaustion from what he'd endured in Cairo and
Yemen—he was glad for a moment in a quiet spot.

Shelves and shelves of books, reassuring and familiar. Ricky
gazed and remembered: the long library tables, the high vaulted
ceiling, the lancet window with its stained-glass lotus motif.

Filled with readers, the last time he'd studied in this room:
Hattie, Iggy, Cindy, Greg, nasty Bob Thwarter; even Frank Hammond the dreamer, pacing about moodily, a *Coffin Text* tucked under an arm. Isolated and competitive, all of them, solitary in their
studies; but bound at least by a common love of antiquity, of pharaonic Egypt.

How long since he'd last been here? A few years, and a thousand lifetimes ago.

He turned to Iggy, breathed a long sigh. "Thanks for hauling
my butt out of there. I was kind'a acting on impulse."

Iggy grinned. "Name me one time you haven't." He was still massaging his arm. "But I'm the guy who should be saying thanks. If not for you, ol' Thwarter would still have his death-grip on me."

"Got something to show you." Ricky unslung the knapsack from his back. "You're not gonna believe what I found."

"Up there." Iggy pointed to the second-floor loft—what students had nicknamed the 'Minstrel's Gallery'—overlooking the main reading room. "Nothing upstairs but back issues of old journals and a couple of spare computers. Quietest spot in the house."

They cleared a scattering of books from a table near the gallery's railing. "There," announced Iggy. "Now we've got space. Let's see what you found."

Ricky laid the knapsack on the table, opened the bag, and produced a three-foot-long cylindrical object that lay shrouded in a cloth.

Iggy stepped closer. "What on earth is that?"

Ricky recognized the expression on his friend's face: doubt, uncertainty, fear.

So intent were the two on the object that they failed to hear the library door downstairs quietly open and close.

Ricky paused, one hand on the shrouded thing. "Before I explain, I guess I should warn you that this could cause trouble for both of us."

"You mean trouble for all three of us," came a voice from the gallery stairs. Harriet Kronsted strode swiftly to the table, eyeing the knapsack and concealed object.

"Hattie!" *Shit, I don't want to get her involved, too.* Hastily Ricky jammed the thing back into the bag. "Oh. Hey. Hi. Been a long time."

"You might have said hi back at the reception."

Ricky didn't note the half-smile on her face that softened the rebuke as she spoke.

"Uh. Yeah. You're right. Sorry." He glanced at his two former companions, reminded himself he was on the cusp of exposing them both to danger and harm. He hesitated, his hand still on the bag.

"I know what you're thinking," said Harriet gently. "But whatever you've got there, I want in on it, too."

Ricky still hesitated. Harriet's presence changed things. *I still like her,* he realized. *A lot. Though from the look on her face I'm not sure she's exactly wild about me. And the same bad things that happened to the Midnight Trio could also happen to her.*

Aloud he said, "It's just that...Well, the, ah, legal status of what I've got might be considered questionable."

"I hope you're not trying to tell us," warned Ignatius Forsythe, "that you're still involved with antiquities trafficking."

Embarrassed silence from Richard Atlas.

"My God." Iggy sank into a chair, clapped a hand to his head. "You mean you've just walked into the University of Chicago's Oriental Institute, in the middle of an ARCE gala, with a smuggled Egyptian artifact in your backpack? Tell me I'm wrong. I beg you."

Silence from Ricky.

"You realize," continued Iggy, "you could get us all arrested? Arrested again, I should say. You do understand, don't you, that the reason I'm a sad-sack wannabe and hanger-on in the field of Egyptology is because of our little Ushabti Incident back when."

His voice rose. "You and I, my man, already have a criminal record. Felony break-in, attempted theft, suspended sentence. End of my career."

"You're not the only one, Iggy," interrupted Harriet. "Being perceived as the girlfriend of a UC dropout and ushabti thief didn't exactly help my career either."

"*Would-be* ushabti thief," Ricky corrected her wearily. "And what's this about being my girlfriend?"

"I didn't say I was your girlfriend." Stiffness now in her voice, and pride. "I said I was *perceived* as your girlfriend."

"Ah." *Shit. What do I say to that?* "Guess I'd probably better not pursue that point."

"That's probably wise of you."

"Okay then."

"Okay."

Prickly silence.

"You guys." Iggy watched them with exasperation. "Could we please get back to the fact that we've got a dubious object in front of us here? An object that I suspect is a real career-wrecker."

"I thought you said"—Ricky couldn't help smiling—"your career was already wrecked."

"Yeah. Well. It's about to get wrecked again." Iggy shook his head. "I don't know what to do. Ask you to leave, or say *show us the stuff*? Why are you back here, anyway? Why didn't you just sell this off to someone, whatever it is?"

"Maybe I could've," acknowledged Ricky. "But what I've got in this bag might be a way of apologizing to Frank Hammond."

This caught the interest of both Iggy and Harriet. "How so?" they chorused.

"After the ushabti business and the arrest and everything, I ran away to Cairo. Tried to start a new life. But even over there I heard about what Frank was going through. His breakdowns, one after another. Being stuck in a locked ward somewhere."

A grimace, and a sigh. "I wanted to get in touch with him. Wanted to. But I never got around to finding out where he was, how he was doing. Too busy. Too busy trying to make money." He grunted a brief bitter laugh, shook his head.

"Make money," he continued. "Yeah. What a stellar success that turned out to be. And then I found something that I knew for sure would interest Frank. Something that might bring Frank back into Egyptology, no matter where they'd locked him away. An artifact bearing the name of the one person he gave his whole life to."

He turned pleadingly to his former classmates. "I know it was crazy, walking in here like this, after all that happened. But I had to come back, had to try to find him, try to show him what I found. It might be a way to make it all up to him. At least," he concluded uncertainly, "that's how I made myself feel a bit less guilty while I was away overseas."

His friends exchanged glances. Harriet stared questioningly at Iggy. A moment's silence. Iggy pushed back his chair and stood.

"Let's take a look at this thing you found."

Ricky gazed appraisingly at each of them in turn.

"You want in on this?"

"Yes." A prompt reply from Harriet. "I haven't changed my mind. I want in on it."

Iggy gulped, nodded. "Yeah. Yeah. I mean, what more can the Institute do to me? Break me further in rank? Reduce me to licking the stairs clean every day? Hell, I want in on it, too, whatever it is."

chapter 38

James Henry Breasted Memorial Egyptology Wing
Oriental Institute Museum, University of Chicago
IF ANYONE WERE to ask him—not that anyone would dare—how he
felt after manhandling pathetic Budge-the-Pudge Forsythe and
bellowing at that other loser, Richard What's-His-Name, Robert
Thwarter could truthfully have said, *I feel fine. Tonight nothing can
touch me, because I've got a big payoff coming.*

He surveyed the ARCE gala crowd and mouthed a mirthless
smile. Students, professors, field archaeologists, departmental ad-
ministrators. *Baboons, jackals, hyenas, apes. Talking, shouting, craving
attention, showing their teeth.*

All jockeying for position, all dreaming of a find—a new text,
a new treasure, a new inscription—that might secure their reputa-
tions.

Well, *he* had scored a find that would secure his reputation
djet er neheh, as the Ancients used to say: *enduringly, through all the re-
curring cycles of time.* A find he was keeping secret for now, that he'd
been persuaded to keep secret, paid to keep secret. *But only for the
time being. Only for the time being.*

They fawned over him now, mentors, colleagues, and students alike, because he'd already scored discoveries aplenty. An
uncatalogued New Kingdom manuscript he'd found in the base
of a Ptah-Sokar statuette at the Ashmolean in Oxford. A Heb-Sed
scarab he'd uncovered on a Karnak Temple dig. A foundation-de-
posit featuring execration tablets and severed Nubian skulls he'd

excavated from beneath the walls of a crumbled fortress on the Egyptian-Sudanese border.

All Nineteenth Dynasty, all contributing to his reputation as North America's—no, make that the world's—outstanding scholar of the reign of Ramses the Second. At 32, he was already tenured, already the holder of an endowed chair in Brown University's Department of Egyptology and West Asian Studies. *Not bad. Not a bad start.*

A start, for there would be more. Just wait until the ARCE crowd learned of his latest coup.

He visited the moment once more in his mind. *Some memories are so luscious, so good to the taste, they have to be relived.*

Upper Egypt, eighteen months ago. Abu Simbel, on the Nile kingdom's southern frontier. The shrine-complex built by Ramses, with four giant statues of the seated king frowning from the cliff-face.

Sinister, that mammoth scale. Meant to frighten all who approached the land of the gods. *But fascinating*, thought Thwarter, *fascinating, for how it projected power.*

Appropriate, had been the joke circulated by one Francis Valerian Hammond, appropriate that Egyptology's greatest egotist should happen to be writing his dissertation on the most egotistical of all Egypt's rulers.

That had scored a laugh at Thwarter's expense, the day Hammond made that witticism during a seminar in grad-school days. Scored a laugh. Yes.

But where was Pharaoh Frank now? Locked away and medicated, the last time Thwarter had checked (and he made sure to check often).

Thorazine and Prolixin: hard to focus on scholarship—hard even to think—when you're tanked up on meds like those.

Neutralized, old Pharaoh Frank. The thought made him smile.

A face passing in the ARCE throng—a pretty young grad student; her badge read *NYU*—thought the smile was for her. Flattered, she smiled back.

Baboons, jackals, hyenas, apes. A hard light came into his eyes. The student dropped her smile, backed away.

Abu Simbel, eighteen months ago. Yes. He'd been studying the wall-reliefs in the sun-chapel carved deep within the cliff-face. The battle of Qadesh, Ramses in his war-chariot, his horses trampling under their hooves the enemies of Egypt.

Then, in a dark corner of the chapel, he noticed a carved scene he'd overlooked: a depiction of Ramses performing a ritual.

Ramses stands before the sacred mountain, within which is seated Amun, the god known as "the hidden one." In one hand Ramses wields a type of scepter called *sekhem* ("the power"); in the other, he holds an incense burner. Incense to charm and flatter the god; a *sekhem* to conjure him forth.

The carving shows the effect of this ritual: a huge crowned cobra emerges from within the mountain, an epiphany of the god, the god made manifest in animal-form, ready to heed the pharaoh's summons.

For a moment Thwarter had stood there, envying Ramses his self-confidence in standing face-to-face with deities, imagining the first explorers who'd come here two centuries ago and stood where he now stood. Burckhardt. Belzoni. Champollion.

Heroic days, back then. They'd each had to hire Bedouins to clear away the wind-mounded desert sand and force open the chapel doors. Champollion had arrived on a day of dreadful heat and recorded a temperature within the shrine—as he sweated and transcribed hieroglyphs—of over 120 degrees.

And now here he stood: he, Robert Thwarter, a man cast in the same explorer's mold, in a place that had long since become an air-conditioned tourist venue, long since domesticated, documented, measured, known.

But perhaps not completely. For even as he contemplated this unfamiliar carving, something called for his close attention. He recognized the feeling, called it his hunter-killer instinct. It had never failed him. He'd learned to trust it, for it led him unerringly to finds.

He heeded the instinct now, stood there studying the picture.

Reciprocal gaze at work here, for he suddenly felt the figures eye him in turn. It was the kind of feeling occasionally voiced by crazy Frank Hammond, the kind of feeling on which Thwarter publicly heaped scorn. But privately he knew that in some ways he and Frank shared almost a kinship of worldview. They saw things other Egyptologists didn't. That's why Thwarter viewed Hammond as his worst rival.

He stepped a pace closer to the wall. Luckily, no tourists here today; all the political disturbances had scared sightseers away. Two guards dozed outside on chairs by the door. Just him and the empty shrine.

But not so empty. No. The feel of a reciprocal gaze grew stronger. But coming from which figure? He reviewed in turn the sculpted Ramses, the seated Amun, the cobra emerging from its sacred mountain.

The serpent. Its eye fixed him, drilled into him with a hollow blank stare.

What would Hammond say if he were standing here now? How would he respond to the scene of a sacred snake emerging from the god's abode in response to a king's prayer?

Hammond would like this, Thwarter guessed, would like this a lot. *It depicts an encounter of the divine and the human. A moment of contact. A feeling we're not so alone in this vast cosmos into which we've been hurled.*

Hammond had blurted out exactly these words in the midst of a seminar, in front of a half-dozen grad-school peers, while translating the Middle-Kingdom text of *The Tale of the Shipwrecked Sailor.*

And once Hammond had started, he couldn't help but babble on: *I mean, why else would we study ancient religion, except for the hope of retrieving such encounters, relieving the cosmic loneliness, touching noses with a god?* Hammond's exact words.

His classmates had looked embarrassed. Professor Thorncraft had choked off crazy Frank with a frosty "Thank you for that bit of wisdom, Mister Hammond. Touching noses with a god. How quaint."

The reproof gave Greg and Cindy license to snicker. Thorn-craft had peered around the classroom disapprovingly from be-hind his bifocals. "And now may we translate the next sentence?"

Yet Thwarter had known Frank Hammond was on to some-thing. And if he were here now inside the Abu Simbel chapel, Hammond, too, would feel the reciprocal gaze, would babble once more of relieving cosmic loneliness by making friends with a god.

Crazy Frank always made these epiphanies sound like some wispy passive love-encounter.

But Thwarter had studied the Nineteenth Dynasty long enough to know that for the likes of Ramses, wispy-passive wouldn't cut it. Ramses the Great, who'd gone to war against Nubians, Liby-ans, Hittites. Who loved to be depicted crushing a helpless cap-tive's head with a mace. Who ruled sixty-seven years, lived past ninety, outlived fifty-plus sons. Who built shrines to himself on a scale never seen since.

No, when it came to religion and Ramses, wispy-passive wouldn't cut it. The operative words would be *coercive, arm-twisting* (if it were possible to twist a god's arm): a summons to appear for the pleasure of a king.

So, friend Cobra—Thwarter almost spoke aloud as he studied the picture, but stopped himself with the thought he might sound like crazy Frank—*what do you have for me? Give it up; give.*

Eyeball to eyeball. And that's when he saw it.

A wind from the open chapel-door had just blown through the shrine. Sand gusted by his feet.

Within the stone cobra's empty eye-socket, something flut-tered, something that was stirred by the breeze.

Thwarter shuddered.

An epiphany.

No: impossible. Don't think crazy thoughts, like Pharaoh Frank.

Steady now. Steady.

He glanced at the door. The guards still dozed in the sun.

From a coat pocket he extracted a penlight, stepped up to the wall, shone the light in the eye.

Something there. Something that still stirred in the wind.

Much too small, the serpent's eye-aperture, for him to explore with his fingers.

But Thwarter in his travels never traveled without certain essential gear. From another pocket he extracted a pair of tweezers.

Another glance over his shoulders. *Guards still asleep. Do it!*

He explored the aperture with the tweezers, seized whatever the shadowy something was, tried an experimental pull. The thing yielded, protruded now an inch's length from the eye.

Enough for him to see what it was.

Papyrus. A scroll.

Gently, disciplining himself not to hurry, but knowing he was in a race against time—the length of the sleeping guards' nap—he teased the scroll forth.

There. Quickly he pocketed it. Inspection could wait.

He resisted the urge to salute the empty-eyed snake—*something only a nut like Hammond would do*—and quietly strolled out the door, past the still-dozing guards.

Yes. A luscious memory, well worth re-living. And worth celebrating now, in this Chicago ARCE gala, with another glass of wine. He beckoned a server.

For months, once safely back on campus at Brown, he'd puzzled over what he called the Abu Simbel Scroll. He'd taken his time with the translation, dribbling out bits of information to the group that had offered him fistfuls of hard cash for his textual skills—a group he knew only as the Corporation. He'd given them just enough information to keep their hunt going—the hunt for the artifact mentioned in his scroll.

For his part he'd agreed to postpone publication of the text until they secured what they wanted. He'd asked their rep—a smooth-talking Egyptian named Hamdi—why the Corporation was so interested in the object described in the scroll. The man had been pleasant but evasive.

Didn't matter. What counted was that Thwarter had just finished the complete translation, had copied the text onto a CD. He could've emailed it but their agreement had been: hard disk for hard cash. Face-to-face handover. Rendezvous innocuously at Chicago's ARCE convention.

Six weeks from now, flush with fresh dough, Thwarter would be free to publish his newly discovered text, and give his colleagues another taste of Egyptological shock-and-awe.

Thwarter surveyed the room. *Baboons, jackals, hyenas, apes.* How little they knew, all of them, as they jockeyed.

He dismissed the thought. For now he sought simply one man.

There he was: Mustafa Hamdi.

"My good friend." Hamdi insisted on a cheek-to-cheek hug. After a loud and effusive display of pleasantries came the low-voiced question: "Professor Thwarter. I assume you have the disk?"

"Of course." Another luscious moment, one he knew he'd relive for years to come: the night he'd finished the translation, when he could look forward to recognition in the form of private cash and public acclaim as the intrepid discoverer—in the tradition of Belzoni and Champollion—of the Abu Simbel Scroll.

For reassurance—as he'd done a hundred times that night—he patted the pocket of his suitcoat, just to feel the hard plastic case secure in its place.

Not there.

Wait. He felt again.

Not there!

He checked his other pockets. For the first time that night, for the first time in a long time, he felt something like a loss of power.

Not there!

Mustafa Hamdi eyed him sharply. "Is anything wrong, Professor Thwarter?"

chapter 39

Minstrel's Gallery, Mezzanine Loft
Oriental Institute Library
University of Chicago

"So THIS IS what you found," marveled Iggy Forsythe. "Looks like a royal scepter, or a wand."

"Part of a wand," explained Ricky Atlas. "My employer—guess I should say my former employer—has the top part, the finial. He thinks this is what medieval Arab legend was referring to in various stories about *'asaayat Suleiman.*"

"King Solomon's wand," translated Harriet Kronsted.

"Exactly." Ricky lifted the object from its shroud. "According to the legends, this is what gave Solomon the power to compel various species of djinns to build his temple and to tunnel for gold in his mines. But the Arabs knew that this object was far older even than the time of Solomon."

"What's it made of?" Carefully Iggy ran a hand along the length of the shaft. "Some kind of gypsum, maybe, like alabaster? It has alabaster's translucence."

Harriet switched on a table lamp and twisted its gooseneck towards the wand. The object refracted the lamplight so thin columns of iridescence radiated and swirled through the hall.

"Whew," breathed Iggy. "Never saw alabaster do that."

"In any case," judged Ricky, "it's much stronger than alabaster or any kind of gypsum. More like very thin steel, some kind of iron alloy. Tough enough to survive a high-speed motorcycle dive into a Yemeni ditch."

"I just hope," reproved Harriet, "you weren't on that motorcycle when it did its little dive."

"Well, it's not like I planned it. I don't go ditch-diving recreationally."

"Stay focused, guys." Iggy tapped the staff experimentally. It gave a faint ring. "Well, if it's a metal of some kind, I don't know where the Egyptians would have found it. Maybe in the mines of Wadi Hammamat?"

Harriet was already scanning the inscription. "You say you've completed a translation of this?"

"A rough draft. Here." Ricky unfolded the sheet containing his translation:

Khaemwaset, prince no longer, sem-priest no longer, beloved no longer of his father Ramses, says the following:

My father has renamed me 'Hateful and Ill-Omened in Thebes.' So be it.

He has stripped me of all princely titles. So be it.

He has cursed me and ordered me to depart from Upper and Lower Egypt. So be it.

For I do not repent. I do not repent. I do not repent.

I have broken the wand; I have separated the pieces; and I have done this to protect the sekhemu.

Let only the worthy know: this crest is to be replaced in the tomb of the son of the nameless king.

The other part of the wand is to be deposited in the Cave of the Sunburst, in the Nile under the stone, atop Crow Mountain, in the northern hills of the Deshret beyond the Sea of the Land of Punt.

May the pieces remain sundered until we are ready once more to revere the sekhemu.

"Wow," enthused Iggy. "You're right. Frank would love this. Wish he were here now. The sight of this would do him good. An artifact containing a text authored by Prince Khaemwaset. He'd eat this up."

"I wish he were here, too," replied Ricky. "Lots of puzzles to this text. This word *sekhemu*, for starters. I know it can mean 'powers,' or 'divine powers,' or even 'gods.' But why does Khaemwaset say the gods need protecting? And why did he have to break this wand to do that?"

"No idea," frowned Iggy. "And here's another puzzle: 'this crest is to be replaced in the tomb of the son of the nameless king.' The crest must be the finial you mentioned, the piece your old employer has. But what's meant by 'tomb of the son of the nameless king'?"

"Nameless king," repeated Harriet thoughtfully. "That term was often used in the Nineteenth Dynasty, in Khaemwaset's time, to refer to the most hated pharaoh from the previous dynasty: Akhenaten. The heretic king."

"And his son would've been..."

"Exactly. Tutankhamun."

"So this wand," said Ricky excitedly, "originally came from Tut's tomb."

"Apparently." Her eyes shone. "And look at this line: 'My father has renamed me *Hateful and Ill-Omened in Thebes.*'" Harriet smiled. "A nice instance of word-play, a curse based on Khaemwaset's own name."

"Oh, I see." Ricky nodded in admiration. "I'd forgotten the literal meaning of Khaemwaset's name in Egyptian."

"Khaemwaset," she said promptly. " 'He who makes an auspicious and well-omened appearance in Thebes'."

"And, according to this text, his father apparently renamed him *Binemwaset.*" Iggy joined in. " 'Hateful and Ill-Omened in Thebes'."

"Pretty strong language for a father to use on his son." Ricky turned the staff in his hands. "The Nineteenth Dynasty isn't my specialty, but I'm not aware of any historical references to tensions between Khaemwaset and Ramses. I know Khaemwaset is supposed to have predeceased his dad, but I've never read anything about his being driven into exile."

"Neither have I," confessed Iggy. "Well, the real specialist on the Nineteenth Dynasty and Ramses, of course, is our own distinguished UC alum, the dearly beloved Robert Thwarter. If anyone could make sense of this text, it'd be Thwarter. Too bad we can't consult him."

"Maybe we can." Sly satisfaction glinted from Harriet's eyes. From her pocket she produced a CD in a clear plastic case.

"What's that?"

"Something that happened to fall from Jolly Thwarter's suitcoat."

"You mean you heisted it?" Astonishment in both men's voices.

"Let's just say I availed myself of an opportunity."

"Harriet Kronsted!" Warm admiration from Ricky. "You are *evil*."

"Coming from a tomb-thief, that's a compliment."

"Bet your ass." He reached across the table and pumped her hand.

"Shall we take a peek?" Harriet sat herself before a computer at a nearby desk, slipped in the disk, clicked on the icon that quickly appeared. Iggy and Ricky peered over her shoulder to read what Thwarter had entrusted to his CD:

To: Mr. M. Hamdi, Cairo

From: Dr. Robert Thwarter, Associate Professor of Egyptology, Brown University

Following is my translation of what I have decided to call the Abu Simbel Scroll. As outlined in a previous conversation, I discovered this scroll while studying the Amun-Ra panel in Ramses II's sun-chapel. Included in this memorandum is a photograph of the scroll, together with my commentary on the text.

But first, a word as to the object's physical condition.

Measuring 21.2 x 25.8 cm, it is made of fine quality papyrus, comparable in manufacture to the very best productions of Ramesside Egypt. If one takes into account the painstakingly articulated handwriting (excepting the subsequent—and startlingly brutal—textual intrusion, about which more below)—reed-brush work inked in a very legible cursive hieratic typical of the Nineteenth Dynasty—then the speculation may be permitted that this piece came from the Theban Per 'Ankh/House of Life. That is to say, what you have before you (please consult the photograph reproduced below of the papyrus) is in all likelihood a text commissioned by the royal scriptorium of Ramses himself.

Paradoxical, then—given its high quality of composition—to ponder the scroll's ultimate fate. Its top is ragged and blackened; faint traces of ash confirm that the papyrus had been scorched by fire. The bottom is torn, so that the text's conclusion is missing. Laboratory tests on the ash confirm that the scroll was set alight only a short while after the initial date of composition. If one may permit oneself a flight of fancy: might the composer have repented of what he wrote?

Here is my translation of what survives of the text:

...discovered by the beloved Prince Khaemwaset, Priest of Ptah, son of His Majesty (all life, longevity, and dominion be his!) and son of Princess Isetnofret; discovered in the tomb of the son of the king who is nameless.

Armed with this scepter, this gift from a dutiful son, His Majesty (all life, longevity, and dominion be his!) will bend the sekhemu to His will, just as He has subjugated all of Libya, Asia, and Nubian Kush.

The sekhemu themselves will say of His Majesty (all life, longevity, and dominion be his!): We bow before the scepter; we bow before this Greatest of Men, Greatest of Gods.

In recognition of the piety of a dutiful son, this text is to be recorded in a place of honor within the Amun-Ra chapel of His Majesty (all life, longevity, and dominion be his!), beside the depiction of the crushing of Egypt's enemies at Qadesh. May the Prince continue to serve...

⌖

My dear Mr. Hamdi, such is the text, as much as survives. But what of the brutal textual intrusion to which I alluded above? Well might you ask.

For, if you consult the photographic reproduction below, you will see that the words 'beloved,' 'Khaemwaset' and 'dutiful son' have been slashed through in angry red ink (the mark of ritual execration). Written above these *words, also in splattered red ink, is the phrase 'Hateful and Ill-Omened in Thebes'—a new and dreadful name for a son, apparently bestowed by a father whose feelings have changed from affection to wrath.*

Why this change? Currently we have insufficient data to furnish an answer. But we have one clue. In the margin of the scroll is a scrawled verse, in a different hand (the hand of Ramses himself?), written in haste:

My son (who will be my son no longer) threatens to break the scepter, to hide it once more in its original resting place. If he does so, he will be made to suffer, even more greatly than have his sekhemu. Let his name be engulfed by the cobra.

⤝⤞

Cryptic, the above, testifying to a father-son conflict hitherto unknown to scholarship. Further proof of this conflict: the symbolic confinement of the son's name to a scroll that has been dishonored—burnt, torn, and imprisoned eternally within the constrictive eye of a carved serpent.

But this much we can say with certainty: the 'scepter' referred to above, with its power to bend the gods themselves to a man's will, conforms to your own theory—that the centuries-old Arab tales of 'asaayat Suleiman, King Solomon's wand, have a basis in ancient fact.

Whatever this wand was, whatever this scepter, Khaemwaset found it in a site described in the text as 'the tomb of the son of the king who is nameless.'

As soon as I read these words, I intuited what was meant (though such intuition, I may add, comes only to those who have endured long years of scholarly studies).

Khaemwaset must have found the wand in the tomb of Tutankhamun, son of the heretic king Akhenaten. Khaemwaset must have forced his way—at the bidding of whom, or of what, I know not—into Tutankhamun's tomb, in search of treasure from a previous dynasty.

Unlikely? Perhaps. But bear in mind that Khaemwaset was known even in antiquity as an antiquarian, who spent much time probing deserted wasteland sites for what secrets they might yield. One thousand years after his death, later generations of Egyptians remembered him as a wizard and necromancer. Anything, any speculation, is possible when it comes to Khaemwaset.

And the scroll's marginalia—the scrawled note by an angry father—hint at an enticing possibility. The lost wand of power—or at least a portion thereof (if in fact Khaemwaset had the courage to break it)—might have been reinterred by the prince in Tutankhamun's tomb, and thus it might still have been hidden there when the site was discovered by Howard Carter and Lord Carnarvon in 1922.

Be that as it may: with Tutankhamun's grave as my only clue, I set about examining all the remaining records from the twentieth-century discovery and excavation of the boy-king's tomb. I examined the catalogues listing all of Howard Carter's finds. No reference anywhere, however, to any artifact from the tomb that might correspond to Khaemwaset's ensorcelled wand.

I almost despaired until I recalled a passing reference in a footnote in a biography of Carter. It seems he had a penchant for forming a 'pocket collection,' keeping for himself from Tutankamun's tomb small treasures that he secreted in his personal belongings—a cigar box or a coat pocket—and then smuggled out of Egypt.

An irascible bachelor and a solitary man, Carter in his last years—exhausted by his efforts in Egypt—lived alone in a London flat, surrounded by bookshelves stuffed with his treasures. On his death in 1939, he willed his pocket collection to his only companion in old age—Phyllis Walker, his devoted niece.

She, for her part, sold most of Carter's antiques to the dealer Spink & Sons. And thus the treasures were scattered to private collectors throughout the world.

But we were in luck, my dear Mister Hamdi; we were in luck. Careful research revealed that Miss Walker—perhaps as a sop to her conscience, having profited from her uncle's thefts?—donated a few of the pieces from Tutankhamun's tomb to the Egyptian Museum in Cairo.

Repeated visits to the Museum have allowed me to ascertain that one portion of Khaemwaset's wand—the finial—is currently on display, in the lower-level Amarna Gallery. It is unlabeled, like many of the Museum's artifacts; I doubt the Egyptian authorities know the full story—or the potential worth!—of this piece.

The question now is one of retrieval. Given the instability of the current political situation in Egypt, extracting the piece will involve some hazard.

Someone will have to be dispatched for this task of retrieval, someone knowledgeable of Egyptian antiquities, but whose career is expendable in case the initial attempt miscarries. Someone who is both unscrupulous and skilled in artifact extraction.

May I suggest a former colleague, one Richard Greyling Atlas? He lacks a doctoral degree, nor does he have any academic affiliation; but this means only that he will not be missed, should something unfortunate befall him after he has served his purpose.

Yours faithfully,

Robt. Thwarter

PS/Addendum/Update: My suggestion above pre-dates current circumstances. Now that Mister Atlas is back in the States, we need only have a quiet word with him and relieve him of the Wand. After that, we must interview Francis Valerian Hammond again—as often as necessary—to pry from him a clarification of what he mentioned in his babblings about a 'Portal.'

I suspect that only then will the reconstituted Wand serve you as you wish.

"Hey." Indignant protest from Ricky Atlas. "This isn't exactly a flattering portrait of me."

"The least of your worries," noted Iggy. "These guys know you're here, and they know you've got the wand."

"And to make matters worse," groaned Ricky, "this note shows Thwarter's been working for my old boss Hamdi. Not good. Not good at all."

"You'd better leave," urged Harriet. "Now. I don't know about this Hamdi, but Thwarter's capable of anything."

"No argument there," agreed Ricky. "But it sounds like they're after Frank, too. I'm worried about him. The problem is, I don't have any clear idea where he's living these days."

Harriet closed the screen, returned the CD to its case. "I've heard he's been drifting around the Southwest. Hitch-hiking. No idea why."

"The Southwest's a big place. Arizona, New Mexico, Colorado, Utah. I can't go driving around hoping to spot him walking down some road somewhere."

"I've got a better idea," offered Iggy. "He's been in and out of psychiatric centers ever since his Ushabti breakdown. Last I heard, he'd checked himself—or somebody checked him—into a place called the Bellevue Clinic."

"Any idea where that is?"

"New England. Rhode Island, somewhere in Providence."

"Strange." Ricky frowned. "That's Thwarter's turf. He's got that tenured position at Brown. Wonder if that's a coincidence."

"Knowing Bob Thwarter?" A grim smile from Iggy. "I doubt it. But I'm not sure what the connection is there."

Ricky re-shrouded the artifact and stuffed it back in his bag. "In that case, I'd better head for Providence. If I find Frank, at least I can show him this. He knows more about Khaemwaset than anyone in the field, including big-ego Thwarter. If anyone can make sense of this mystery of the wand, he can."

"With Thwarter's crowd after you, you could get hurt," Harriet warned him. "Which means you need someone to watch your back."

"Since when do I need someone to watch my back?"

"Since you developed a habit of flying motorbikes into Yemeni ditches. Come on." She plucked him by the arm. "No time to argue."

"And since both of you are gonna need looking after," added Iggy, shepherding Ricky by the other arm, "I'd better come along, too."

"I won't argue then," surrendered Ricky with a grin.

"It'd be a waste of your time," Harriet assured him.

"But just one thing." She snapped her fingers. "Wait here a sec. I have a small chore to take care of."

"What's that?"

Again a sly look in her eyes. "I need to return this little CD I borrowed."

"Return the CD?" Real alarm in Ricky's voice.

"If I play this right, Thwarter might not even know we sneaked a peek." She gave her friends an elaborate wink. "I'll be right back. Then you gentlemen had best be ready to scram."

chapter 40

James Henry Breasted Memorial Egyptology Wing
Oriental Institute, University of Chicago
AGAIN THE INSISTENT question from Hamdi. "Is anything wrong, Professor?"

"No. No, of course not. Everything's fine." Robert Thwarter contorted his lips into a smile.

Again, and yet again, he patted his suitcoat pockets. *Not there! What's happened to my freaking CD?*

He glared around the crowded hall. *Who could've taken it?*

"Say, I wonder who dropped this." A woman beside him stooped and plucked something from the floor.

"That's mine. Gimme that." He caught her wrist, wrenched the thing from her hand.

The dish. Still intact, still safe in its case.

"Where'd you get this?" He kept his hand on her wrist.

"I just found it here on the floor." Startled innocence in her eyes.

"You're lying. You stole it from me." He tightened his grip.

"I said I just found it." Loud indignation as she tried to twist away from his hand.

"The lady's telling you the truth." A stranger had appeared by Thwarter's side.

Red face; white hair. Older guy, but muscled, well-built. He laid a hand on the younger man's shoulder as if he were refereeing a foul in a basketball game. *Where did this clown come from?*

"The lady's telling you the truth," the stranger repeated. He said it with a smile, but Thwarter sensed behind the smile a sharp watchful mind.

"And who the hell are you?" He met the stranger's smile with a scowl.

The woman was trying to twist away again. Thwarter tightened his grip all the more.

"Alastair Wilcox." Another smile.

Wilcox. Not wearing an ARCE convention badge. Not an Egyptologist—Thwarter knew all the players. *Hence not a rival. Insignificant.*

"Professor Thwarter." A discreet cough from Mustafa Hamdi. "We're drawing attention."

So they were, Thwarter realized. Hangers-on and sycophants—Greg Holman, Cindy Lynch, his whole entourage—seemed startled by his outburst.

He turned his attention from the disk and the seized wrist to the woman herself.

A server, a waitress, was his first thought: dressed in black trousers, white shirt, black vest. *Cocktail help.*

Her face. *Wait.* He knew her. *One-time grad student, classmate years ago.*

Can't place her name.

A clerk nowadays at the Institute museum.

Kronsted. That's it.

A part-timer. Not a threat. A non-entity.

"Professor Thwarter?" Hamdi stirred by his side.

Yes, he remembered: Harriet Kronsted. That was the name.

Not a threat. A non-entity.

Slowly he released his grip.

All about him, people watching.

Things were back under control; under control. He had the disk.

For the onlookers' benefit, he forced another smile. "Fine," he said aloud. "Everything's fine. Just thought for a second I'd misplaced something." One more smile for the crowd.

Sycophants, all of them: they smiled back.
Baboons, jackals, hyenas, apes.
The non-entity retreated through the crowd.
No damage done. No info leaked.
He had the disk. He had the disk.

chapter 41

Corridor outside the ARCE gala
Oriental Institute, University of Chicago
HARRIET KRONSTED TOOK a deep breath, let out a sigh. *Whew. Thought he'd wrench my arm off.*

"Neatly executed." A man blocked her way.

Wilcox again.

"What do you mean?" *Best to feign ignorance.*

"I mean the way you dropped that disk on the floor, then pretended to find it. I've seen it done by professionals, and you rank as one of the best."

"Don't know what you're talking about." She hurried past him. "Have to meet some friends," she called over her shoulder. "Please excuse me."

"Certainly."

chapter 42

Delta Flight 4273
En route Chicago O'Hare-Providence

"THE CAPTAIN HAS switched off the Fasten Seatbelt sign. You may now move about the cabin."

Richard Atlas unclipped his belt and allowed himself to begin to relax. He turned to his seatmates. "In the air, and out of Chicago. Feels good, let me tell you. I wasn't sure we'd make it out of the Institute with the wand."

"Not so loud," urged Harriet Kronsted. "After my last run-in, I'm ready for creepy-crawlers to pop up anywhere."

"And what's the name of this psychiatric facility we're going to investigate?"

"Bellevue Clinic," came Iggy's prompt answer. He explained that Professor Thorncraft had given him the name months ago. "Said he'd heard that Frank had experienced yet another in a series of breakdowns, and so he'd had to be hospitalized again."

Ricky glanced at Harriet, who was seated between him and Iggy, and he knew she was thinking the same thing he was: *Grim, grim fate. And the same fate could have befallen me.*

Iggy was apparently thinking along the same lines. "There were some days, after that Ushabti blowout, when I couldn't drag myself out of bed, couldn't make myself go to class. Wondered if I'd end up like Frank."

Harriet asked softly, as if to avoid making her question sound like a rebuke: "Why did you two go along with Frank's loopy scheme to break into the museum and grab that ushabti? Why didn't you guys try to talk him out of it?"

"A long story," mumbled Ricky. *Can hardly explain it to myself,* he thought; *the whole thing's heartbreaking to remember.*

Iggy was more forthcoming. "Frank believed so much in the possibility of bursting through the barriers of time. All you had to do, he insisted, was touch an object that had been handled by someone you loved; and no matter how far away that someone was, in space or in time, you could commune with them somehow. Psychometry, he called it: 'the measurement of souls.' Remember, Ricky?"

Ricky bobbed his head.

Iggy spoke faster as he warmed to his subject. "When he was in what he called his theosophical-philosophical moods..."

"Which was often," interjected Ricky.

"Granted. Which was often." Iggy laughed. "Anyway, Frank liked to claim someone someday would invent instruments and gauges to measure the residual psychic imprint left on ancient artifacts by the individuals of four thousand years past. Until that day, we humans of today would have to use our own sensitive psyches to serve as the gauges."

Ricky nodded. *Impossible to forget. How many evenings, hunched together at a table over coffee at Florian's, did Crazy Frank lecture us on psychometry and its possibilities?*

Epiphanies; theophanies; breakthroughs. Heady stuff.

After talk like that, as we walked back to campus through the late-night streets, the vistas seemed limitless.

Iggy smiled. "I'll never forget how excited Frank got the day Thwarter told him an ushabti with Khaemwaset's name on it had just been loaned to the Institute. Frank wandered around saying over and over, 'The prince himself might have handled this statuette once, might have gazed into its eyes!' Remember, Ricky?"

Ricky nodded yes. *How could I not? Pharaoh Frank had a way of making horizons seem bigger, of making time feel like something infinite, open-ended, amenable to travel.*

"Making contact with ghosts, with great-hearted spirits from the past: Frank loved all that." For a moment Iggy watched clouds stream by the plane's porthole. "Hattie, I know it sounds loopy. You're right. But Frank believed it all so much, Ricky and I wanted it to be true for him, wanted it to be real. It meant so much to him."

Iggy smiled a sad smile. "And then one day Frank announced he was going to steal the gallery keys and creep into the Institute at midnight and open the vitrine so he could have five minutes, just five minutes, to hold the ushabti and dial up Khaemwaset—remember that, Ricky? His exact words: 'dial up Khaemwaset'—and that way commune soul-to-soul, or whatever you do when you have a mystical moment, or nervous breakdown, or whatever. And he said he was going to do it with us, or without us."

A shrug of helplessness, or resignation. "Well, there was no way Ricky and I were going to let him traipse solo into the museum for a midnight ushabti tête-à-tête on his own. We figured somebody'd better be on hand to keep him from tripping an alarm or tripping over himself. And in the end of course we all got nailed."

He paused, rubbed his chin. "Well. You can't help but feel protective about a guy like that. Fragile, you know? But I always felt he could see things we couldn't. We wanted it to be true for him. For that matter, we wanted it to be true, period."

Ricky tilted back his seat. *The old days. Grad-school days.*

When Frank was still in the picture, the world felt like a bigger place. Pharaoh Frank and his visions.

The world does somehow feel bigger if we're not forced to live only in a narrow sliver of time, if we can feel the doorway to the past, to ancient times, is somehow open just a bit.

The feeling came over him strongly. He missed Frank Hammond. Missed him a lot.

"This Bellevue Clinic." He pushed his seat back to the upright position. "Have you found out anything about it so far?"

"Checked online. Private facility. 'Residential treatment center,' the website says, 'with professional individualized attention in a quiet garden setting'."

"Sounds charming," came Harriet's ironic commentary. She plucked an in-flight magazine from the seat-pouch in front of her, idled through the pages. "Do you have the address?"

"Prospect Street. According to Google Maps, it's supposed to be on College Hill, near downtown Providence. Next door to Brown University."

She made a face. "Brown. Thwarter's turf."

"Thwarter. Ugh." Ricky muttered, "Let's pray we don't run into him again."

"Amen, Reverend." Iggy made a face, too. "Amen."

Harriet stuffed the magazine back into its pouch. "Never anything to read in these stupid things."

"Oh, that reminds me." Iggy suddenly stood and clicked open the overhead bin. "Speaking of reading matter." He pulled a folder from his overnight bag.

"Wha'cha got?"

"So much has happened, I forgot to show you guys this." Iggy opened the folder, produced a sheaf of yellowed crumpled papers. He riffled the sheets. Each was crowded with writing, penned in black ink in a tightly packed scrawl.

"I know that hand," exclaimed Ricky. "Frank must have written it."

"I made photocopies for each of us." Iggy passed them over to his friends.

Harriet turned to the first page. "Where'd you find this?"

"Remember that crappy room Frank used to have in Hyde Park?"

"Sure," said Ricky promptly. "Over on East 55th, between Stony Island Avenue and South Woodlawn."

"Exactly. Last week I got a call from his old landlady. She remembered I'd been the one to clear out his room when he took off so abruptly after that Ushabti meltdown."

"A meltdown for all of us," commented Harriet, "one way or another."

"Very true. Anyway, the landlady was throwing out an old bed in the room he used to rent. And she found these, didn't know what to do with 'em." He lifted the yellowed sheaf. "Frank must've stuffed them under the mattress."

"What is all this?" Harriet peered at the minuscule writing. "Notes for that article for *JEA* he was always talking about submitting?"

"*The Journal of Egyptian Archaeology*? Are you kidding? After that talk he gave at ARCE a few years ago—what did he call it?"

" 'Alternative Interpretations of New Kingdom History'," said Ricky drily.

"That's the one. After that, *JEA* wouldn't even consider anything he wrote. No, this is something else. I think..." Iggy hesitated. "I think it's supposed to be fiction, maybe."

"Fiction?"

"Maybe a fragment of a historical novel. Something like that. But I'm not sure. Anyway," added Iggy, "Hattie was saying the in-flight magazine's no good, and I'm betting whatever Frank wrote is going to be a lot more intriguing."

"Fair enough," said Harriet, and the three of them each turned to the first page of what their old colleague had written and hidden under a Hyde Park mattress:

FROM THE PSYCHOMETRIC NOTEBOOKS OF FRANCIS VA-LERIAN HAMMOND

The first thing I want to explain, in case anyone ever reads these ravings—no, not ravings, they tell me I shouldn't talk about myself and my work that way.

Let me start over:

The first thing I want to explain, in case anyone ever reads these writings (better, Francis; see: you're making progress already!): the first thing I want to explain—not that anyone's ever going to read this crap (not crap, Francis; think of it as 'first steps in therapeutic self-aware-ness').

The first thing I want to explain (even if I end up entombing these notes under the mattress on which I'm now perched—meaning that this bed could serve as the East-55th-Mausoleum of F.V. Hammond (a.k.a. Fe-ral Frank the Pharaoh—and yes, colleagues, I know all about the names you cruelly pin on me—cruelly, yes, but the pins don't stick, because my *flesh is time-resistant, like good-friend Khaemwaset's); this bed could serve as the East-55th-Mausoleum of the intellectual relicta of one F.V. Hammond—*

Lost the thread; start over.

Curious, isn't it, how the psychometric sciences can be traced (by those who know where to look) back through the dragon-whorled mists of time to ancient, ancient Egypt; and yet the term 'psychometry' first became popular in America only relatively recently, in the nineteenth century, through the speculative efforts of a humble Kentucky physician, one Joseph Rhodes Buchanan.

If you are separated from a loved one, preached Doctor Buchanan, whether by distance, or time, or death, then you may ease that separation and re-establish the intimacy for which you long, by handling an object that your beloved once touched: a bit of clothing, a favorite hat left behind on a rack, a brush that retains stray strands of hair. Your inner 'psychometer' will detect the trace-element residue of your beloved's soul on that once-frequently-handled relictum; clutching that hairbrush, that hat, that bit of clothing, you will recapture the presence you crave.

Mesmeric fraud; spiritualist chicanery: such were the scornful responses when Buchanan first presented his speculations. But with the American Civil War, when thousands perished in war, when thousands more disappeared nameless and without trace on smoke-swirled battlefields, wounded and left crawling endlessly for aid, or held captive as anonymous prisoners of war, or abandoned as rotting corpses in a night-shrouded ditch—then, at that moment in our history, when families in their thousands longed to embrace their missing loved ones once more, then did Buchanan's psychometry begin to attract widespread attention.

Think of it! Merely through handling an object that had once been handled by a beloved, we might break the barriers that hem in our puny lives: time, distance, death itself. All broken, all shattered, all…all…

Losing the thread again. Start over.

What I want to say is:

What I offer below is not to be submitted to some journal (I know— so no one needs to tell me—this won't be considered scholarly); knowing this in advance, I am immune to rejection. What I offer is a jeu d'esprit, a bagatelle, a psychometric trifle.

Call it disposable; call it fiction; call it play.

And yet: every word is true.

For what is depicted below is what I witnessed.

Or saw. Or had communicated to me.

Sometimes I'm not sure.

But of this I'm very sure: I'm not gonzo, mad, bonkers, what you will. Too easy, much too easy, for gentle readers to flip this off, dismiss what's to follow as insane ravings.

But not ravings, no. Recall, if you will, what Nijinsky wrote in his diary: "I have made many mistakes; but I have corrected them, I have paid for them, through my sufferings and sorrows." Something to that effect; I lost his book, I think, the night I became sad and threw many things out the window.

Nijinsky the ecstatic Russian; Nijinsky the mad dancer. Yet through his madness, in his diary, come lightning-bolts of insight: "I have made many mistakes; but I have corrected them, I have paid for them, through my sufferings and sorrows."

True for me, too. True for me, too.

For I, too, through my sufferings and sorrows have paid for my many mistakes.

Sorrows that helped me gain solidarity with the Seraphim in their torments here on earth (Seraphim/Seraphs: more on them anon, should I develop a scintilla of trust in you, O potentially-kindred-spirit Reader!).

Mistakes that toppled my career and leveled it like the sand-whipped ruins of the Serapeum. Mistakes that estranged my friends— yes, I once had friends!—and hurt their lives.

And yet, what the world calls mistakes were twisted paths that led me to things, to glimpses, to glimpses...

Hard to explain. Let me instead illustrate one glimpse—from among many—in the form of a tale.

Let the time be fourteen centuries before Christ, or more precisely, 1336 BC.

Let the setting be the Central Nile Valley, the city of Akhetaten, what today is called Amarna.

Let—and here I'll confess I'm sounding grandiose; I look at what I've written and I sound like a voice-over for some Cecil B. DeMille 10 Commandments epic.

Enough. Now I'll share the glimpse, the vision.

Ricky looked up from the scrawled sheet. In the plane-seats beside him, Iggy and Harriet were engrossed in their copies. *This writing,* he thought. *Sounds exactly as if we're back at the Florian Café, and Frank's saying he'll buy everyone another coffee and pizza-slice if we'll just bear with him one more half-hour and listen to his latest idea.*

Well, go ahead, old friend. He silently addressed the page. *You've got my attention. You've got the attention, I think, of all three of us.*

He turned back to the scrawled page and surrendered to Pharaoh Frank's tale.

chapter 43

From the Psychometric Notebooks of Francis Valerian Hammond:

Amen-em-het knew the king's secret. Knew everything there was to know. Everything. Not bad for a mere servant, an underling, a young no-body the pharaoh never troubled to acknowledge.

"Everything?" Ay stopped him in the temple corridor for the fourth time that day.

An old man, this Ay, bent with years, but still strong. A sudden thrust with his walking stick in the deserted corridor, and Amen-em-het found himself pinned by the throat to the wall like a bird on a fowler's lance. "Everything? Are you sure?"

The young man gagged but didn't dare push the stick aside. Ay, after all, was Commander of Chariots and Privy Councillor and more: he kept an eye—a leeringly more-than-protective eye, whispered some—on the most luscious of the king's daughters.

The jewel on the tip of the stick dug grooves into Amen-em-het's throat. Amethyst. A pretty stone, pricey and maybe worth stealing, if one could only find a gem dealer willing to take chances in this newly built City of the Sun. Amethysts kept one sober even in the worst drinking bouts. A good stone for Ay, who was known to like his beer.

Another jab with the stick. "I said, are you sure you've spied out everything there is to know?"

Amen-em-het said he was sure. "The king carries the object, whatever it is, all the time. Except when he prays at the Dawn Altar."

"Choose that as your moment, then." Ay darted looks up and down the corridor. " 'The One Living in Truth,' this king of ours calls himself.

Hah." A low laugh from the old man. "Say rather, the Living Insult to the Gods. Imagine the arrogance. To abolish all cults save one, to outlaw all gods save his, to abandon all shrines save those dedicated to his One and Only." He made a sign to avert evil. "Amun and the pantheon must be restored."

Another look up and down the corridor. "You have what I gave you?"

Amen-em-het showed him what he concealed beneath his cloak: a knife with a honed ten-inch blade. He knew this knife, had seen it used at the altar set aside for the foreleg-dismemberment ceremony. He'd heard bulls cry out at the mere sight of this tool.

Ay saw him wince. "You are being well paid. And you will have help. I've also given gifts to the inner sanctuary guards. All of them loathe him. This pharaoh of ours. This Akhenaten."

A sound of footsteps, and the echo of laughter. "Ah. The voice of youth. How welcome to an old man." Ay turned and offered a courtier's smile to the group advancing along the corridor. Ay and Amen-em-het both bowed low to the crown prince and his entourage.

"Greetings, your highness." Amen-em-het marveled at how skillfully Ay could switch tones. Only a moment earlier the old man had been plotting against this youngster's father.

Ay saluted the prince. "A joy to greet you, O Living Image of the Aten."

The young prince—diminutive, frail, with a thin sensitive face— smiled trustingly up at the Privy Councillor.

Ay asked after the prince's health. "We must guard you well, my son. After all, you will one day inherit your father's throne."

"May that day be distant." A pious exclamation from the prince.

"Of course, my son." Ay bestowed a smile worthy of any loving uncle.

Amen-em-het studied Ay's face and knew at once his thought (he'd heard the old man boast in private all too often): when that day comes, the real power will be standing a discreet pace behind the throne. A power which will see to it that the Living Image of the Aten changes his name to coincide with the restoration of Amun-worship: from Tutankhaten to Tutankhamun.

A power which will arrange two things for this young prince: an early death and a hasty burial.

Another loving-uncle's smile from Ay. "Long life to you, my son."

⟨⟩

Enough scribbling; night descends, the vision wobbles, and I must away for refreshment (pizza, pepperoni, extra cheese) to wherever I can score some grub.

Thus endeth the day's Psychometric (not Psychotic!) jottings.

⟨⟩

Ricky smiled. So clear, this voice from the page. It was as if they were all back at the Florian, Frank gesticulating, Iggy rolling his eyes in protest at some verbal extravagance, Hattie taking a careful bite of her pizza slice so grease wouldn't drip on her chin.

Ricky turned to the next page—another chapter, it seemed, in the story; another visit with his old friend.

chapter 44

F.V. Hammond: **more psychometric verbiage (I use the word 'verbiage' in acknowledgement of my literary self-indulgence)**

Akhenaten lingered in his favorite place at this, his favorite time of day. The chapel of the Aten, the sacred sun-disk, as the god rose from the east.

This chapel was simply an outdoor altar, with no roof save the open sky. The altar faced the Mountains of the Dawn and was aligned with a cleft on the horizon where the god bestowed its first appearance every morning.

Akhenaten breathed thanks to the Aten for this day, this silence, this solitude.

For to be pharaoh meant to be surrounded by noise, unmastered chaos, beings numberless, all petitioning him for favor.

Not that he disliked these beings. No. They were his charges, his cattle, and he loved them.

At least from a distance. From a distance, he could pen hymns with his reed stylus to the Aten, thanking the god—*his* god—for giving the Nile and all its animals and humans into his care. From afar, yes, he loved them, loved the vision of order.

But close up: they all appalled him. Made him crave solitude, silence, such as he could enjoy only here at this moment of dawn.

Not that he truly had solitude even here. Councillor Ay had insisted on hand-picking a retinue of attendants for even this most private of rituals. "To increase the Aten's honor, O Great One," and Akhenaten had *given in, just as he'd given in to the old man's incessant badgering to be appointed Commander of Chariots.*

Fine: he'd given him the title, just so he could enjoy a moment's peace and pen another hymn.

Ay thought him a fool, he knew. Thought he couldn't see the ambition glitter in his councillor's eyes. Thought he couldn't see the hunger for titles.

Commander of Chariots. Fine. Let Ay have the precious title; let him scheme.

For Akhenaten knew that schemes and titles were what people made do with if they lacked any true vision of the Aten. Other individuals had to live without revelations, without direct contact. But not he. Akhenaten raised his hands in thanksgiving.

Not for nothing did he call himself Solely Beloved of the God. Let others consult their sand-gazers and entrail-diviners, their scorpion-men and dog-stranglers, their sorcerers who caught boys by night and jammed their heads face-down over candlelit oil pools until the child-eyes swam with the wake of demons and marsh-things in greasy liquid spirals. Let them. Let them. No one had a source of revelation like his.

Behind him, a scuff of sandal on stone.

He knew who it must be: the sulky servant with the offensive name. Amen-em-het: "Amun is at the forefront."

Didn't this wretch know such a name belonged to the old order? Akhenaten had suppressed the Amun priesthood years ago.

He could have made the man change his name, could have banished him to the Sand-Wastes or fed him to the crocodiles. Sycophants and opportunists had suggested all these remedies.

But no. He, solely beloved of the Aten, loved his subjects, his cattle. It was enough to feel the strength of the Sun Disk as it rose, to sense its rays pervade the earth and crush the forces of Night that opposed the Pharaoh of Light.

Rays pervading the earth. The thought reminded him of the wand he always carried as he wandered about his palace.

Always carried; always. Yes. For it was through the wand, and what it showed him, that he experienced the Aten on earth—the Aten, as made visible in its ethereal Emissaries, the Sekhemu.

It was the Aten that had first led him from the palace and far into the desert, one glimmering transcendent dawn, the Aten that had guided him in discovering the precious substance from which he had made the wand.

Carefully he relinquished the sacred object and placed it on the altar.

The first rays of the sun struck the wand's shimmering surface, strengthening it, strengthening its ability to make manifest the Emissaries of the Aten. Akhenaten gazed on it and smiled.

He gazed, too, at the upright carving propped atop the altar: a giant image of the sun disk. Sculpted at the disk's base was a cobra, its neck ringed by an ankh. Ankh: hieroglyph of life, life bestowed on Akhenaten, and through Akhenaten, bestowed on all his cattle. The image, made of dark obsidian, was polished so highly that its mirrored surface undulated with shadows.

As he did with every sunrise, the king leaned forward and peered at the disk, studying these shadows, hoping to divine what the dawn might bring.

One shadow loomed larger than the rest: a being of some sort, garbed in a cloak. Akhenaten stooped forward to see more clearly.

Yes, a cloak. The cloak concealed something.

From beneath the garment emerged a hand, and in the hand—this the disk showed him clearly—was a knife.

Again, from behind him, a scuff of sandal on stone—but this time from no more than two paces behind him.

Akhenaten saw death in the mirror, heard death in the sound.

Most men, he knew, would panic at the breath of death on their necks. Not he. He loved risk, throve on it.

Call the guards? No; he knew their disaffection.

Run, and lose his dignity? No. He loved risk, loved horizons where possibilities radiated beyond even a pharaoh's sight.

"Amen-em-het." One word, pronounced without deigning to turn, articulated with all the authority belonging to only the Beloved of the Aten.

"Yes, O Great One?" Akhenaten could hear the surprise in his servant's voice, knew the wretch was startled into a guilty bow.

"Did you wish a closer look," and now Akhenaten turned, "at this?" He plucked the shimmering wand from the altar.

The knife had been hastily concealed once more beneath the cloak. Akhenaten caught the acquisitive flash in the servant's eyes.

"Great One." The wretch, unsure of himself, bowed and bowed again.

Calmly the king announced he was about to visit the Aten's inner sanctum. "Would you like to join me? Just the two of us? Would you like to glimpse the Sekhemu? You've never seen them, have you? They love to emerge in settings of tranquility such as my private shrine."

"The Sekhemu? What do you mean, O Great One?" The man's voice quivered between ambition and fear: a chance to murder his monarch, Akhenaten knew, but the danger of whatever lay in the sanctum.

And Akhenaten himself didn't know how the Sekhemu would respond to such impiety, to a knife raised against the Aten's beloved. They would be provoked; it would be risky.

Would they protect him? Would they strike them both dead?

A rare epiphany, to be sure. And Akhenaten lived for such moments.

"Come." He took his would-be murderer by the arm as if out for a stroll with a friend. "Let us see what mood awaits us in the sanctum."

⎯⎯⧳⎯⎯

Let us see...

Vision fading. Suddenly very tired. Seraphim withdrawing into their vessels. Wings. Multiple wings, folding, at rest.

Dark again. Night.

Sadness, at the withdrawal, after this intimacy of the vision.

Mad Nijinsky. The mad dancer. He had it right when he wrote: "They'll call me crazed, demand I be confined, because I speak of things I can't understand."

True, I don't fully understand. But I have seen, even if only intermittently, through the most opaque-smoked glass; and what a blessed visitation: In illo loco stabant seraphim et volitabant et clamabant alter ad alterum et dicebant: Sanctus sanctus sanctus.

Tired now. Seraphs fled. Darkness through my window.

Sanctus sanctus sanctus.

Thus endeth today's Psychometric jottings.

⎯⎯⧳⎯⎯

Ricky looked up from the page. His friends had both finished their reading. "What's this bit in Latin?"

"From the old Vulgate Bible," explained Harriet. "The angels in attendance around the throne of God: 'In that place stood the seraphim. They hovered and cried, each unto each, and they said: *Holy, holy, holy*.'"

"An old habit of Frank's," smiled Iggy. "If he felt strongly about an experience he couldn't put into his own words, he'd fall back on some ancient holy text. He knew 'em all."

Ricky studied the scribbled-over page. "Okay. But what kind of experience is he trying to talk about? He starts out with Akhenaten and ends up with angels. I don't get it."

"Not sure I do either," replied Iggy slowly. "He presents it as a story—historical fiction of some kind—and he makes sure to tell readers it's just a bagatelle. A jeu d'esprit. Nothing to be taken seriously."

"Except," intervened Harriet, "it's clear Frank himself takes all this very, very seriously."

"Yeah," agreed Iggy, "to the point that he feels depressed and worn out when what he calls 'the vision' fades."

"But what's strange," insisted Ricky, his mind on the pragmatic dimension, "is how Frank brings a wand into the story. A wand, like maybe what I've got right here in my carry-on bag. But how did Frank know about this thing? None of us has had any contact with him or any chance to tell him about this discovery."

"If Frank were here," grinned Iggy, "I bet he'd say some seraph told him. Or maybe he had a psychometric breakthrough."

"Maybe," grunted Ricky. "I guess if we find Frank, we can ask him."

"A big if," added Harriet. "Let's just hope we can track him down."

The intercom voice told them to prepare for landing in Providence.

chapter 45

Department of Egyptology
Charles Edwin Wilbour Hall
Brown University, Providence, Rhode Island

THE VIEWS FROM his spacious third-floor window were a small but delectable part of what pleased Robert Thwarter about his tenured perch at Brown.

Cobblestone streets, that rippled unevenly above ancient tree roots. The campus green, set among lecture halls built of stone and ivied brick and Doric Greek columns. The eighteenth-century gables and gold cupolas and church spires of College Hill. Street names—Merchant, India, Packet—that survived as reminders of this city's past as a seafaring colonial New England port.

Steeped, steeped in the past, all this: precisely to the taste of an antiquarian. He stood at the window and contrasted this with his alma mater:

Set above the doorway of the University of Chicago's Oriental Institute—and positioned so that Egyptology students couldn't help but see it every day—was a sculpture on the theme of 'The Old Gives Its Gifts to the New.' An Egyptian scribe yields a scroll (*the Wisdom of the East*) to a broad-shouldered Man of the West. Behind the Westerner is a horizon that includes a Parthenon and skyscraper; by the Westerner's feet reposes an American bison. The catchy attractiveness and dominance of the New: all of a piece with the newness of the Chicago campus, broad-shouldered, post-World War Two, and industrial-grey, much like its host-city.

What was it Pharaoh Frank Hammond had said years ago? *Enough of Chicago! If I ever manage to pass myself off as normal and get a fulltime job, Brown's the place for me; it's easy to get lost there in a dream of the past.*

Thwarter's sentiment exactly. Astonishing, was his reaction when he'd heard Hammond's burblings, how much Crazy Frank mirrored his own mind.

That had been the day before Thwarter lectured his fellow seminar students on the under-appreciated qualities of Ramses the Great, and Hammond had interrupted with the petty witticism at which Thwarter still smoldered: *Appropriate that Egyptology's greatest egotist should take as his specialty the most egotistical of all Egypt's rulers.* Everyone had laughed.

Yes, laughed. Thwarter pushed back the office curtain further and looked to the right, down Prospect Street. From this third-floor office he could see the entrance of another ivy-clad building: the Bellevue Psychiatric Clinic.

"*And thus the whirligig of time,*" he murmured with quiet glee, "*brings in his revenges.*"

"I beg your pardon?" This from the man standing just behind him.

"Sorry." His savoring of vengeance had made Thwarter forget there were others in the room. "Just a verse from Shakespeare. Appropriate, considering what's going on down there in the street."

Mustafa Hamdi, senior executive of the Egyptian Heritage Corporation, stepped to the window. "What is it?"

Thwarter tapped the glass. "There. All three of them. I knew they'd show up sooner or later."

"Indeed." Hamdi contemplated the scene. Three individuals stood in front of the Bellevue Clinic, looked up and down the block, seemed uncertain what to do. "I recognize my former employee of course. Mister Richard Greyling Atlas. And the other two: I saw them in Chicago the other day, at the American Research Center's gala."

"The woman in black is named Kronsted. The fat guy's named Forsythe. But I prefer to call him Budge the Pudge."

The pair watched as the trio below studied the Bellevue Clinic's door.

"I am just a touch concerned," confessed Thwarter. "I know they'll learn nothing here. But what if they hear about the clinic's unlisted branch in Warwick?"

"It won't matter." Hamdi spoke with an assurance at which the American had to marvel. "They'll discover nothing worthwhile. I've paid out enough cash to make sure of that."

From the shadows at the back of Thwarter's office stepped forth another man, someone whose presence Thwarter preferred not to note. Hamdi had insisted he be included in the operation. From Yemen, he explained, a surviving member of a largely exterminated al-Qaeda affiliate known as Ansar al-Din. Zubayr, was the man's name. Hasan Zubayr.

To Thwarter's way of thinking, Zubayr wasn't a good fit. The jut of the man's jaw, the continuous glare in his eyes marked him as too pugnacious for the slow and subtle dagger-work preferred by Thwarter.

But Hamdi had said Hasan Zubayr would have his uses.

Zubayr stepped beside them and watched, his gaze fixed on one of the trio in the street. "*Atlasss,*" he hissed. "*Atlasss.*"

The trio had apparently made up their minds. They opened the door and disappeared within the Bellevue Clinic.

Zubayr pressed his face to the third-floor window, hissed again. He looked ready to lunge at his prey through the glass.

Hamdi spoke to him sharply in Arabic, pulled him back. *Istanna shwayya. Al-sabar gameel.*

Thwarter's Arabic was good; he'd done his share of dig-time in Egypt. He understood Hamdi's warning: "Wait a bit. Patience is a beautiful thing."

Walakin lil-sabar hudood came the impatient reply: *But there are limits to patience.*

"He, too," explained Hamdi, "awaits your whirligig of time. He wants revenge for the loss of his colleagues in a Hellfire Predator strike in the highlands of Yemen."

"Someone who wants revenge that recklessly," warned Thwarter, "could get out of hand."

"He'll have his uses," said Hamdi firmly.

Zubayr kept his face to the glass. "*Atlasss.*"

chapter 46

Parking lot of Exxon-Mobil Rest-Stop
Highway 17, near the junction with Route 179
Verde Valley, Arizona

ANITA MARTINEZ WOKE with a start. *Where am I?*

The dream had been so vivid.

She'd had it before, many times. It always came to her more clearly after time spent in the cave. Especially after handling the seraph-sherds.

She kept her eyes closed a moment, to fix the details in her mind.

Confusion, smoke, tumult. An island in a lake. Towers and temples, rising from the water. Market stalls: tobacco, chocolate, silver, slaves.

Stairways red with the blood of slain captives. A dismembered goddess. Stone skull-racks; the skewered heads of the sacrificed.

A royal causeway; a palace. And a name: Aztlan, 'the realm of white herons.'

Men. Priests parading in the flayed skins of victims. Warriors. Eagle feathers and circular wicker-reed shields. Cumbrous clubs studded with obsidian blades. Warriors, awaiting their enemy, the enemy of Tenochtitlan.

Hatred, anger, fear.

The enemy: here they came. Bearded, capped in steel. Metal breastplates. Firearms. Gunpowder. Cannon. Horses.

Hatred, anger, fear.

Confusion, smoke, tumult. The end of Aztlan. The ruin of Tenochtitlan, and great sorrow.

But out of the smoke:

A solitary figure, injured, limping, making slow progress—painfully slow! Injury must be part of his story—up a thick jungle path. The shredded remains of a gaudy knit kilt mark him as a member of royalty.

But like a laborer, on his back he bears a slatted wooden cage. Squalling within heralds the contents: bright birds that flap their wings.

So vivid, this dream, that Annie sees how the sun shines on his face, so she knows he's walking north. And as he walks, despite his pain, he smiles.

And that smile fills her with hope.

⧖

Curious. Before she opened her eyes, Annie realized—as she had when she'd dreamt this dream before—she'd been given a glimpse of the last days of the Aztec empire, of conquest by the Spanish conquistadors.

"Maybe some kind of Mexican ancestral memory, passed on through the genes?" had suggested Tomasina over at the Sonic Drive-In a few weeks ago, the last time the dream had come to Annie.

"Yeah, except my folks are from Costa Rica."

"So the Aztec-memory part doesn't work so well," conceded Tomasina.

And who was the man in her dream with the birds on his back? *Always so tired, always so hopeful, his face set to the north.*

A stirring beside her brought her fully awake. A furred presence. Presences: make that plural. Two, to be precise.

"Gabby, Micky." She heaved the dogs off her chest. "You don't have to sleep on top of me."

She sat up. Now she knew where she was.

The night had been spent in her car. She'd taken the front.

Sprawled asleep across the back seat: Francis Hammond.

What had he called himself? *Nuthouse escapee.* She still thought of him as Mister Gaunt the scarecrow.

Luckily the car was big enough: a vintage '66 Oldsmobile. Dynamic 88. Four-door, eight-cylinder.

"Your yacht," her grandfather had said when he'd given it to her as a dented and aged—but still serviceable—gift. "Your land-yacht." A yacht that still smelled of cigar fumes. Maybe that was one reason she'd kept it all these years: it reminded her so strongly of him.

As a teen—many, many years ago now!—she'd left her family rather than marry a man she didn't want. Wrath from her parents, of course.

But her granddad had stood by her, had driven with her all the way up the Pan-American Highway to Nogales. A long, long time ago, when border crossings had been easier on immigrants hoping for work.

Still asleep, Mister Gaunt. *Let him rest another minute. He needs it after last night.*

They'd had to run, and run hard. Flashlight beams had flickered on their backs as they bobbed among the pines. They'd splashed across Beaver Creek, heard one cop behind them slip and fall among the water-slicked stones.

They'd climbed a ridge, then circled and eventually descended, making their way back to the Sonic parking lot where Annie had left her car. A burst of speed onto Highway 17, then she'd pulled over at a rest-stop.

"Sun's up." She reached back and tapped Gaunt's knee. "You feel like some breakfast?"

A 24-hour diner right beside the gas station. Rather than have Micky and Gabby stare at them through the window, she ordered take-out and the four of them ate outside by the curb.

Her scarecrow seemed famished as usual. *Good thing I ordered the works.* Bacon and scrambled eggs. Pancakes in dark pools of maple syrup. Hash browns and ketchup.

She ate her own meal—oatmeal and plain yoghurt—in a few brief bites, which gave her time to study him.

Felt good to watch him eat. He seemed a salt-and-sugar man: he liked to push each bacon strip deep into the syrup before wolfing it down.

Wordless, true, but not unaware of her, she noted: Gaunt paused now and again, paper plate balanced on his knee, to offer her a bit of maple-slathered meat. Each time she smiled no. Solemnly he turned to Micky and Gabby—who'd swallowed their assigned dog food in breathless gulps—and fed them each morsels in turn.

She reached into the paper bag beside her on the curb. "Wasn't sure if you'd be wanting dessert." Hot fudge brownie sundae. "Amazing that I-Hop offers these things at seven in the morning." She didn't mind doing the talking for both of them.

Apparently also a dessert-at-breakfast man. But polite. Carefully he scooped a large spoonful that included ice cream, fudge, and brownie, topped by a sprinkling of pecans, and extended it to her mouth.

"Hey, the nuts at least are healthy," she said, and she accepted the bite as Gabby and Micky looked on.

"And coffee, of course." She pulled two cups from the bag.

As they drank she saw he still wore that blue plastic wrist tag. Faded now, the lettering, but still legible. *Bellevue Clinic/Psychiatric Unit/Francis Valerian Hammond.*

The thought hit her again. *I don't know this guy at all. How bad off is he? Unbalanced? Unstable? Unhinged?* Strange, how comfortable she felt around him.

"Hey," she offered. "How about we cut this thing off?"

Between sips he suddenly spoke. "No."

First word out of him all morning. A crow's croak.

"No," he said again, and then the crow seemed to realize it should practice being human, that some explanation might be in order.

"It reminds me." He flicked the tag on his wrist.

"Reminds you of what?" *This guy needs some prompting.*

"Reminds me I'm not normal."

He went back to sipping his coffee. End of conversation.

A truck passed on the freeway. Dishes clattered inside the I-Hop.

Guess that's it on crow-talk for the morning.

She was wrong. The crow wasn't done. "Do you remember that little thing," he resumed, "you left me in the cave? The Jurassic plant, with the picture on the label?"

"Yeah. I remember. The label showed a dinosaur. With wings."

"I don't know how you knew, but that's me." He sipped more coffee.

"What do you mean, that's you?"

"The pterodactyl. My giant wings"—he extended a long bony arm—"are well suited for flight. Soaring high in a huge desert sky. Open horizons everywhere. Limitless."

A pause. Then he continued. "But pterodactyl wings"—he flicked the tag again—"make me ill-adapted for walking this earth. The little blue label here reminds me there's no use trying."

"I don't know if that's the most constructive attit…"

"When you were a kid, you ever see those picture-books with names like *Prehistoric Monsters from 100 Million Years Ago*? They'd have diorama-type scenarios: a little flying lizard flitting about in the sky, enjoying its liberty. Then some gargantuan tyrannosaur stomping around on the ground—all teeth and gaping jaws the size of a steam shovel—rears up and snaps the flitterling for lunch."

He stared into his cup. "This coffee's pretty good. Anyway, I need reminders. It's dangerous for winged creatures to land on earth. Wings get burnt. It's happened before."

He rose from the curb. "Which reminds me. I promised to show you something." He strode to the car. "You know a place called the V-Bar-V?"

"Sure. It's an old cattle ranch. Been deserted for a hundred years."

"You know how to get there?"

"Yeah. It's not far."

"I said something to you last night about portals. The V-Bar-V will show you something of what I mean." He retreated into silence.

Rather than ask for more explanation, she drove, Gaunt beside her in front, the dogs breathing companionably on her neck from the back.

A quick phone call to Tomasina. "Girl, can you cover for me today?"

"Sure can. You feeling sick?"

"No. No. Actually I'm feeling fine."

"Well all right then. You have yourself a good day."

Feeling fine.

It was true, she realized. Wheeling up 17 in a big car that reminded her of home. For company, an early-morning high-desert sky; Micky and Gabby; and Gaunt the pterodactyl-crow.

A crow that had consented to fold its wings a moment and sit in the front seat of her '66 Olds.

chapter 47

V-Bar-V Ranch
Off National Forest Path 618
Verde Valley, Arizona

RED DUST ROSE in clouds as the Oldsmobile jounced along the trail. Annie pulled over where Francis Hammond motioned her to stop.

She stood and stretched, still stiff from a night curled up on the driver's seat. The dogs leapt about her, glad at the prospect of a walk.

Quiet. Behind her, the pinging of the car's motor as it cooled. Around them, the insistent shrill whir of cicadas.

A tumbled wooden-rail fence. A boulder-and-brick chimney—the remains of a ranchhouse.

Before them, a narrow track—a band of copper-orange dirt—amid dusty green shrubs, sycamore, and oak.

In the distance, a range of bright tawny hills.

Gaunt stood beside her, abruptly told her thanks for the meal. "Junk food fights it out with the sludge-residue of meds. Food's winning today. Which makes it a superlative morning."

He downed the last of his coffee, lifted his head high. "Pulse is up. Sugar's kicked in. Now I'm ready for any and all manner of beings"—he threw his arms wide—"whether they be animal-headed shamans stammering blessings as they emerge sun-dazed from the bush, or strange-limbed mutant zoomorphs wandering in open fields as the tree-life sings."

"Mutant zoomorphs?" This cascade of talk startled her—a rushed croak of caws from her crow. "You sure you feeling okay?"

"Fudge sundae meets maple syrup. Makes my blood smoke." He startled her again: his unshaven face creased into a smile. "Forgive me. I gibber."

He took her by the hand, pulled her along the dirt path. "Come."

The dogs ran before them, sniffed the air. A sweet breath of sage blew about them.

Junipers clustered along the path, trunks contorted, branches twisted.

"Note their motionless writhing." Gaunt suddenly paused. "Locals say this is a vortex spot."

"I've heard of that," said Annie. "A place where some kind of energy surge in the earth affects everything growing in the vicinity. Some folks up in Sedona claim there are so many vortex points around here that they've drawn visits from UFOs."

And in fact—though Annie had never told anyone, not even Tomasina, who was tolerant about this kind of talk—it was the half-formed hope of UFO-spotting that had first impelled her to this part of Arizona, to her cave, to her castle.

"Unidentified flying objects," said Gaunt, with an expression she took as half-meditative, half-crazed. "Except maybe we can identify these objects that fly, give them a name, you and I."

He paused to pat a juniper trunk. "And these trees in their writhings. It's their way of saying: *We, too, give witness to the ecstasy, to the glory.*"

He strode away up the path, apparently eager to show her his revelation.

Annie hesitated before the juniper: *These trees in their writhings give witness to the glory.*

One side of her—the hard-headed side, the side that had gotten the assistant-manager job at the Sonic and saved money for a double-wide trailer and made sure her Remington stood always loaded and handy by the front door, the side that kept her independent and safe and strong—that side of her screeched a warning.

He's wearing that tag for a reason. Not normal. A nuthouse escapee. He said so himself.

Then the dogs rushed up to slobber their joy and wag their tails and invite her to join them in following the other human who hurried ahead down the trail.

"Gabby, Micky. Give a gal a minute to think."

Not normal. A nuthouse escapee. He said so himself. Is it safe to stay around him?

But then why did I name these two Gabby and Micky?

Gabriella and Michael.

I named them in honor of angels. In honor of the ones I call seraphs, for want of any better name.

The ones whose presence I felt from the first night I entered the cave.

A presence that puzzled and thrilled me so much I scooped up some of the seraph-stones and laid them out in the shed that I gave the grand name of 'Museum.'

Girl, if he's a nutcase, then what does that make you?

Impatient, the dogs turned and tore after the fast-receding figure of Gaunt.

Not normal.

Well, neither am I.

"Hey, wait up." She ran after them all. "I'm part of this too."

chapter 48

V-Bar-V Ranch
Verde Valley, Arizona

SHE CAUGHT UP with him where he paused with the dogs before a soaring cliff face. To a height of twenty-five feet the rock was incised with markings, some identifiable, some deeply strange.

Mazes, whorls, spirals. Gouges and errant squiggles. Tortoises, horned quadrupeds. Archers and humpbacked flute-players.

"See." Francis Hammond pointed. "The figures are thickest here, along this big crevice in the rock."

He tapped a lichen-filled marking. "This one's my favorite."

A standing anthropomorph of some kind, from whose head unspooled a tapering ropy filament. This appendage twirled around pictographs of a pair of long-beaked spindly-legged avian shapes. The shapes faced each other.

"A priest, or a shaman," exclaimed Gaunt, "having a vision. And look. His brain's coming uncoiled from the overload of it all. Boy, I know that feeling—when your head's so full of thoughts your brain comes unglued."

"Petroglyphs," breathed Annie in wonder.

"Not just petroglyphs. Look here." He jabbed at the rock. "Hieroglyphs. Egyptian hieroglyphs."

"Egyptian?"

"See this incision here? And here? Right beside the shaman, and the birds. *Netjer nefer, netjer 'a'a*: 'The beautiful god, the great god'."

"Wait. Egyptian hieroglyphs? Here? In Arizona? I don't get it."

"Look. Look." Impatiently he pointed to the pair of avian shapes. "A vision of an encounter. A hitherto unknown moment in history. The ibis of Thoth meets the heron of Aztlan."

"Aztlan. Hey, wait."

"Pharaonic Egyptian meets Aztec Mexican. Right here."

"Hey, hang on. Let me catch up with you. Who's this guy having the vision?"

"You mean this shaman, the individual whose head is all but melting, poor guy? A long-ago Aztec emperor. Montezuma. He holed up here a while."

"Not possible." She laid a restraining hand on his arm. "I know something about that history. Montezuma got killed down in Tenochtitlan, when the conquistadors invaded. Killed either by Hernando Cortez, or by his own people, because he didn't want to go to war."

"Killed, according to what the history books claim. But they're all wrong." His eyes shone with assurance. "Here. Let me show you something I wrote after my first night in the cave. I wrote it while the vision was fresh. It's one of my psychometric jottings."

"One of your what?"

"Just read this page. Here, right here":

From the day of his birth, his people marked him for war. They wanted him to fight other tribes, to take captives that could be butchered, their hearts as plucked offerings, on altars whose spilled blood sped the sun through the sky.

His people wanted him—jaguar-robe on his shoulders, flint-knife in hand—to consecrate his life to Tezcatlipoca, god of combat and sorcery. A god ready to drink blood—blood of the Spanish, blood of rival tribes. It mattered not. What mattered was war.

He wanted none of it, he, Montezuma Xocoyotzin, Montezuma the Young, the Youth Montezuma. Rather, he sought meditation, sought ancient codices, ancient myths, ancient tales.

Among all the gods, the one he loved best was Quetzalcoatl, the Feathered Serpent. And among all the myths, the one he loved best to hear was the tale of how Quetzalcoatl once saved humankind:

The creator gods were casual in their cruelty, willing to create beings of flesh, unwilling to share with them food. Maize, corn, cereal: these the gods hoarded in a silo in a mountain within the forbidden world underground.

Quetzalcoatl, his heart touched by pity for humans as they starved, braved the underworld and found the forbidden mountain. Unable to penetrate the storehouse in his feathered-serpent form, he transformed himself into an ant—a creature so minuscule it went unregarded by the puma-headed demons that guarded the hoard.

Grain by grain, with great labor, the ant brought forth food from the silo. And thus he saved humans from starvation.

This was how the Youth Montezuma saw himself. Not as a warrior, but as a solitary quester, a wanderer, willing to brave strange lands to discover rare things of value he could bring home, things with which to astonish his people.

From merchants he'd heard of how tribes to the Far North—Pueblo Indians, mesa cliff-face dwellers—loved the bright-plumaged birds of the south, were willing to trade precious stones for these birds.

And this was all the vocation Montezuma longed for: to be a wanderer and trader, a solitary shaman, bringing scarlet macaws and blue-and-yellow parrots to the Pueblo and Sinagua folk, returning south with turquoise.

And when the Spanish came and wanted war, and when the Aztecs also wanted war, Montezuma refused any part of it. 'Enough blood,' he cried, and he prepared to flee.

History says they killed him. My vision says they failed.

⇥⇤

"Wait," exclaimed Annie, looking up from the scrawled notes. "I saw him."

This got Gaunt's attention. "You did?"

"In my dream. After I'd been handling the seraph-stones, you know, the potsherds in the cave. A tired man, with birds on his back. Walking north. Limping, but with a smile on his face."

"Yes. Yes. That sounds right," he agreed. "And when he reached Arizona, reached the place that later generations called Montezuma's Castle, he was welcomed by the *sekhemu*."

"By the what?"

"The Egyptians called them *sekhemu*. Seraphim is how they're named in the Bible."

"Whew. I feel like my own head's unspooling." She sat abruptly by the cliff-face. Gabby and Micky pawed her knee for attention. "But what were Egyptian seraphs doing in the American Southwest?"

"They were in exile, somehow, from Egypt. Spirits in exile are drawn to certain places. Kindred spirits," he smiled. "Like Prince Khaemwaset. Montezuma. Pterodactyls, like me. And you," he added, "with your museum of seraphs in torment. Because believe me," and here his smile faded, "the seraphim have suffered. And I'm afraid they may suffer more."

She wanted to hear more—so many unanswered questions crowded her mind—but both dogs suddenly voiced low throaty growls, their heads pointed stiffly along the trail.

"Someone's coming. And to judge from the dogs, someone unfriendly. We'd better get back to the car."

No sooner had they reached the Olds than they saw in the distance a pair of approaching vehicles.

"Yavapai County sheriff. Get inside." She opened her car door, thrust the scarecrow inside. "With all that dust they're raising, they probably haven't seen you yet."

She pushed him to the floor. "Get under these dog blankets. Gabby, Micky: you lie on top of him and keep still. You hear?"

The dogs settled atop the unprotesting scarecrow.

Casually she posed by the Olds as the two police cars churned to a dusty halt. She knew one of them. Big Bartholomew Kincaid. He stopped by the Sonic often for burgers.

"Morning, Annie. Thought you'd be at work serving coffee this time of day."

"Day's so nice"—she was impressed at how casual she kept her tone—"just had to take it off."

The deputy showed her a flier—a photo beneath the words *Wanted: Interstate Fugitive.*

"We've got roadblocks posted everywhere for this individual. Wanted on a number of charges."

"Haven't seen him. What's his name?"

He read it out painstakingly. "Francis Valerian Hammond."

Carefully he folded the flier. Then he stooped to the window to look in her car.

chapter 49

Department of Egyptology
Charles Edwin Wilbour Hall
Brown University, Providence, Rhode Island

"THAT'S NICELY SETTLED, then." Mustafa Hamdi clapped his phone shut with a satisfying snap.

He looked across the office. The American was still staring out the window as if he hadn't heard.

"I said," he repeated more loudly, "I've settled things nicely."

"Hmm?" With obvious reluctance Robert Thwarter turned from the window. "Oh, yes, sorry. To whom did you place a call?"

"Calls. Plural." Hamdi allowed a reproving tone into his voice. "While you were enjoying the view, I've been phoning Highway Patrol centers and county sheriffs' offices in four different states."

"I'm not simply enjoying the view. I'm keeping an eye on the Bellevue down there. I want to see how soon our little trio emerges. I'm worried they might discover something. Especially that Richard Greyling Atlas. He's clever, and persistent enough as a snooper that he might pick up Hammond's trail."

"Atlasss." Hasan Zubayr, like Thwarter, remained fixed in place by the window.

The Yemeni and the American: from Hamdi's point of view—who prided himself on his cool pragmatism—both were too headlong, too passionate in their hatreds.

"I told you"—Hamdi allowed a greater note of insistence to enter his tone—"there's no need to worry. They'll learn nothing useful at the Bellevue."

"How can you be so sure?" Thwarter kept his back to Hamdi as he stared at the street below.

"Because I've made generous cash payments, as I told you already, to Ms. Orloff, the head psychiatric nurse, and to every staff member who could possibly know something relevant at the Bellevue."

"And suppose our trio down there makes a more generous cash offer?"

"Unlikely, Professor. Unlikely." Hamdi permitted himself a small smile at Thwarter's back. "You, as a member of academia, know what small salaries scholars earn. None of the three below is likely to have the money to better our bribes."

He stepped to the window. "Besides, I've an agent in place at the Bellevue. Someone who's been working there in the guise of an administrative assistant for the past several months. One Nadia 'Ateeyah."

A skeptical grunt from the American. "This 'Ateeyah. Is she reliable?"

"Absolutely. She's a graduate student in Egyptology at Cairo University, with hopes of being hired someday by the government's Supreme Council of Antiquities. I myself, as you know, in my capacity as a senior executive at the Egyptian Heritage Corporation, am also an SCA affiliate with considerable influence in the Council's decisions on hiring."

He permitted himself another smile. "Which means she knows she mustn't displease me. Which means I'm very, very confident she will behave precisely as instructed."

"Well thought-out." Another grunt from the American. He remained by his station at the window. "But I'm still worried they might find Hammond before we do."

"This," replied Hamdi firmly, "will not happen." He reminded Thwarter that the Corporation had confirmed the rumors: Francis Hammond had indeed been sighted at various places in the Southwest. "Colorado, Utah, Arizona, New Mexico. He's somewhere out there. We know he escaped from the Bellevue some time ago."

"But why did you call the police?"

"If you'd been listening just now," explained Hamdi—*I am a very patient man*, he told himself, *considering what headlong and headstrong youngsters I have to deal with here*—"you'd know that I just told the various major police departments in those four states that an antiquities thief is on the rampage somewhere in the Southwest. A convicted felon with a suspended sentence from his break-in at Chicago's Oriental Institute. Someone who has also very recently stolen a valuable artifact from the Haffenreffer Museum here on Brown's campus."

Thwarter's head half-turned from the window. "Now that's a clever move. And let me guess. You made up that crime and told the police we didn't want to report it yet because Francis Hammond, after all, is a beloved but unfortunate colleague, someone with a documented history of mental illness, whom we wish to locate and bring back to Bellevue before he obsessively commits more antiquities thefts in the Southwest, crimes from which we wouldn't be able to rescue him. We want to keep him from falling further afoul of the law. Hence our appeal to the authorities."

"Bravo, Professor. And now we must leave."

"Leave?" The American sounded annoyed.

"You and I and our Yemeni friend here"—Hamdi chose a peremptory tone now; he wanted no more arguments—"have flights this evening for Albuquerque. I anticipate that Hammond will be found shortly. We need to be on hand so we can interrogate Hammond as promptly as possible."

"Why the rush?"

"Because"—Hamdi was becoming a bit tired of these petty questions—"my colleagues in Firthland Oil are growing impatient. They want to locate this 'Portal' that Hammond referred to under the influence of our medications. The location of this Portal, whatever it is, and wherever it may be, is apparently more crucial to our venture than the two halves of the wand."

"I still say"—Thwarter spoke with a vehemence that Hamdi privately catalogued as borderline-insubordinate, to be dealt with later—"we should snatch the half of the wand that Atlas is carting around."

"It will keep," Hamdi reassured him. "If somehow we miss Hammond, I'm counting on Atlas and his crew to lead us to him. Let's do nothing till then to increase their vigilance. And don't worry. Orloff and 'Ateeyah will keep track of our friends down there. We can seize the other half of the wand any time we wish."

"I still say snatch it *now*."

Definitely insubordinate. Hamdi was becoming displeased.

"Professor, like so many archaeologists, you've become fixated on one material object, when you need to keep in view the big picture: the two halves of the wand, plus the Portal. Plus, I suspect, Francis Hammond, who in the end may be the only person, the indispensable person, to unlock this riddle of the *sekhemu* and how we can make the *sekhemu* serve the purposes of our Corporation and Firthland Oil."

"Pharaoh Frank Hammond isn't the only Egyptologist who knows something about the *sekhemu*." This in the tone of someone whose pride was injured.

"Now don't sulk, Professor, just because your little sessions with Hammond at the clinic's branch in Warwick haven't yielded what we'd hoped."

"You should've increased the level of his meds, the way I suggested."

"And have him brain-dead, which is what I suspect you secretly want? No, Professor. We need his brain functioning. At least until we've teased from that brain the information we need."

He handed folded sheets of paper to Thwarter and Zubayr. "Our flight itinerary for Albuquerque. Time to leave, gentlemen."

"Atlasss." The Yemeni still stared down the street.

"Gentlemen. Time to leave."

The American took one last look at the clinic. The trio still hadn't emerged.

"Time to leave." Hamdi closed the office curtains, switched off the office light. Still the two hesitated.

"Time to leave." He guided them both out the door.

chapter 50

Bellevue Clinic
51 Prospect Street
College Hill, Providence

IGNATIUS FORSYTHE HAD expected some resistance, invocation of privacy rules and so forth. But not to this extent.

"I'm afraid we can't help you." The office manager—a massive pale blonde, who eyed them from behind gold-rimmed spectacles with a gaze that warned *No nonsense, now* and *Please don't make me pitch you out the door*—straightened files as she spoke. Her name tag read *Stark*.

Richard Atlas tried again. "Francis Valerian Hammond."

"Yes," said Nurse Stark. "You already gave me his name."

"But we know he was a patient here," said Harriet Kronsted, "maybe multiple times."

"Sorry. I checked through our files. No record of any Francis Hammond."

"Maybe under a pseudonym?" suggested Ricky. "He's a skinny red-haired guy, scraggly looking. Really tall, too. How tall would you say, Iggy?"

"Huh? Oh, six-three or so." Iggy had become distracted.

The other Bellevue employee at the reception desk hadn't said a word. She'd stayed seated behind her computer screen in the far corner of the room, apparently typing.

But she kept eyeing them, then glancing at Nurse Stark. *It's as if she wants to say something,* thought Iggy.

Petite, and quite pretty. Dark brown eyes, long black hair, olive complexion, all of which contrasted strikingly with her white clinician's uniform. Her name badge read 'Ateeyah.

'Ateeyah: an Egyptian name. *Funny coincidence.*

Nurse Stark was saying no one of that description had been checked into Bellevue Clinic over the past five years. "And I should know," she announced with a prim pursed set to her mouth, "because I've done all the intake listings for just that length of time."

Harriet and Ricky asked if they could review with her the list of all clients admitted over the past few years. Nurse Stark said loudly it was out of the question.

More darting glances from 'Ateeyah. She lifted her head as if to say something, then bit her lip and turned back to her screen. *Agitated; torn about something; conflicted, maybe.*

If anyone had asked Iggy Forsythe to rate himself as a potential date for a Saturday-night-out (which he'd done once, for an online matchup service, only to lose his courage and hit *Delete* instead of *Send*), he would have classified himself under the heading *'depressingly timid.'* And that, he would've added, was even before the Ushabti disaster and his latter-day tendency to curl up fetal-style in bed whenever the world proved to be too much—which lately it mostly was.

Nonetheless he could see this 'Ateeyah wanted to say something and Hattie and Ricky hadn't noticed—they were still arguing with Nurse Stark—and if he waited the chance might pass and he'd better do something *now.*

She definitely looked Egyptian. *Perhaps an Arabic speaker? And if so, perhaps here was an opportunity to communicate and get in some questions Stonewall Stark wouldn't understand?*

Take a chance, man; take a chance!

He leaned across the counter, braced himself to do the bravest thing he could remember doing since joining Frank and Ricky in that Ushabti break-in. *Which had been crazy and ill-advised, and maybe this is, too.*

Just do it, man.

Lau samahti, ya anisa. He whispered the Arabic words hesitantly; he hadn't used the language in years. *Hal anti Misriyah?*

She said nothing but stiffened. The words—*Excuse me, Miss. Are you Egyptian?*—had definitely caught her attention.

Nurse Stark was still arguing with his friends. Good.

Ihna nakhuf 'ala sadeeqina. Nakhuf annahu mat.

She kept her eyes fixed on her screen. But he could tell she'd heard, and understood him, too: *We're worried about our friend. We're afraid he's dead.*

"Out of the question," Nurse Stark was saying.

"What about your Psychiatric Unit?" asked Hattie.

"I checked that intake list as well. No one by that name."

"Well, we'd like to visit that unit, take a look around. Could you please give us the address?"

"I'm afraid that's also out of the question." A hard glint from behind gold-rimmed glasses. "We reserve the address for patients and their families. A matter of privacy and strict confidentiality."

Sadeequna—Iggy saw 'Ateeyah fix him suddenly with her deep-brown eyes, which made him blush madly but gave him hope to plunge on—*Sadeequna al-habeeb, fayn huwa? Arguki!*

Flowery talk, this, but Iggy figured *Why not go all-out?*

Again she stared at him as his words seemed to hit home: *Our friend, our beloved friend: where is he? I beg you!*

Suddenly she ducked her head decisively, wrote hastily on a notepad, then stood and made her way to the counter. She took an armful of manila-folder files from the counter and as she did so she slipped the note into Iggy's outstretched hand.

"…confidentiality," repeated Stark loudly.

Neatly lettered on the bit of paper was an address:
Psychiatric Unit
27 Cole Farm Road
Conimicut, Warwick

And beneath that, a bit of Arabic: *wa-Allah ma'akum—May God be with you!*

He couldn't help look at her again. A pretty face. Pretty eyes.

But now her attention seemed fixed once more on the screen. Nonetheless, even though Iggy Forsythe had never classed himself as a person blessed with intuitive insights, he had an intuition now. Her averted gaze contained the message *Best to get out now.*

"Guys. Hey, guys." Ricky and Hattie were still at it with Nurse Stonewall. "Let's go get something to eat."

He didn't dare look back, but he was sure—or almost sure— that 'Ateeyah gave him a quick hidden smile as the trio walked out the door.

chapter 51

Bellevue Clinic
51 Prospect Street
College Hill, Providence

NADIA 'ATEEYAH'S TIPPING point had come only yesterday.

Up until then, she'd been submissive and cooperative enough. Admittedly, she'd never liked being bossed around by Mustafa Hamdi. Wasn't the whole point of the Arab Spring, the Lotus Revolution, and Egypt's democratic uprising to get rid of men like him? Corrupt, opportunistic, always ready to use their political appointments for personal advancement.

The way Hamdi had. An important member of the Supreme Council of Antiquities, an executive in a new and shadowy—but very influential—group known as the Egyptian Heritage Corporation, he wasn't someone a young Egyptian graduate student could afford to cross—not if that student wanted a career in Egyptology.

And she did, badly. She'd wanted that life since she was a child, introspective and bookish, on a primary-school bus trip to see the pyramids of Giza. The other kids had run about, screaming and chasing each other. Nadia 'Ateeyah had wandered off. When her teachers found her, she was standing alone, head craned back for the view, in front of the stone fore-paws of the Sphinx.

At first she'd noticed how the Sphinx's tail curled around its body—so true to feline format. Just like her kitten at home, she thought; and that delighted her.

But what commanded her attention had been the statue's limestone visage—a face full of remote wisdom, of mystery, of promise. The promise, perhaps, of something larger than the incessant blaring noise of present-day Cairo.

That had done it. She'd been hooked right there.

She'd stayed loyal to that dream, through all the maneuverings and joustings involved in her undergraduate and subsequent graduate studies. She'd accommodated herself to the patronage system: in a field as small as Egyptology, where the SCA's directors controlled every excavation and the appointment of every field director, one had to learn to cultivate backers—or at least avoid antagonizing them.

And so when Mustafa Hamdi had approached her with an offer—the promise of a secure perch in the newly reorganized, post-revolutionary SCA, with the prospect of someday heading a dig anywhere she liked in the Nile valley—naturally, she'd jumped.

"Of course," he'd said smoothly, "you'll have to serve an apprenticeship."

Of course. That was natural. She'd asked where that apprenticeship would be.

Overseas, he'd explained, on the campus of one of America's most prestigious Egyptological programs. Brown University, in a city called Providence, in a locality with the appealing name of College Hill.

Brown: well known, a splendid reputation. It offered one of the world's best programs in her field. She hadn't hesitated a moment. The Sphinx was smiling on her now, she'd thought gladly at the time; smiling because she'd stayed loyal to that lofty dream of wisdom.

Except the job had turned out to be not in Egyptology and not at Brown.

In Providence, yes, and on College Hill; but that was all. "You'll be working next door to Brown," Hamdi had said to placate her when she'd protested the deception, "but before you do anything at the university itself, I need you—the Egyptian Heritage Corporation needs you—to take a position at an off-campus posting. An administrative position, at a clinic. A mental-health clinic. Just for a few months. An interim job."

"A mental-health clinic? But this isn't what you promised me."

"Of course," Hamdi had continued, as if she hadn't spoken at all, "should you lack the flexibility to handle this assignment, you're free to pay your own way home. I'll find someone else with the flexibility to succeed in Egyptology. Someone who understands what she needs to do to succeed."

He bestowed on her a crafty little smile. "Yes, feel free to fly home. I'm sure you'll be able to find lots of work in our field on your own."

So of course she'd stayed.

Humdrum, was the worst at first she could say of the job. Shuffling files, answering phones. With only one proviso: if anyone contacted the clinic wanting to know about a certain former patient, she was to say that no such person had ever been treated there. A patient named Francis Valerian Hammond.

A strange business. But she told herself to be patient. A strange apprenticeship, no question; but if it led her back to the Sphinx, to a career in Egyptian archaeology, it'd all prove worth it.

Hardest part of the job: the other staff, especially the office manager, Antonia Stark. Too grumpy, too humorless.

But Nurse Stark was a sunbeam compared to Barbara Orloff. She ran Bellevue's residential-psychiatric branch, in a locality known as Conimicut, in the city of Warwick, some ten miles south of Providence.

Nadia had worked there just once, on a day several staffers were out sick and she'd had to fill in.

A nice setting—right on the water, an inlet of Narragansett Bay, the feel of a village to the locale.

But oppressive, this workplace. Bellevue's psych unit consisted of a small one-story office—the administrative center where Nadia had spent that work-day—plus a half-dozen cottages set back from the road on a big wooded lot. Trees obscured the cottages from the road.

An uneventful morning, until the phone rang.

The voice on the other end asked if they had any record as to when and how long a certain patient had been treated at Bellevue.

"One moment, please." She put the caller on hold.

The receptionist working at the next desk—a nervous and fussy-minded old woman named Marie—worriedly asked, "Whom do they want to know about?"

"Someone named Hammond."

"Francis Valerian Hammond?"

"That's it."

"For goodness sake," shrilled Marie with surprising vigor, "tell them we've got no record of any such person. No Hammond here; never has been. Get rid of whoever it is, fast."

Only when she'd fended off the query and hung up had she remembered that *Hammond* was the name she'd been cautioned about.

The trouble with being an archaeologist, she thought a moment later when Marie went to the restroom, leaving her briefly alone in the office, *is that one always feels the urge to dig around for possible finds.* In other words, she had to admit with a private half-smile, she was incurably nosy.

Quick: she stepped to Marie's desk and clicked on an icon that said *Intake—New Residents.* Hurriedly she scrolled down the alphabetized list, until: yes, there it was—the name *Hammond, Francis V.*

The flush of a toilet in the restroom. She had sixty seconds, tops.

Many, many documents in his folder. She clicked on the first, skimmed it.

The rush of water in a sink. *Good thing Marie's the type to wash her hands.*

A long intake document. No time to read it properly. She could hear her co-worker cranking a length of paper towel from the dispenser.

Dissociative thought processes...psychotic episodes...confinement... continuous supervision...increase level of medications...create mock-conference space for 'therapeutic' purposes...

Mock-conference space? Nadia paused in puzzlement.

The lock on the bathroom door flipped to 'Open.'

Click: she closed the Intake screen. Click: she restored Marie's screen. A lightning scoot back to her own desk.

With just enough time to greet Marie's return with a radiant smile.

Whew.

For the rest of the morning, part of her mind played with the thought that she'd been coerced into taking part in a lie. *Who is this Hammond?* She knew she'd best leave it be, if she didn't want to fall foul of Hamdi; but still it bothered her.

At lunch she'd drifted out back to smell the air. She breathed deeply. A taste of salt on the breeze—she guessed there must be a beach nearby. *It'd be nice to see the bay,* she'd thought, and set out on a path that led through the trees.

Pretty, these cottages, though each of them was windowless, shuttered tight, lifeless. Beyond them stood what looked like a neglected greenhouse.

She hadn't gotten far.

"Who authorized you to poke around here?" A loud unfriendly voice.

Head Nurse Barbara Orloff, a stout sturdy woman with muscled biceps big enough to make Nadia think this individual must've been a washerwoman in a previous life.

"I'm not poking. Just on my lunch hour."

"Off-limits here. All of it." From Orloff's thick waist dangled a dense clump of keys.

"What're these?" Nadia pointed to the secluded tree-hidden cottages.

"Locked wards. Residences, for our more challenging patients."

"Oh."

"You always ask so many questions?"

"No. No."

"That's good." Orloff fingered the keychain. "Employees that ask questions don't stay employed long."

From behind Orloff approached two male orderlies, as if they'd just scented a disturbance. Big, each of them, in crisp white hospital garb—the mark of the healing profession.

What didn't look so healing was the bulge under the lab coat by each man's left shoulder. A firearm, she guessed—and each of these men seemed ready to use it. They scowled at her as if awaiting word to propel her off the property.

A relief, after that, to return to Providence and work quietly for Nurse Stark.

Things had stayed humdrum after that, with Nadia wondering how much longer she'd have to serve this 'apprenticeship,' until the humdrum was broken just yesterday.

Into Bellevue's College Hill office had walked three men. Mustafa Hamdi, flanked by two individuals she'd never seen before.

Hamdi, smug and domineering as ever, had made the introductions. "This is our young apprentice. Nadia 'Ateeyah. Nadia, I'd like you to meet Dr. Robert Thwarter and Mister Hasan Zubayr."

Thwarter she'd heard of—who in Egyptology hadn't?—a gifted philologist and textual scholar and field-digger, with an uncanny knack for discoveries, and of course a tenured professor here at Brown. Thwarter gave her barely a nod and then joined Hamdi in a lengthy conversation with Antonia Stark.

The other man she disliked at once. He'd lingered by her desk, staring and staring at a photo she'd propped up by her computer screen: a pair of puppies—wrinkly-faced pugs—a reminder of home. She'd named them Wepwawet and Anubis, in honor of her favorite ancient jackal-gods. Her mom was looking after them back in Cairo while Nadia slaved through her time in this foolish apprenticeship.

"Aren't you Muslim?" he'd begun accusingly.

"Yes, I happen to be."

"Then you should know dogs are unclean. A touch of their tongues, or a drop of their saliva, is enough to invalidate one's prayers."

Great. Just what she needed: being lectured by a zealot.

"I hate dogs," he continued. "You know what *najis* means?"

"Yes," she said wearily, "I know what it means."

"It means ritually impure. One touch of a dog, one lick from their tongues, and you're *najis*. Which means you have to start your ablutions all over again if you want your prayers to be valid."

"Isn't it just possible"—she knew she shouldn't get into a fight with an associate of her patron, but she couldn't help it—"that God cares more about the purity of our hearts than what shows on the outside?"

"And how come"—this, as if he hadn't heard a word she'd said—"you're not veiled? Where's your Islamic modesty?"

"Miss 'Ateeyah." Mustafa Hamdi had stepped forward. Rarely had she been so glad for his intervention. Hamdi turned to Zubayr, muttered something. Zubayr backed away.

Hamdi handed her an envelope. "For you."

"What's this?"

"Open it." He beamed like a kindly uncle.

A thick sheaf of American currency. Twenties.

"One thousand dollars." He beamed again.

"For what?"

"A present. *Eid al-Fitr.*"

"What?"

"*Eid.* To celebrate the end of Ramadan."

"I'm Muslim," she said stiffly. "I know what *Eid* is. And I know Ramadan ended three months ago."

Still beaming: "Just consider it a thank-you for how deftly you handled a phone inquiry not so long ago at our branch in Conimicut."

"You mean that man Hammer? No, that's not right. *Hammond.*"

"We don't mention that name around here."

She closed the envelope, tried to hand it back to him.

"Keep it, as a token of your bright future in Egyptology."

"But I..."

"Keep it, Miss 'Ateeyah." With a nod to Nurse Stark, he'd left, trailed by Thwarter and Zubayr.

A bribe, pure and simple, to pay for my continued silence. What have I gotten myself into?

She thought of the wise stone face of her Giza Sphinx. *What would it think of such goings-on?*

And then, just today, had come the visit from that woman and those two men. Graduate students, like her, she guessed—or former grad students. And clearly very worried about this Hammond, whoever he was. Frantic to locate him. Worried something bad had happened to him. Worried he was dead.

She particularly liked the young man who'd surprised her with his Arabic. An unthreatening individual. Plump, with a sweet face and earnest eyes, full of entreaty—all of which reminded her of her wrinkly pugs back home.

And she'd responded to that entreaty by acting impulsively and jotting an address and thereby jeopardizing her career—and who knew what else besides.

But—and she tilted her head proudly as she thought this—*I have no regrets. That thousand dollars is some kind of hush money; and I won't let Hamdi's cash buy my silence. No regrets.*

"Antonia," she announced, "I have a bit of a headache."

Nurse Stark was in a good mood—she, too, had received a cash-stuffed envelope—so she expansively suggested, "Little to do here today. Why don't you give yourself the rest of the day off?"

"Think I'll go for a drive. That always helps my headaches."

"Why don't you do that, then."

"May I borrow one of the staff cars?"

"You go right ahead."

If I drive fast, Nadia calculated, *and the traffic's not bad, I can be in Conimicut in twenty-five minutes.*

Stonewall Stark didn't even look up as she left.

chapter 52

West Shore Road, near Bellevue Clinic's Psychiatric Unit
Conimicut, Warwick, Rhode Island

"WELL, THAT WAS one hell of an exercise in futility." Bitter frustration in Richard Atlas's voice. *The same tone,* thought Harriet Kronsted, *that became his habit after the Ushabti Incident and his decision to drop out of grad school.*

Ignatius Forsythe joined in the complaint. "Those goons certainly hustled us out of there fast enough."

No sooner had they entered Bellevue's Psychiatric Unit and mentioned the name *Hammond* than they'd been told to leave. When they said they'd driven all the way from Providence and they were pretty sure Francis Hammond had been a patient here at least once, if not several times, then Barbara Orloff had dismissed them with a careless rebuke: "You should have phoned first. Saved yourself the drive."

When they'd remained at the reception counter, insisting Bellevue must have some record of a Francis Hammond, then she reached for a whistle on a cord around her neck. Two shrill blasts, and a half-dozen plus-sized orderlies had appeared from the back and shoved them right out the door.

Now they stood about on the street. Ricky stormed away from the clinic, heading for West Shore Road, Conimicut's main traffic artery. Harriet and Ignatius hurried after him. "Looks like he's gonna punch the first person he sees," worried Iggy.

Just what I'm afraid of, thought Harriet. *Ushabti Meltdown all over again.*

On the corner Ricky spotted an empty beer can in the gutter and gave it a vicious kick across the street.

"Why didn't you just pick it up," suggested Harriet, "and put it in the trash instead of knocking it into traffic?"

"Because I needed to see something get squished," snapped Ricky, "and I wasn't sure I could get away with tearing Nurse Orloff's head off—not with all those goons in attendance."

He glowered at the can in the street. "*Should have phoned first,*" he continued, mimicking the nurse's voice. "Right. We've phoned who knows how many times, and they've always, I mean always, dead-ended us."

A passing car crunched the beer can flat. Ricky hailed the crunch with a "Now *that's* what I'm talking about."

A bad mood all right. How best to channel that energy?

Iggy came to the rescue. "Let's think this through, shall we?" He reminded his friends that the rumors they'd heard in Chicago indicated that Frank had been in and out of Bellevue several times. "And the latest rumor had to do with the possibility that he'd recently escaped from one of Bellevue's locked wards."

"So?" Ricky glared at the gutter as if he needed another beer can to bash.

"So I'm thinking it's just possible folks in one of these shops here might've seen him. I mean, he is kind of distinctive looking."

"You mean strange and freakish."

"Yeah," agreed Iggy. "Like us."

That made Ricky laugh.

"I'm going to try asking around in this hardware store," said Iggy, "for starters."

"And I feel like having ice cream," announced Harriet. She pointed up the street to a Dairy Queen.

"Let me buy you a cone." Ricky seemed to be coming out of his mood. "You still like chocolate-vanilla swirl?"

"You remember that? It's been a long time."

"Yeah, I remember." He held the door open for her as they entered the shop. "I also remember you used to like Drake's Coffee Cakes."

"I still do."

"Then I'll have to buy you another one some time."

"I'd like that very much."

"I also remember you used to razz me about my coat. What'd you call it?"

"Ratty. A coat you're still wearing. And it's still ratty."

"Not ratty. Lucky."

"Ratty."

"Tell you what. Can we agree to call it both ratty *and* lucky?"

"Fair enough."

"Okay then."

"Okay."

A friendly freckle-faced teen took their order.

"Let's see," began Ricky. "We'll have a medium chocolate-vanilla swirl eat-it-all cone."

"Not medium," Harriet corrected him. "Jumbo."

"Living large! I beg your pardon." He started over. "A jumbo chocolate-vanilla swirl for my friend...Hey, does this outing qualify as a date?"

"I'd say it does."

"Okay then. A jumbo chocolate-vanilla swirl for my date, and for me"—he scanned the overhead menu—"hey, I haven't had a Banana Boat in ages. I'll go with that."

"You got it, mister."

Harriet licked her cone and they watched as the boy fixed the Boat. Three scoops of ice cream nestled in a crescent-shaped dish, flanked by a lengthwise-sliced banana and topped by whipped cream, strawberry syrup, and a dusting of chocolate powder.

"Frank loved this stuff, too," reminisced Ricky. "After he finished eating one of these babies, he used to say he was 'fueled and stoked, fueled and stoked.' He said he was powered-up enough to take his Banana Boat dish down to the Chicago River and shrink himself to bug-size and climb aboard and keep paddling until he reached Central America."

He chuckled at the memory. "And he said once he made port he'd show the dish-boat around as proof of his love of all things Banana and on the strength of that get a job in Honduras or someplace with the United Fruit Company. And I'd always say, 'Frank, when I listen to you on one of your sugar-riff highs, I realize you make me look normal'."

"Hey," said the server. He'd apparently been listening in. "That's a coincidence."

"What's a coincidence?"

"A few weeks or so ago," explained the server, as he placed the completed confection on the counter, "can't say exactly when, there was a guy in here, and he ordered the Banana Boat, too. And he kept saying 'Fueled and stoked,' like you just said. Except it was hard to make out what he was saying," he added, "because he was mumbling. Drooling, too."

"Drooling?"

"Yeah. You could tell he was doped up. One of the head-jobs from the nuthouse over on Cole Farm Road. Right near here."

"You mean the Bellevue Clinic?"

"That's it," smiled the boy. "You could tell he was from there because there were a couple'a guys in white coats staying close by his side the whole time and reminding him what a privilege it was they let him out for air. Shit, I hope I never end up in a place like that."

"Do you remember"—Harriet had stopped licking her cone— "what this fellow looked like?"

"That was a while ago. We get a lot'a customers."

"Try. It's important."

"Is he a friend of yours? Wait. Yeah, I remember. Red-head. A tall dude. Real tall. And skinny. Like he hadn't eaten for a long time."

He rang the sale on the register. "And here's something else. He started saying—just like what you were saying—the first chance he got, he was going to bust out and sail down the coast in his Banana Boat dish. But not to Central America. Some other place."

"The Southwest?"

"Yeah. That's it. Colorado, New Mexico. Can't remember. Someplace like that. And then one of those dudes keeping an eye on him says if he keeps talking like that they'll have to increase his level. I think they meant upping his dope. Nasty."

"You know what?" said Ricky. "You've been really helpful." He stuffed dollar bills into the tip jar.

"Hey, thanks, mister." A big smile accompanied them out the door.

"Are you thinking what I'm thinking?" This, as they stood on the street and Ricky scooped up the last of his ice cream.

"That since the bay is so close by, we should see if there's a dock around here?"

"You know something, Hattie? You're awfully good at reading my mind."

"I'm good at many things. You're just slow to notice."

"Hey. At least I remembered about you and the Drake's Coffee Cakes. That's gotta count for something."

"It does." She slipped her arm in his. He looked surprised but pleased.

"I get to do that," said Harriet, "because this is a date. Now let's go find that dock."

chapter 53

Rexall Drug Store
West Shore Road
Conimicut, Warwick, Rhode Island

THE FIFTH SHOP he'd stopped in, and nobody recalled seeing anyone who might have been Francis V. Hammond. Ignatius Forsythe was getting discouraged.

He stopped by the magazine display and surveyed the comics rack. *Green Lantern. The Flash.* He flipped through the pages.

Back in Chicago, whenever he felt blue, he'd curl up in bed with old comic books. *Feeling blue now,* he realized. *Something awful could be happening to Frank right at this minute,* he thought, *and I'm accomplishing diddly to help him.*

"There you are." A voice behind him. "I was hoping I'd find you."

He turned. "Hey! Hi." That young Egyptian woman, from College Hill. "Uh, 'Ateeyah, right?"

"My first name's Nadia."

"Ignatius Forsythe." He wasn't sure if it was okay to shake her hand. She solved the problem by extending hers. "Iggy. Though some people call me Budge. Or Pudge."

"Which name do you prefer?"

"Oh, definitely Iggy."

"All right, Iggy."

He stood and stared. *Even prettier than I remembered. What a beautiful sweet face.*

"...Hammond?" She was saying something.

"Oh, sorry." He giggled nervously. "Spaced out for a second there."

"I said, would you like help finding out what Bellevue knows about Francis Hammond?"

"Wow. You bet."

"Well, come on then." She tugged him by the hand.

"One sec. Gotta put *Batman* back on the rack. Okay."

She led him out onto the street.

"Uh, let me just find my friends, okay?"

"No time." She hurried across West Shore Road, then led him at a trot down Cole Farm Road. "The head nurse has just gone home for the day. The rest of the staff is busy with dinner for the patients. We've got a perfect opportunity to snoop around in the files."

Trying to keep up with her gave him little breath for protest. "My friends..."

"You can report to them later. Come."

She bounded up the steps of the office, gave a glance left and right, then unlocked the door.

"Good. Just as I hoped. No one here." She took a seat in front of a computer, clicked open a screen, motioned Iggy to sit beside her.

"Here's his admission record." Iggy peered over her shoulder.

He gasped as he skimmed the file. "We were right. He's been admitted here four times. The last time just a month ago. Quite a list of symptoms."

Beside the name *Hammond, Francis V.*, some intake clerk had typed: *Paranoia. Dissociative thought. Behavior symptomatic of incipient schizophrenia. ADHD.*

"ADHD?"

"Attention deficit hyperactivity disorder," she explained.

After listing Frank's alleged symptoms, the clerk had typed *Recommendation by B. Orloff: confinement in Cottage #6, with Greenhouse Privileges to be allowed only if Patient proves cooperative.*

"Bad." Iggy shook his head. "This Cottage Six, whatever it is, sounds like the equivalent of a locked ward. But look at this." He jabbed at a line in the file: *Unauthorized departure. Current whereabouts uncertain.*

"So he busted out. Good for him!"

"He's not here, then." Nadia sounded disappointed. "Looking at this material will do you no good."

"Not necessarily," he reassured her. "I'm hoping to pick up a clue as to precisely where he might've gone once he escaped from Bellevue. Let's try this one here." He indicated a file entitled *Hammond, F.V.: Creative Writing Task—'Psychometric Notebook.'*

"Psychometry again," whispered Iggy. "Okay, Frank, old friend. Let's see what you've got for us today."

chapter 54

From the Psychometric Notebooks of Francis Valerian Hammond:

I suppose I should be grateful for this chance to write—I should say, 'for this imperative to write,' since Nurse Orloff et al. seem most anxious to induce me to set pen to paper—and Ms. Toohey says if I write something especially illuminating—whatever that means—they might even let me go free some day.

Free: a lovely word.

Ms. Toohey. Linda Toohey. My dear, dear therapist. She's the one who arranged to let me sit in the Greenhouse and write instead of being shut up in windowless Cottage Six all day. They say I'm schizo, paranoid, you name it. Who wouldn't be, I say, after staring at a blank wall all day?

Tumbrel Toohey, I sometimes call her; and when she asks 'What's a tumbrel?" I smile and say it's a cart for conveying aristocrats to their place of execution. And she says, Oh no, I'm here to hasten your healing; and I say Of course and when you've squeezed me dry you'll haul me off for disposal.

But the Greenhouse is an improvement. Warm in here, too warm, really, but this is not a complaint; the windows are scuffed, as if to block the view, but I still get sunlight and some of the panes are broken. Which is good, because the breaks let in air, air with a salt-smell, air which tells me I'm near the water. Banana Boat special, with all its attendant promise!

Immediate environs, immediate view within my Greenhouse: plants, potted, hanging on hooks, dangled and stran-

gled. Did they agree to this confinement? Did anyone consult with them before imposing this potting? Unlikely. The cruelty, the thoughtlessness, of humankind beggars description. These ferns, violets, what have you: one can hear them cry: Place us outside, in the earth, not dangled and strangled—Please! But does anyone listen? In their fate they are much like the Seraphs.

Seraphim: dear, dear Miss Toohey wants me to write about them. Why? Not sure.

Says she wants me to play a word game: write something that links the following terms: 'Seraphim'—'Sekhemu' (how does she know about the Sekhemu??!!)—'Khaemwaset' (again, I find it odd to be quizzed— here, in a loony bin/sorry, in a therapy session—about a 3,200-year-old pal of mine)—'Solomon's Wand' (the less written the better, as to its—fragmentary—whereabouts)—and, finally, the term 'Portal' (an ambiguous and innocuous-sounding vocabulary item, but I know better than to ascribe this assigned word to happenstance; fine, call me paranoid, but again I say: Someone's digging).

They're digging, and I'm trying to keep them from sinking holes in my (psychometric) turf. If they want so badly to set shovel to earth, let them liberate a few of these sorrowful plants that keep me company: these green citizens of Earth want so badly not to be dangled and strangled.

But dear Miss Toohey—who keeps inspecting what I write—is getting impatient, says to stop going on about stupid things in pots.

And of course she warns that if I'm not productive they'll have to up the meds. So I'll give them something, and let them see if they can sift it for clues.

Even here, in confinement, with no more than a smudged view from this shattered Greenhouse—and maybe it's because the potted plants remind me of suffering Seraphs, and hence provide me with a glimmering—even here, I feel I'm granted a vision, even under the baleful gaze of Tumbrel Toohey.

So, then: let the setting be that most glorious of all Egyptian venues: the Valley of the Kings, on the west bank of the Nile, opposite the city of Luxor.

Let the time be November 1922.

And let the hour be midnight.

But soft! The mists disperse, and we become privy to voices, to hidden thoughts:

⧱

This, complained George Edward Stanhope Molyneux Herbert, fifth Earl of Carnarvon, was an altogether beastly hour to be dragged back to the tomb for another furtive look-round.

Howard Carter wouldn't tell him the true reason for this outing. Couldn't, really. Carter might have reminded his patron that tomorrow morning, at first light, would be the official opening. That meant government inspectors from the Antiquities Service, with their endless questions and all-too-evident eagerness to criticize Carter's methods.

Plus Egyptian officials from Cairo, pompous in tarbooshes and suits. Plus photographers, and nosy newsmen, and avaricious villagers, and holiday-makers from London and Paris and Nice, each demanding a private viewing.

Howard Carter frowned at the thought, frowned deeply.

All of them—and Carter scowled as he visualized this—all of them, all those visitors, wanting a glimpse, a word, a revelation: a chance to see something of the golden boy-king. All poised to swarm.

Yes, to swarm. Like feral dogs. Like flies, round the waste-leavings from that smelly butcher's shop in Carter's poxy boyhood hometown of Swaffham. Swarming round Tutankhamun. His Tutankhamun. His.

"But you still haven't told me, dear chap"—Lord Carnarvon stifled a genteel yawn—"why the need to roust me from my room for this secret mission." He peered over the stern as the boatmen rowed and murmured to each other.

Black Nile water by starlight. Usually the sight was enough to make Carnarvon burble about the romantic setting and all that, but this night air made his chest hurt. The cough was coming back. He hadn't been well for years.

"You know, dear man, you've just forced me to abandon the most enchanting whisky-and-soda. Hearthside, in the Winter Palace. And still not a word of explanation from you."

All Carnarvon got by way of explanation was a mumbled muttering from Howard Carter. Something about a last chance, or maybe it was a lost chance.

Rum chap, this Carter. Touchy. Suspicious-minded. Right as rain one moment, then ready to jump down a fellow's throat the next.

Talented, of course. Oh my. Brilliant. Yes. No one to touch him in his chosen field. Not another excavator like him anywhere. Lucky to have found him. But cursed with a simply beastly temper. Beastly.

"A last chance, did you say?" Carnarvon coughed again. The boat touched the Nile's west bank, and the boatmen jumped out to hand the two Englishmen ashore. Good. Away from the water, the air would be less chill.

Donkeys awaited them. Carnarvon had hoped for a horse and carriage—perhaps the loan of that very comfortable sporting calèche owned by the resident Inspector at Gurna—but Carter would have none of it. Oh no, that might prompt questions. Secrecy, secrecy. Carnarvon coughed again.

"I suppose," offered Carter, settling atop his diminutive donkey with the ease born of long practice, "one might well call this a last chance."

A tap of the stick, an impatient <u>hut hut</u>, and the donkeys were off. "Yes, let's call it that. A last chance."

He said he wanted to enjoy a final private hour with Tutankhamun before the swarm arrived.

This was true, as far as it went; but it wasn't Carter's real reason.

"Well. Yes." Carnarvon sat awkwardly astride his mount, his long legs dragging.

A cheerful sort (ill health and cough notwithstanding), the aristocrat soon found a thought with which to console himself—and with which to rouse his archaeological employee to more conversation. "In any event this may be just the opportunity to add to one's pocket collection, what?"

Normally this would have provoked a conspiratorial chuckle. Whenever Carnarvon sponsored a dig, he had a habit—as did Howard Carter—of palming small finds—votive statuettes, faience beads, ivory figurines the size of a chessman—for his private enjoyment in Highclere Castle. Such pieces—never reported, of course, to the Egyptian government's Antiquities Service—simply vanished from the archaeological record.

But all Carter said in reply was, "Hmm. Of course," and he hurried his donkey along the trail to the Valley of the Kings.

Could he, Carter wondered, share with his patron the real reason for this mad midnight trip? It was Carnarvon, after all, who'd had faith in him when no one else did, who'd offered him work as a private excavator after Carter had gotten into that sorry brawl with those French tourists at Saqqara and subsequently found himself stripped of his government post as Antiquities Inspector.

Carter the brawler. How his rivals had sniggered. But Lord Carnarvon had taken him up, sponsored him, kept faith.

Carter said <u>hut hut</u> to his mount and reviewed the events that had led him to his Tutankhamun.

How, for seven very long years—seven years!—he'd persisted in digging in the Valley of the Kings.

How all his colleagues—Maspero, Davis, Newberry, Gardiner, Weigall, the lot—had stood about and said there was nothing further to discover in the Valley of the Kings, that the valley was played out, would yield no more mummies, no more finds.

How they'd told him he was wasting his sponsor's wealth.

And how they'd doubtless all sniggered about his obstinate folly behind his back as year followed fruitless year.

Sniggered. Yes. That was their way. They had their university degrees and fine manners, whereas Howard Carter: he'd been no more than an uneducated boy from poxy Swaffham, who'd had to make his own hard way in a very hard world. Self-made, he was.

Well, his obstinacy had paid off, with his discovery just days ago of the long-buried staircase, leading deep into a bare rocky hillside in the valley. Sixteen stone steps, hastily uncovered as he'd urged on his dozens of Egyptian workmen.

Then: the finding of the outermost doorway, hidden far within the hillside. A doorway stamped with a seal showing nine crouching captives surmounted by a crouching jackal.

Nine: the number that for the ancient Egyptians symbolized infinity, a limitless number. Egypt's limitless enemies, held in check by the jackal-god Anubis.

Excited as he was by the discovery, eager to tear down this doorway and see what lay beyond, Carter nevertheless restrained himself, contemplated the find.

Nine captives plus jackal: the royal necropolis seal.

Like the vanished pharaohs, Carter, too, believed he had an infinity of enemies. He contemplated the nine bound captives and gave them names: Gardiner, Weigall, Winlock...Well, he had them by the throat now.

Impestuous and short-tempered, yes; but Carter had been professional enough to wait to see what lay beyond that door until Lord Carnarvon could be summoned by telegram from Cairo: <u>At last have made wonderful discovery in valley: a magnificent tomb with seals intact; recovered same for your arrival; congratulations.</u>

Then, with Carnarvon and his daughter Lady Evelyn beside him, Carter had had his workmen demolish the doorway, which revealed a rubble-choked tunnel leading to a second door.

Quickly the rubble had been cleared, and then—carefully, ever so carefully, for Carter had known that something splendid had to be awaiting them—he'd dug out a small aperture in the upper left corner of the second door.

Riding now by donkey with Carnarvon, Carter relived the moment, that supreme moment of his life:

How he'd widened the hole until he could reach within with a candle.

How Lord Carnarvon and Lady Evelyn had crowded beside him, hoping for a glimpse.

How the candle had guttered and almost gone out from some draft within the tomb.

How Carnarvon had asked him—the longing clear in his voice—whether he could see anything.

How at first Carter had seen nothing, just the blank darkness of death.

How—his eyes now accustomed to the dimness—he'd begun to see things.

The gleam of gold. Strange shapes. Guardian statues. Animals. Monstrous heads. Men. Gods. Gold.

How Carnarvon—frantic now, his hand on Carter's shoulder, voice rasping in his cough-racked chest—had pleaded, "Well? Can you see anything?"

How at last he'd replied, "Yes. Wonderful things."

But—and this Carter had told no one—before he'd yielded the view to his patron, he'd seen something more. Movement.

Yes. Movement. A shadow. A silhouette. Nothing more, glimpsed by candlelight.

A silhouette, that had emerged from the tumble of gold and grave-goods.

It had seemed to grow, to darken an entire wall, and then to advance on him.

He'd staggered back, heart hammering. Afraid.

Lord Carnarvon had apparently thought his employee was graciously yielding him a view. "Thanks, dear chap."

Carnarvon had taken the candle, exclaimed as one might expect, said nothing about out-of-place shadows or silhouettes, then given his daughter a chance to look in.

Afraid. Yes. As Carter recalled that moment now, he could find no better word to describe how he'd reacted.

Foolish, really. He, a foursquare no-nonsense sort, had let himself go, let himself be frightened.

And of what? A shadow. Trick of the light, no doubt. That, and the fact that in the weeks leading up to the find his nerves had played the very devil with him.

Lanterns ahead. Low voices and hushed conspiratorial greetings.

Mahmoud Badawi, Carter's <u>rayyis</u>, a strong squat Gurnawi villager who'd worked alongside the Englishman for ten years. Mahmoud had always displayed the great virtue of shrugging off Carter's frequent temper-storms with a shrug and a placatory <u>Zayy-ma anta 'ayz, ya Effendi. Zayy-ma anta 'ayz</u>: 'Just as you like, sir; just as you like.' The foreman's son was there, too: an eager twelve-year-old named Hassanein.

The villagers lit the foreigners' path, past the soaring black cliffs, past Hatshepsut's temple and the Ramesseum, to the mouth of the Valley of the Kings.

Carter's donkey twitched its ears suddenly, as if it, too, were shaking off thoughts of shadows and the dark. Its harness-bells jingled bravely.

He realized suddenly that Carnarvon, riding beside him, was studying him. There was a kindly gaze in the aristocrat's eyes, the look of a man willing to be another man's friend. The gaze, too, of a man awaiting a reply to a question.

Well, thought Carter, he could try telling him the truth. He could say out loud, right now: I, Howard Carter, want to prove something to whatever it was in the tomb that frightened me. I, Howard Carter, gentleman-archaeologist, am not the type to be afraid. I, Howard Carter, confront and overcome anything and everything that block my way. I am not the type to run from a shadow.

But part of him recalled how the shadow had grown and filled the whole wall. The part of him that was a discoverer wanted to find out what it was that had moved among the gold of the boy-king. A guardian spirit?

Superstitious rot. This, after all, was the twentieth century, the year of our Lord 1922.

Still, something in Carter told him that with daylight and the hubbub of dignitaries and newsmen and flashing cameras, something would be lost, something would vanish from the tomb of Tutankhamun. Tonight was his moment to catch that something.

Carnarvon on his donkey coughed, continued to give him that kindly gaze.

Should Carter confess all this, trust the other man with his thoughts?

Surely his employer would simply say, "Nerves, dear chap," and then privately snigger. Yes, snigger, as so many of Carter's rivals had done.

Aloud Carter said, "Just hoping, sir, for a last quiet moment with my...with our Tutankhamun. You know, before the descent of the swarm and all that."

"Yes, yes. Of course." Carnarvon seemed a bit disappointed. Saddened, even.

Carter felt an urge to reassure the other man. This moved him to do something he did seldom. He made himself smile, or try to. It came out as a grimace.

Carnarvon wondered if his employee was feeling dyspeptic again. Rum chap.

Surely it'd been just a trick of the light, Carter told himself. Shadows, and superstitious rot.

Whatever it'd been, he planned to confront it head on, as he'd done with other threats in his life. Fear. Rot. Sniggering.

He, Howard Carter, would show them. He'd show them all.

Another <u>hut hut</u>. He urged his donkey on, into the mouth of the black valley.

⊰⊱

The mists gather again, and the vision fades. We must away...

Whoops. Dear Miss Toohey's unhappy. Consults her clipboard, says the writing guidelines clearly stipulated 'a creative exercise linking the words Seraphim, Sekhemu, Khaemwaset, Solomon's Wand, Portal.' Says I don't seem to have done that. Says the clinic's corporate sponsors still haven't seen the results they urgently require.

She's so displeased she stamps her foot. No kidding: stamps her foot. I thought only Rumpelstiltkin-dwarves in fairy tales did that.

But then again, here in this Greenhouse-cell, maybe I truly am in such a tale.

Displeased: there must be a raise, or bonus, or promotion for Tumbrel Toohey in all this, depending on what I scribble. Can't help feeling sorry for her.

In reply I tell her that with all the drugs they've pumped into me, I can't help but comply with their orders. But I can only jot the vision I've been given.

End of session, says dear Toohey. Angry clack-clack of her clipboard.

Back to windowless Cottage Six. And no, I don't get to say goodbye to the plants.

Guess she really is displeased.

chapter 55

Conimicut Beach
Warwick, Rhode Island

TOBY PRIDEAUX, SKIPPER of the skiff *Don't Give A Damn*, sat glumly on the dock, the evening sea breeze on his face, and counted up the links in his chain of bad luck. To console himself in his count he took frequent pulls from a pint-bottle of Jim Beam that stood ready to hand on a plank by his feet.

Link one: The formerly proud owner of two vessels, he'd been effectively reduced to one because of an incident some months ago. His sixty-foot commercial fishing boat, the *Defiance*, had had a little accident out in Narragansett Bay.

All right, all right: not so little. He'd been checking his lobster pots on the east coast of Prudence Island when the *Defiance* had drifted just a bit and tapped a competitor's boat (even if the police report later claimed "a gaping hole" had been torn in the other guy's vessel—*hey, shit happens*).

Link two: Ten minutes later, just after backing away—amid much hooting and hollering—from the damaged boat, the *Defiance* had gone aground on the rocks off Prudence Island. Damage to the hull below the water-line in ten different places. A mess.

Link three: The subsequent police report had cited him for "irresponsible piloting while under the influence of alcoholic beverages." *Okay,* he thought as he relived that day, *so I enjoy a little nip now and again. Was that any reason to suspend my commercial fish-*

ing license and impound the <u>Defiance</u>—which'd had to be dry-docked anyway for repairs—*until I pay for damage to the other guy's boat?*

Link four: That left him the *Don't Give A Damn.* Sourly he eyed it as it rocked in the water by the dock. License or no license, he could slip out once in a while on a foggy night to try his fortune.

But here, too, his luck was bad. The bay was mostly fished out. Forty-five years he'd worked these waters, and a catch these days wasn't what it used to be.

Striped bass, bluefish, quahogs, clams. He'd tried them all, and lately it all scarcely seemed worth a try. Or maybe it was because he'd just turned sixty-six and he felt tired.

Link five: To top it all off, a few weeks ago Aggie had upped and left him. Just like that. Married how many years—he could never keep track—and she walked out.

You sober up, I'll think about coming back. Meantime I'm sick of your drinking, sick of your feeling sorry for yourself, had been her parting words.

I got reasons to feel sorry for myself, came the thought—which came often—as he took another pull on his bourbon. *Five links in a bad-luck chain.*

Funny how when it comes to people you're sore at—and he was definitely sore at Aggie—what they've said tends to stick in your mind.

How about instead of tallying up all your bad luck, you try remembering some of the good things in your life? Such as four sons you ought'a be proud of?

True. True. But they'd long since grown up and moved away and didn't phone much anymore. No time for their old man.

He rubbed his bristly chin (*no sense shaving regularly, with Aggie gone*).

But she'd had a point. There were one or two things in his life it felt good to recall. Like the time he labeled in his mind as *Coyote Day at the Lighthouse.*

He'd been out lobstering—years ago, when he'd still had the *Defiance*—nice morning, nice slap of the waves against the bow, and he passed the lighthouse on Conimicut Point Shoal.

Usually lifeless. Just an old warning beacon in the bay.

But that day a Coast Guard launch had tied up by the lighthouse. And a half-dozen crewmen were running around shouting on the shoal.

Curiosity had gotten the better of him. He tied up by the government boat, clambered ashore, grabbed a seaman by the arm. "What's all the fuss?"

The launch had stopped for a routine lighthouse maintenance check and had found something strange. A coyote had gotten itself stranded on the shoal.

"Must'a swum out here," said the crewman. "Now it looks like it's afraid to try swimming back. We've been trying to rescue it. Bring it back to the mainland." His informant looked nineteen, twenty—a kid with a bad case of sunburn. "But man it keeps outfoxing us."

So it was. The animal raced around the shoal, zipped up the lighthouse steps, whirled along the railing, jumped back onto the sandbar. The crew huffed and puffed and tripped over each other.

"I say shoot it," wheezed one of the crew. "List it as vermin in the report. Probably rabid anyway."

"Rabid. Shit." Toby Prideaux had gone back onto his boat and returned with a bucket of fishbait. He called to a petty officer. "How about you boys stay still a minute."

From its perch on the lighthouse veranda, the coyote eyed the bucket.

Toby knelt, reached into the pail, held out his hand.

The coyote's ears went up.

Delicately it descended the steps, approached to within ten feet of the human.

"Go on. Chopped fish. You gotta be hungry."

It advanced a few paces. Young: Toby guessed it to be little more than a pup.

Wild-eyed and frightened: sure. But Toby sensed an independence of spirit, something inherent in creatures that know how to live on their own.

Whatever accommodation I make with you now, said that spirit, *it's only so I can continue to live free.*

Then the beast took the food from his hand.

"Atta boy." Toby reached in the bucket for more.

The coyote allowed itself to be picked up. And Toby held it in his arms on the launch all the way back to the mainland. He grinned at the crew. "Rabid. Shit."

Once ashore, he'd knelt on the beach—not far from where he sat now—and the coyote sprang off into the coastline woods without a backward glance.

Would'a been nice if the Coast Guard boys had bought him a bottle of something afterwards by way of thanks. But drink or no drink, it'd been an outstanding moment.

Aggie was right—good to remember the good things. Which reminded him of a different memory—much more recent—one that truly made him count his blessings.

Just a few weeks ago, he'd been sitting right here on the dock, enjoying the water, having a little nip, feeling a touch sorry for himself, when out came a line of folks from Cole Farm Road.

Didn't know the faces, but he'd known who they were all right: nuthouse inmates from that place set back in the trees up the road.

Bellevue. That was the name. Locals knew to keep away.

Fifteen of them, shuffling in line, one behind the other. Striped tunics, loose flapping striped trousers—like prison garb.

All of 'em tied in a string: a thick rope knotted around their waists looped them all together.

Men in white coats herded them from the tree-line, out onto the beach, then along the wooden planks of the dock. The individual in charge was a big tough-faced female with a whistle on a cord around her neck.

As the procession neared his perch—and no one seemed to see him sitting quietly on the dock—he saw the name-tag on her uniform. *Orloff.*

A nod from her, and the procession shuffled to a stop. Orloff blew on her whistle—a blast that hurt his ears, must've hurt the inmates', too—and then gave a speech.

Something about how going out for a walk was a privilege, and all you resident patients should be grateful, but keep in mind privileges can be revoked, so you resident patients should make sure to mind your behavior.

Through the talk all the residents kept their heads down. Doped up, he guessed, to the max. They looked defeated. Beaten down by life.

Oh, he knew that look. Knew the feel of it.

Defeated. All except one.

A tall, tall, skinny guy, red-haired, who swiveled his head around and sniffed the air with a wild-eyed gaze that reminded Toby of somebody.

Reminded him of his lighthouse coyote.

Wild-eyed and frightened, just like that pup. Roped by the waist, like all the other inmates. But Mister Slim had something else in his gaze that reminded Toby of the coyote: despite the dope pumped into him, there still seemed some trace of independence of spirit.

Another blast from Big Whistle. She was trumpeting something about how all you resident patients ought to blah blah blah.

Toby had tuned it out, because something smart-ass to say had popped into his head. Should've kept his mouth shut of course; but sometimes the drink did this to him.

And so, nice and loud, he'd called from his perch: "Resident patients? They look more like convicts on a chain-gang."

Big blast from Big Whistle, and one of the white-coats—biggest guy in the bunch—rushed up to where Toby sat.

The man stood over him and growled, "Another word from you, and you'll find yourself going for a swim."

Toby had assured him he wasn't in the mood for no swim.

Final blast from Big Whistle. The chain-gang turned and shuffled back towards the tree-line and Cole Farm Road.

But Mister Slim had twisted his head in Toby's direction. A twitch of the inmate's face. Toby realized with a start what the man had done.

He'd given him a wink. A way to say thanks.

Which was why Toby hadn't been so surprised, a week or so after that, when his old friend Al LaCroix dropped by to tell him about something strange that'd happened the other night.

"I'd just tied up at the dock when this guy comes out'a the woods onto the beach. Staggering. Kind'a dazed. Woozy. Wearing striped pajamas. Knew right away he had to be on the run from the Bellevue."

"What'd he look like?"

"Red hair. Tall fella. Real lean. Underfed."

He knew it: Mister Slim.

"Did'ja take him back?"

"Back to that shithole? No way. Said he'd busted out and was desperate to get away from the coast."

"So what'd ja do?"

"Ferried him down to Watch Hill."

"That's a hell of a long ways."

Al said he'd felt sorry for the guy. "Gave him a spare jacket'a mine from the cabin locker to wear over that pajama getup so he wouldn't look so out'a place in the world."

Al said the escapee had some notion of walking over to 95 and then thumbing a ride out west somewheres.

"All the way to Watch Hill. How much did'ja charge him?"

"Not a nickel. The guy was piss-poor."

Toby had said charity's fine but it doesn't put food in your mouth.

"I just felt bad for the guy is all." Al stuck his hands in his pockets. "What would you have done?"

"Me? I'd'a made sure he paid cold cash. Up front."

"The hell you say. You ain't that hard-hearted."

"I don't stick my neck out for nobody. Not for nobody."

Well, now at least he had two memories that made him feel a bit less at the bottom of the heap (*Aggie ought'a be proud of me*).

One, the coyote. For some reason he liked remembering that day (even if he hadn't made any cash out of the business).

Two, that Bellevue chain-gang. No matter how bad off he was, unemployed and close to broke, at least he wasn't roped by the belly to a string of sorry-ass nutjobs.

Toby Prideaux was approaching a moment of philosophically derived contentment.

It burst a moment later when he saw two strangers approach.

Youngsters, a couple, arm in arm. The girl said something and the guy laughed.

That's how he and Aggie used to be. Arm in arm. Happy.

Other people had no business going around in public looking so glad when his license had been suspended and the bay was fished out and his wife had left him.

The young woman waved in his direction. He emitted a go-away scowl.

On the other hand:

His bottle was near-empty, and he just might be able to sweet-talk them into standing him the price of a drink.

The scowl changed to a smile. "Howdy."

chapter 56

Conimicut Beach
Warwick, Rhode Island

THE DOCK LOOKED deserted. Only one boat, a small one, tied to the pier.

"Nobody here," complained Richard Atlas.

"Yes, there is," Harriet Kronsted corrected him. "But he doesn't look friendly."

A surly-faced whiskery man in a battered sea-captain's hat sat on the planking, a bottle by his side.

"You've certainly got that right," agreed Ricky. "Don't know if we can learn anything from him. Probably half-drunk."

"Worth a try." Harriet waved a hello.

Bristly frown in reply.

"So much for that." They stood about, undecided.

Must've had second thoughts for some reason, thought Harriet: now the man was smiling, giving them a friendly "Howdy" and a boozy salute with his bottle.

"Nice boat you've got there." Ricky nodded at the vessel.

"You folks like to go for a spin, help an old fisherman earn a few bucks?"

"Maybe."

Harriet didn't find reassuring the name stenciled on the stern: *Don't Give A Damn*.

The man saw her dismay and gave a raspy laugh. "Don't let that put you off, Miss. The *Don't Give A Damn* is the fastest vessel in Narragansett Bay. Eighteen-foot skiff. Brand-new Evinrude motor."

"But that motor doesn't look brand-new," objected Ricky. "Lots of wear and tear on that engine."

"Well, it's almost brand-new. Got it just two years ago from the Marine Salvage yard down on Rocky Point. You know the place?"

"We're from out of town."

"Tourists, huh? Well, if you want a tour of the bay, let me tell you this is a fine craft. This Evinrude's a twenty-five horsepower four-stroke engine. It'll deliver thirty knots and take you anyplace you like to go in a hurry."

Ricky turned to Harriet and murmured, "That could be useful, if we get into a jam."

"Actually," confessed Harriet, with a smile she hoped would keep the man from relapsing into a scowl, "we're not really tourists. We're searching for news of a friend."

"What sort of a friend?" The skipper's expression shrank from expansive to guarded.

The couple exchanged glances. "A patient," continued Harriet. "At the center up the road."

"The nuthouse?"

"Bellevue Clinic."

"People around here stay away from that place, know better than to ask questions. Bellevue ain't friendly."

"They gave us that impression, too."

The skipper grunted agreement. He drank off the last of his liquor—Jim Beam, read the label—and pitched the bottle into the bay.

"Well, what's your friend look like?" He belched into the back of his hand.

"Red hair. Tall. Very thin. Thoughtful looking." She paused, then added, "Stands out in a crowd."

"Mister Slim."

"Beg your pardon?"

"That's what I call 'im. Mister Slim. Yeah, I seen him. Right here on the dock." A calculating expression came into his eyes. "But he ain't here no more."

"He's not?" This in unison from Ricky and Harriet.

"Nope. Busted out. Vamoosed."

"Where'd he go?" A pleading tone in Harriet's voice.

"Hard to recollect." The whiskered man gazed out over the water where Jim Beam had sunk with a splash.

Ricky reached into his shirt pocket and extracted a ten-dollar bill. "Will this help your memory?"

"Shit."

Ricky rolled his eyes but extended an additional ten.

"It all comes back to me now." Whiskers pocketed the cash. "My friend Al—my name's Toby, Toby Prideaux, by the way, pleased to meet you both—my friend Al, he found him here on the beach and gave him a ride in his boat down to Watch Hill."

"Where's that?"

"On the coast. Near the state line. Almost into Connecticut."

"Did our friend tell him where he was heading from there?"

"Something about thumbing a ride out west."

"That figures," said Ricky. "Heading to old haunts. He never did explain exactly why he kept going to the Southwest every chance he'd get."

He turned back to Toby. "How long ago did our friend escape?"

"Maybe three, four weeks ago."

Harriet whispered, "That's probably as much help as we're going to get from this guy."

"He might just possibly be helpful in one more way," Ricky whispered back.

He turned again to the skipper. "We appreciate all the information."

"No trouble at all."

"One last question. Say we wanted to hire your boat at short notice, in case difficulties arose here. How much would you charge?"

The skipper rose to his feet, belched again. "What kind'a difficulties? You mean with those Bellevue folks?"

"Possibly."

"Bellevue. We're talking mean-hearted. Messing with them in any way: I'd have to charge a premium."

"How much? Just hypothetically."

"Hypothetically? Let's see." Toby scratched his chin. "Just you and this nice girl?"

"Plus a friend of ours. He's asking around about the Bellevue up on West Shore Road."

"In fact we'd better go fetch him," urged Harriet, "before he gets into trouble out there on his own. I think maybe…"

She was interrupted by sounds from the woods on the shoreline.

A gunshot. Then another, and a third, followed by the high shrilling blasts of a whistle.

"I think," commented Toby Prideaux, scratching his whiskery jowls anew, "your friend's already bought himself some trouble."

More gunfire inland. But closer now.

And then came the sound of persons thrashing through the woods, pounding towards the beach and the dock, but still shrouded from view.

More blasts of the whistle.

Behind Hattie and Ricky, another belch and a rasped suggestion: "Maybe we should talk about the *Don't Give A Damn*."

"The what?" Ricky, like Hattie, was straining to see who was about to burst onto the beach from the treeline.

"My boat. Because things aren't so hypothetical anymore. Because I think you're gonna want to get offshore fast. Which means," he added with a smirk, "we need to calculate just how much you're ready to pay."

chapter 57

Inside the Bellevue Clinic's Psychiatric Unit
Cole Farm Road
Conimicut, Warwick, Rhode Island

NADIA 'ATEEYAH LOOKED up from the computer and glanced about the office. "Before we check any more files, let me do something I should've done the minute we snuck in here." She stood on a chair and flicked a switch on an overhead wall-mounted screen.

"Split-image display," she explained.

"What are we looking at?" asked Ignatius Forsythe.

"The upper-left part of this screen gives us a live webcam view of Cole Farm Road and the main entrance." She pointed out each quadrant in turn. "Upper right shows the rear entrance of this building and the locked-ward cottages just behind us."

She paused and studied the display. "All quiet there. The lower-left part of the screen shows the woods leading out to the beach, plus the Greenhouse and Cottage number Nine. Nine's bigger than the other buildings. I think they use it for staff meetings, things like that. Quiet there, too. Good."

Turning her attention to the lower-right quadrant, she concluded, "And here's our busy-bee hive, the dining facility. Lot of coming and going at the moment, what with staff feeding the patients. Okay. As long as we remember to keep an eye on this live feed while we're spying out stuff, no one can catch us by surprise in here."

But Iggy had listened to little of this. His attention was fixed on Bellevue's computer files about his old friend Frank.

"Let's try this one," he urged: *Hammond, F.V.—Mock-Conference.*

"This intrigues me, too." Nadia clicked on the file. "I'd like to know what they mean by 'mock-conference'."

The file proved to be a digital video recording. It began with an introduction by someone Nadia recognized. "Doctor Linda Toohey. One of the staff psychoanalysts."

Iggy remembered the name. "Of course. Frank mentioned her in that other file. The 'creative writing exercise.' Tumbrel Toohey. So that's what she looks like."

Hair pinned back in a severe bun, narrow chin, sharp nose, thin nervous lips parted in a smile that seemed an attempt at empathetic warmth. Iggy chuckled at the enamel brooch pinned atop the lettered *Bellevue Clinic* logo on Doctor Toohey's coat: daffodils flanking a Happy Face.

"Turn up the sound. Let's hear what she's saying."

"...mentioned earlier, it's with some trepidation that I've agreed to have our psychiatrists prescribe Adderall for Francis. It's true he presents symptoms of ADHD, and our Aderall dosage will allow—perhaps I should say *compel*—him to speak more directly and succinctly to the topics that today's visitors insist that he address. But as his therapist, I must note that since being made to ingest the Adderall dosage, Francis has been experiencing nausea, sweating, and tachycardia—precisely the adverse effects associated with this medication."

She paused and from her lab coat produced a flower-patterned handkerchief, with which she dabbed at her face. "My larger concern—and I insist on saying this for the record—is that in prescribing Adderall for a client who has also been subjected to antipsychotic medications such as Prolixin and Thorazine, we are entering uncharted medical waters. The overall effect—physiological, psychological, and neurological—of these drugs in concert has yet to be determined. And the fact that our client has been spotted occasionally palming, spitting out, or otherwise rejecting our dosages makes it all the harder to provide a precise metric as to the psychophysical factors at play in his body at this moment."

A voice off-camera—indistinct but impatient in tone—triggered a swivel of the lens. Now Iggy and Nadia were presented with a view of a small auditorium of some kind.

"Probably Cottage Nine," whispered the Egyptian. Some twenty persons—most in white Bellevue uniforms, a half-dozen in suitcoats and ties—sat on folding chairs before the podium at which Toohey spoke.

Iggy leaned closer to the screen to identify the audience members. But the video had smudged each face into a pixelated blur.

"Yes," acknowledged Toohey in response to the blurred face—and now the camera had swung back to the podium—"I know we should get on with the 'conference' and let our client give his lecture."

Again she dabbed the handkerchief at her lips. "By way of introduction, let me remind everyone that the purpose of today's mock-conference is to help ease Francis's re-entry into society at large and, more particularly, his reintegration into the community of academic scholarship. If he can successfully give a presentation here, in Bellevue's intimate and supportive environment, on the topic for which he has won international recognition, the life of Prince...Prince..."

Here the video showed her consult the clipboard she clasped to her chest. "Sorry. Prince Khaemwaset. If he can give a presentation on this prince, and do so in a satisfactorily focused, coherent, and intelligible fashion"—here she paused and looked to her right, to beam what Iggy interpreted as an attempt at an encouraging smile at her patient—"then Francis has every prospect of being allowed more sessions in the Greenhouse that he enjoys so much, and more likelihood of an expedited release, the expunging of his criminal record for attempted antiquities theft, and his eventual welcome back into academia by his many friends in Egyptology."

Another off-camera voice, peremptory in tone.

"Yes, I'm almost done." She fingered her Happy-Face brooch. "In the interest of a successful mock-conference, let me remind

Francis that he'll have the comfort of the same format he used to enjoy: a brief lecture, followed by collegial questions and answers. But my patient is to keep in mind—and I trust the Adderall will help him stay focused—that, purely as a test of his re-emergent cognitive skills, he is to treat all the following terms in his speech: 'Seraphim; Sekhemu; Khaemwaset; Solomon's Wand; and Portal'."

Again she looked to her right, essayed a smile. "You'll do that for me, won't you, Francis?"

Once more she faced the camera. "Ladies and gentlemen, it's an honor to introduce tonight's speaker. A distinguished scholar and a promising student, formerly of the University of Chicago, winner of a Dean's fellowship, a Fulbright grant, and a stipend from the National Endowment for the Humanities: Mister Francis Valerian Hammond." She stepped away from the podium.

Slowly the lecturer stepped to the stand.

Iggy gasped as he watched. "What have they done to you, old friend?"

Tall and thin, yes, and the same shock of carrot-flame hair Iggy'd always remembered. But his eyes, puffy and red; the shifting stutter-blink of his gaze; the rounded, sagging stoop of his shoulders—the posture of a sleepless vagrant hounded by cops from bench to bench in a park: this was a husk of the Frank Hammond he'd once known.

The speaker's hands trembled as he shuffled the papers on the podium. Head down, he began in a mumble. "…honor…old…topics…racing…"

A loud disgusted voice from the back. "Make him speak up."

Linda Toohey, who'd taken a seat on stage beside the podium, chastised her patient. "Francis. Remember what we rehearsed. Your freedom's in the balance. Also your reintegration into the Egyptological community."

The last word briefly snapped him into focus. "Community?" A throaty rasp from the lowered head. "Say rather snakepit. Reintegration: not sure how ardently that's to be longed for."

"Francis!" His therapist flashed a look of reproof.

"Sorry. Sorry." Still he kept his head down. But at least he positioned himself closer to the mike. "Starting to say, just now... an honor, I guess, or something like that. Heart's racing. Head's racing, too. Don't feel too good."

Pause. "Sorry. Trying to think here. Hold it together."

The page in his hands shook with such palsied force the mike picked up the sound.

"Guess it all started," he resumed, "when I began thumbing around the Southwest on breaks in grad school. A month in the summer, three weeks at Christmas. Anytime I wasn't working in Egypt, anytime I didn't have the dough to fly out to Cairo, I'd just hitchhike, beg my way out west. Landscapes down there—the air, the feel of it, the feeling anything could open itself up as an epiphany under skies that big, that open...Anyway, all of that reminded me of the places I loved best in Egypt—the Sahara west of the Nile, the wadis and canyons near the Valley of the Kings. That love was what led me to the Portal."

Here his voice tapered off. "...and what I found..."

Another shout from the back: an indistinct command.

"Sorry. Portal. Right. You want more, of course. I'll get back to that."

Silence from the podium.

Head still lowered, hands still trembling, Frank Hammond began anew. "You know, of all Egyptian tales, I always liked 'The Shipwrecked Sailor' best."

Iggy smiled. They'd translated the ancient text together in a seminar back in Chicago.

"You may or may not know this four-thousand-year-old story," resumed Hammond. "A sole-survivor sailor, cast away on a desert island far from Egypt, awakes one morning to find himself confronted by a gargantuan talking winged cobra umpteen cubits long. Flesh of gold, beard of lapis lazuli: clearly the cobra's divine.

"The poor sailor's terrified, grovels on the sand, begs for mercy. The snake reassures him, tells him it got separated from its friends, fell from the sky. Manuscript breaks off; tale's incomplete."

"You're wasting our time." Another voice from the back. "We know the story."

"Do you?" The head lifted; the red eyes flared straight into the camera. "Well, this you don't know. A winged serpent—even a divine one, of lapis lazuli and gold—can get just as lost in the cosmos as any human. Nobility of origin is no protection from coming unmoored, from falling through alien skies. In 'The Shipwrecked Sailor' we have the first recorded instance—rendered of course in traditional Egyptian mythic symbolism—of contact between humans and Seraphim."

Loud stirrings in the hall.

"Proof? You ask for proof?" Again the red eyes flared into the camera. "My epiphanies, and the portal I found, are proof, sufficient for me if for no one else."

He coughed. "But I suppose I should start to read the paper I'm supposed to present."

Fervent whispered encouragement from his therapist onstage.

"Dear Tumbrel Toohey up here is begging me to get on with this. So be it."

He cleared his throat, seemed consciously to try to control the paper that trembled in his hand.

"Anyone wishing to understand the *sekhemu*—the 'divine powers' known elsewhere in the ancient and medieval Mediterranean world as seraphim—would do well to begin with Akhenaten and Nefertiti's Amarna Revolution, for it was Akhenaten who first actively cultivated intimate friendships on a sustained basis with the seraphs, not trusting to chance encounters with lost wayfarers from the skies.

"It was Akhenaten, studying the clues encoded in tales such as 'The Shipwrecked Sailor,' who first began to attract seraphs from the skies. Through rituals, songs, and chants, recited outdoors under open skies, encoded as hymns to the Aten sun-disk, he issued invitations: *Descend! Descend!*

"And they did. The seraphs—*sekhemu*, as they were then known—themselves ethereal, consented to take up temporary residence in vessels—pottery, vases, ceramic jars—so that humans could clasp such vessels and feel the warmth of each seraph's longing for contact, for friendship. Even today, psychometrically sensitive souls who come upon these ancient vessels can still feel the residue of that seraphic presence.

"Akhenaten—a leader yet a recluse, a pharaoh yet a far-faring wanderer—wanted more than the warmth. Others before him—like the shipwrecked sailor—had sensed the presence; he wanted to see the seraphs, behold them in their true form.

"So as a gracious favor they directed him to travel afar, to Wadi Hammamat, where in deep-veined quarries he found an unknown mineral out of which he built a wand. It was a thing constructed in two parts, a staff surmounted by a finial that was embossed with the Aten—a sundisk symbolizing the seraphs' celestial origins."

"Wait'll Ricky hears this," enthused Iggy. He turned to Nadia. "My friend's been carrying half of Akhenaten's wand in his backpack all this time."

Nadia nodded, her eyes on the quadra-format security screen. "We're still good," she said. "The Bellevue crew is still busy feeding patients."

Hammond's speech continued. "…voluntarily resided within the wand, where their ethereal splendor shone in a display that gladdened Akhenaten's heart.

"He kept the wand with him always, delighting in its cracklings, surges, lightning bursts—signs of the seraphic presence. He rejoiced in the corona of light with which the wand surrounded him. A corona that sufficed him as a crown—a kingdom truly not of this world.

"Historians claim Akhenaten outlawed the old gods, the old faith. The truth is simpler: he lost interest in them.

"Disruptive was the descent of the *sekhemu*, like any intrusion of extraordinary Presences into the day-to-day routines—routines held together with the pharaonic equivalent of scotch-tape, paperclips, and chewing gum—that constitute what we call the Real World."

Hard for Iggy to understand this last statement, because someone in the audience interrupted. "You mentioned, and I quote, 'cracklings, surges, lightning bursts.' In your opinion, could such an energy-source conceivably be containerized and harnessed in a reliable fashion?"

"Oh, some have done so already." A sly knowing look entered the red eyes. "I come to that in a moment."

Hammond's voice grew in confidence.

"All Egyptologists know Akhenaten's revolution failed upon his death. But they don't understand the nature of this failure. The earthward seraphic migration faltered when Akhenaten died. His son Tutankhaten would gladly have continued the rituals to guide more seraphs earthward. But the boy was forced by his power-mad councilor Ay to abandon the seraphic Amarna Age and restore the worship of Egypt's old gods. Nevertheless, some seraphs still lingered among us, but not so abundantly as before.

"And when Tutankhaten died—his name contorted to Tutankhamun—his wand was buried with him, a discarded relic of discarded worship.

"There in Tut's tomb did it stay, for some decades, until the reign of Ramses the Great. And here we encounter one of the noblest spirits in history's pageant—young Prince Khaemwaset, son of Ramses.

"A hitherto neglected area of scholarship has been the troubled relationship between Khaemwaset and his father.

"Scholars such as Wilkinson have recently drawn attention to the authoritarian violence and coercion that underlay the decorum and eye-pleasing beauty of ancient Egypt. Among all Egypt's pharaohs, none was more aggressive in his exultant display of coercive violence than Ramses. And among his many sons, none was more averse to such use of force than Khaemwaset.

"Small wonder, then, that the young prince became a priest and scholar, an antiquarian. He visited the pyramids and Sphinx, sand-swept temples that even in his day were fifteen centuries old. He found treasures he kept in a private chapel, treasures he mentioned to few. He wandered alone as much as he could, trudging desert paths, outpacing the royal guards assigned him by an increasingly exasperated father.

"For he knew well that his father expected him—a crown prince—to practice the arts of one who would succeed Great Ramses. Chariotry. Archery. Conquest. War.

"Nothing Khaemwaset did, it seemed, could please his father—until the day Khaemwaset uncovered a neglected site in the Valley of the Kings: 'the tomb of the son of the nameless king,' as it was then called—the tomb of Tutankhamun.

"Within this tomb, the prince found the wand once prized by Akhenaten. Khaemwaset took it to his favorite hermitage—a desert-retreat on a stony ridge he called his 'Falcon's Perch,' in the wastelands of Abu Sir. There he studied this treasure from Egypt's past, handling it, meditating and praying over it, inviting whatever *sekhemu* might be dormant therein to make themselves known.

"And they did. As I noted earlier, seraphs, too, yearn for kinship, for contact, as truly as do humans. They were comforted to discover in Khaemwaset a kindred soul, a fellow pilgrim, just as the gold-and-lapis-lazuli serpent had been comforted to share his exile with the shipwrecked sailor.

"For months the prince remained secluded at Abu Sir in his Falcon's Perch, surrounded by winged seraphs, having ceramic vessels made for them as homes, inviting them by turns to inhabit the wand and please him with their radiant effulgence.

"But an impatient Ramses summoned his son to Thebes, demanding an accounting. Why had the prince neglected statecraft, the royal councils? Why was he not practicing the arts of javelin and sword?

"Abashed before his father, Khaemwaset held forth the wand. He presented it as a gift, something that might make Ramses think better of him. An object that Khaemwaset loved so dearly—surely the king would prize it, too.

"Prize it he did—but for different ends.

"Ramses had his scribes from the House of Life study the wand and so he soon learned how to attract the trusting seraphs, as Khaemwaset—and before him Tutankhamun and Akhenaten—had done.

"But Ramses went further: he altered the wand.

"No longer a voluntary abode, it became a prison, a cage for captive angels. And their radiant pulsations of light—once a display to gladden kindred hearts—now became an energy source controlled solely by the Pharaoh. A source that explains much that is mysterious in the reign of Great Ramses.

"Consider this.

"In an age when most men died by the time they were twenty-five or at best thirty, ever-vigorous Ramses throve into his nineties.

"He reigned sixty-seven years.

"He outlived fifty sons.

"He built fortresses, temples, shrines—Abu Simbel, Karnak—sites that astound us even today.

"He waged relentless war in Asia, Libya, and Kush, crushing enemies wherever he trod.

"It seemed to his subjects he might live forever.

"What they didn't know was that their pharaoh had harnessed the *sekhemu*. Once-joyous celestial entities, descending here freely, had become enslaved, had become seraphs in torment."

"Wait!" A raucous interruption from the audience. "Enslaved seraphim. Seraphs in torment. This is insane. And Bellevue's actually thinking of letting this guy back out into the world?"

The camera had stayed fixed on the podium, so Iggy couldn't see the heckler's face. But this was a voice he certainly knew: Cynthia Lynch, one of Frank Hammond's old rivals, last seen at the Chicago gala.

"Now, now." Another voice, in a tone both smooth and authoritative. "Let's let our speaker finish. We're fostering collegiality and so forth, aren't we?"

And *that* voice, of all voices, was one Iggy knew all too well. A voice that had labeled him Budge the Pudge. The voice of Robert Thwarter, seated with Cindy Lynch at Bellevue.

"Unbelievable," breathed Iggy.

Hammond, in any case—whether because of the Adderall or Prolixin or his own sheer stubbornness—seemed undeterred.

"Sick at heart because of the sufferings he had unwittingly brought upon the seraphs, Khaemwaset one night crept into his father's quarters in the palace at Thebes and made away with the wand.

"No threats from his father—not even exile, which to an Egyptian was worse even than death—could induce him to reveal its whereabouts. He broke the wand, sending one half far away to the East, in the desert highlands beyond the Red Sea, and secreting the other half in Tutankhamun's tomb, in the hope that the wand would be reconstituted in an age more kindly disposed to human-seraph friendship.

"After which, Khaemwaset went into exile, left the Nile valley, and was never seen again in Egypt."

For the past several minutes, Hammond had spoken in an Adderall-propelled rush of words. Now he stopped, chewed at his lip, and ran a hand agitatedly through his hair, as if torn between the drug-fueled temptation to talk on about his favorite topic and the instinct to keep secret the mysteries of his ancient friend's life.

Silence at the podium; nervous smiles of encouragement from Linda Toohey; the sound off-camera of increasingly impatient listeners in the audience.

Nadia and Iggy, captivated by this drama, hunched close to the computer, their noses almost touching the screen. But this would have been an ideal moment to check the overhead security monitor. The lower-right quadrant showed that staff members had finished feeding the patients and were now herding them back to their cottages.

Into Hammond's silence broke a voice from the audience.

"Excuse me, but you've overlooked something important." Another member of Thwarter's claque: Iggy recognized the voice of Gregory Holman. "No matter how reclusive he might have been by temperament, Khaemwaset—and the archaeological record confirms this—fulfilled the royal duty of serving as high priest of the cult of the sacred Apis bull at the Serapeum. As part of his..."

"I'm aware of that," interrupted Hammond. "And I'm also aware he only accepted this duty because the Serapeum was located at Saqqara, which was close enough to his hermitage at Abu Sir to permit him to return every night to the seraphs who were staying as guests at his Falcon's Perch."

Greg Holman made no attempt to hide his annoyance. "Your arrogance is breath-taking in presuming to guess the psychological motivation underlying choices made by a personage who lived thirty-two centuries ago."

"I don't *guess*. I happen to *know*. That's because *I'm* the one who's had the epiphanies. You haven't."

"You also happen to be living in a locked ward. That undermines your scholarly credibility just a bit." Greg Holman emitted a dry *heh-heh-heh*, which Iggy remembered as his version of merriment.

Having scored his witticism, Holman added, "We're wasting our time here."

"I'm beginning to think the same." The camera pivoted to the audience, settled on the pixelated blur of what had to be Robert Thwarter's face. "But let's squeeze him for a minute or two more before we break for something to eat. Greg, go ahead and continue your line of questioning."

"If Pharaoh Frank will be gracious enough to let me proceed"—Gregory Holman apparently couldn't resist taunting Hammond with his old nickname—"I'll point out he might want to reconsider his claim that Khaemwaset fled Egypt and never returned. Because I happen to have extensively studied the Apis-bull cult at the Serapeum in Saqqara, and I'm aware, as I was trying to point out just now, that Khaemwaset served as high priest of this cult.

"What our *colleague*"—Holman poured contempt into the word—"at the podium seems to have forgotten is that as far back as 1851, Auguste Mariette excavated the Serapeum and discovered artifacts directly relevant to the issue at hand. He found a nearly-intact coffin containing a royal mummy.

"Its face was covered with a gold mask—indicating that the deceased was of very high rank—and its body was protected by amulets inscribed with the name of none other than the person under discussion: Khaemwaset, son of Ramses. Which squashes underfoot any notion of the prince having died in exile, as Frank the Pharaoh claims in his little fantasy."

"What's getting squashed underfoot right now," retorted Hammond, all hesitation gone from his tone, "is any notion of your competence in the field of Khaemwaset-studies. Because more recent research—the result of work done by a team of oste-ologists and Egyptologists—has demonstrated that what Mariette had *thought* to be the corpse of Khaemwaset was actually the mum-mified remains of an Apis ox, a combination of animal bones, res-in, and linen-wrappings. So your theory, dear Holman, is—excuse the clowning, but I get to do this seldom—a load of sacred bull."

Greg Holman sputtered, but Hammond pressed hard now. "*My* theory, backed by my epiphanies, is that Khaemwaset knew he would continue to be hounded by his father's agents, who were eager to force him to reunite the wand's scattered fragments. Knowing this, the prince deliberately staged a false burial with a mummy made up to make onlookers think—as Mariette later did—that Khaemwaset had truly died and been buried at Saqqara. That would end the hounding, end the persecution, allow Khaem-waset to flee the Nile valley in peace."

"In that case"—Thwarter's voice again—"where did Khaem-waset go in his exile?"

"Oh," replied Hammond airily, "his friends the seraphs took him away."

"Fine." Growing irritability in Thwarter's tone. "His friends the seraphs took him away. But where did they take him?"

"*Er ta djeser, er imenet.*" Hammond suddenly switched to an-cient Egyptian.

Linda Toohey onstage looked baffled.

"*To the sacred land, to the west,*" translated Thwarter aloud. "Fine, fine. West of the Nile valley, we assume you mean. But where precisely in the west? The Valley of the Kings? Dakhla Oasis? The Oracle of Amun?"

Sly guardedness appeared in Hammond's bloodshot eyes. "Oh, much farther west than that."

"Don't play games, Pharaoh Frank. We need the information. Where did Khaemwaset go? Did he take refuge among the tribes of Libya?"

"Oh, he sought refuge all right. But much farther afield. Much farther west."

"Let me be blunt. Either you give us straight the information we need—no riddling references, no cryptic tricks, no codes—or I'll see to it you rot here forever in your little greenhouse at Bellevue."

Thwarter's face in the film might have been a blur; what remained clear was the over-spilling anger in his voice. "We pumped you full of Prolixin and Adderall for a reason," he cried. "Now deliver!"

The overhead security monitor, had Nadia and Iggy checked, would have shown them that the staff had locked away the last of the patients and were now heading back to the reception area where the two sat.

But the film was too riveting to allow for any vigilance. The camera showed Hammond hesitate again, his mouth aquiver, biting his lips as if to hold back words that might betray his thirty-two-hundred-year-old friend.

He balled the conference papers in his fist, let them drop to the floor. His hands gripped the podium as sweat poured from his face. A drop of blood sprang from where teeth had bitten through lips. And then the words came forth.

"Slipstream tendrils...the six-winged...the ecstasy...enraptured, aloft...and now I see it, see the castle even now from the clouds..." Still Hammond, eyes shut tight, fought against every utterance.

Thwarter, again, in the last stages of impatience: "Where did Khaemwaset go? Did he ever find the Portal? You've referred to it before, Frank Hammond: tell us where it is. Did Khaemwaset ever bring the wand to the Portal?"

"Slipstream tendrils...the six-winged..."

Another voice, unfamiliar to Iggy: "Slipstream tendrils; six-winged somethings: gibberish. I remind you, Professor Thwarter, that Firthland Oil has paid good money to Bellevue to extract what we need from the individual on that stage."

"Tezcatlipoca...Xoco...Xoco..."

A loud scraping of chairs throughout the auditorium. Faces still blurred, visitors streamed from the room.

A command was bellowed at Hammond's therapist from an angry Thwarter as he exited: "Next time, increase the dosage. More Thorazine, more Prolixin, more Adderall. Hell, more everything. Fry his brain if you have to. But we have to have that information."

The video showed only two persons remaining: Linda Toohey at her seat onstage, and Francis V. Hammond, still standing, chest and head slumped forward over the podium, cheek pressed against the mike, arms dangling over the sides, Prometheus bound to his rock.

"I'm very disappointed in you, Francis." She turned to someone out of the frame. "You may as well turn that thing off."

"Yes, Doctor."

The screen went black. But the cameraman had inadvertently left the audio function on: Iggy and Nadia could still hear what came forth from the eyeless screen.

"Jungle trails...northward bound...scarlet-feathered birds...hope of friendship."

Words from torn lips, from an exhausted captive, coughed forth into a dark empty room.

"Quetzal...Quetzalcoatl...Mon...Mon...Montezuma..."

Iggy slapped the table. "Got it!"

Nadia turned to him. "What're you talking about?"

"I've figured it out. I know exactly where we can find Frank. I know just where he's run off to!"

And that's when the evening-shift team of Bellevue staff workers opened the rear door and chanced to walk in on Iggy and Nadia.

chapter 58

Conimicut Beach
Warwick, Rhode Island
A DAY OF surprises for Toby Prideaux. Two more now burst through the treeline.

A pair of figures, running across the beach, making at top speed for the dock, where their friends waved them frantically on.

One of the runners: a nice-looking dark-skinned young woman, shouting encouragement to her companion, who lagged, panting, behind her.

The second: a rotund young man, who waddled frantically forward, slipping in the sand, picking himself up, slipping again.

Harriet Kronsted and Richard Atlas sprang forward to help him to the dock.

"What's happened to you?" cried Hattie. Iggy's face streamed blood from scalp to chin.

"I'm okay," he gasped. "Whiplash. Tree branch. Back there in the woods. Just help me get up."

They hurried him across the beach, reached the dock, just as a dozen white-jacketed individuals emerged from the trees. A moment's hesitation, then a shrill whistle blast.

"They've spotted us," groaned Ricky. He turned to Toby Prideaux. "You've got to get us out of here."

A gratifying feeling burst over Toby: *Time for payback against the world. Here's where I get mine.*

"Not so fast," he grinned. "I have to collect ferry fees first."

"Ferry fees?" Harriet turned her head, saw the Bellevue mob sprint along the beach. "How much?"

"Three hundred bucks. Apiece. Up front. Cash only."

"But that's twelve hundred total!" objected Ricky. "We don't have that kind of cash."

Nadia 'Ateeyah thrust her way forward. "I'll give you nine hundred."

The others looked at her in amazement. Iggy, bent over double, still wheezing, straightened and spluttered, "You're carrying that much cash?"

"Hush money." A tight-lipped smile. "I'll explain later."

She confronted the skipper. "Nine hundred."

More whistle blasts. That would be Nurse Orloff. Her security thugs tore past her.

"Nine hundred? Shit. I said twelve."

"Nine," she said evenly—impressive, given how close the mob was coming—"or else we run off and do the best we can and you don't make a dime."

"Eleven hundred."

"One thousand."

"Eleven."

She pulled an envelope from her coat. "Exactly one thousand dollars in here. You want the cash or not?"

"Shit." He snatched the envelope. "Hop aboard, all'a youse."

Gunfire. A bullet splintered wood from the dock.

"Best lie flat, I'd say." Toby fired up the Evinrude. A nice smooth ignition, and the *Don't Give a Damn* pulled away with a roar.

Gunshots from the quickly-receding pier. The skiff spun fast S-curves out onto the bay.

"Never hit us in a million years." Toby Prideaux laughed. He felt good.

"Iggy's been hurt!" Nadia quickly took charge of him.

"Told you," he gasped in reply. "Just a scratch from some twig. I'm fine."

"No, you are not. You lie still." She turned to the skipper. "Captain, where's your first aid kit?"

From his perch by the stern Toby motioned with his head. "Forward. In the locker."

"Nasty cut on your scalp. Hold still while I bandage it." Nadia seemed to enjoy fussing over Iggy, and Iggy seemed to mind not at all.

Toby watched these four youngsters. Once they realized they were beyond gunfire-range from the shoreline, their fear changed to joy. They whooped and hollered and hugged each other and hugged him, too, and called him the best skipper of a Dairy Queen Banana Boat they'd ever seen. *Whatever the hell that meant.*

Shit. Outracing bullets, doing thirty knots in his skiff, having the feel of a thousand bucks in his pocket—*enough to make Aggie maybe think about coming back.*

Hell, let the kids whoop. He felt good. *Shit, why not run them all the way to Watch Hill? Nice night for a coastline spin.*

He rounded Conimicut Point Shoal, passed the old lighthouse, could all but see the coyote pup from years ago eye him from the stairs. A good moment recaptured, back with him now.

Waves plumed from the hull.

Hell yes he felt good.

chapter 59

ANITA MARTINEZ WATCHED as deputy sheriff Bartholomew Kincaid stuck his head inside the open back window of her '66 Olds.

A quick silent prayer: Dear God, don't let him look under the blankets.

She also prayed that Francis Valerian Hammond—aka Gaunt the Scarecrow—would have the sense, under all those covers, to lie still.

Not so easy, considering that both her dogs were squirming about atop the blanket-pile.

"Well, what do we have here?" Deputy sheriff Kincaid stooped nose to nose with Micky and Gabby. "I'm looking for a fugitive from justice, and instead I find myself a pair'a canines."

"They're very friendly," said Annie, trying to sound at ease and unhurried. "Guys, show him how friendly you are."

They needed no more urging than that. Their eager tongues slobbered him with dog-drip from nose to chin. He sputtered and backed out of the Oldsmobile. The other deputies stood by their patrol cars and laughed.

"Whew—ee." Kincaid wiped his face with a bandana. "Think I've had my bath for the day, thank you very much."

Gabby bounded through the open window, danced about him. "No, girl, I've had enough. Down, now." Hastily he folded his *Wanted* flier.

"Can I help you gentlemen with anything else?" she called out as the deputies got back into their cars.

"Nah." The doors slammed and the cars sped away in a cloud of red dust.

"All clear." She saw Gaunt lift his head from the blankets. "But you might just want to keep out of sight while we're on the road."

He asked her to drive back to Montezuma Castle. "With police looking for me, and my face on those fliers, it won't be long before they ship me back to Bellevue," he said.

"I'm not going to let anyone ship you off anywhere."

As she got behind the wheel and closed the front door, she saw him give her a long silent look from the blanket-pile—*a pterodactyl-crow trying to show gratitude.*

"Thank you," he said finally, as the dogs hopped back inside and the Olds spun up the trail. "Thank you."

"Don't mention it. No friend of mine will get locked up if I can help it."

"Friend," he repeated slowly. "Friend," as if tasting the word.

"So, back to Montezuma's Castle?"

"While I still have my freedom, I want to show you the Portal."

"In the cave? I've been there I don't know how many times, and I have to admit I never saw any such thing."

"It's easy to overlook."

It was afternoon by the time they neared the Visitors' entrance. They parked off-road, then hiked up through the hills in a long looping circle, not descending till sunset. The dogs followed happily, sniffing mesquite and yucca on the cool evening air. Silently she saluted the mudbrick Castle on the cliff-face as it reflected the last of the day's light.

Twilight under the pine trees, as they came down the slope. By now tourists and rangers had left for the day.

"There." At the cave-mouth—*a second home now,* she thought, *for both of us*—they switched on their flashlights.

Once inside, he led her to the very back, the darkest corner of the cave. "Put your hand here."

She crouched where he indicated. A draft of air near the grotto's floor. "Come on." He stooped and disappeared into a hole she'd never seen.

She had to crouch, head lowered, to follow him. Gabby and Micky thought it all a game and bellied in after her.

A short crab-walk, and suddenly the space opened out. She stood upright, the dogs pressed against her, and gazed about in wonder.

A natural hollow of some kind, a chamber, rich with stalactite-pillars that reached to the floor from far overhead. Deep within the cliff-face they must be, yet this inner place pulsed with light. Soft effulgence pulsed from the rounded stone walls. They clicked off their flashlights.

"My cathedral, I call it," he whispered. "My secret."

The light seemed to radiate from one point in particular, a recess—a natural alcove, flanked by tall stalagmites—set deep within a far wall. Its glow illumined what lay piled before the alcove: hundreds of artworks.

Some were Amerindian, Sinagua, Aztec: terra cotta pots painted with whorls and spirals, flute-players and shamans, pumas, jaguars, feathered serpents.

Others were from a far distant land: clay figurines of Anubis jackals, Osiris, ibis-headed Thoth; statuettes of Isis and Horus the falcon.

"What are all these?" wondered Annie aloud.

"Offerings, I think. For safe journeys."

"Journeys?"

"Yes. Don't you understand? This before you is the Portal."

"How do you know?"

Gaunt the scarecrow's haggard face shone in the glow. "I never stepped within that alcove—knew there'd be no stepping back—but when I sat and handled these clay bits, these little pots and statuettes, I knew, from the psychometric message each one bestowed, they'd been left by persons who'd prayed for safe passage before stepping through."

"And where did they go?"

"I'm not sure entirely. This much I can say: Khaemwaset, and the most loyal members of his Egyptian retinue, stepped through this Portal. So, too, later, I suspect, did Montezuma and some of his like-hearted followers.

"In each case the seraphs guided them, guided them along what I call the slipstream tendrils beyond that entrance, guided them home. Wherever home was."

"Home." A look of longing shone in his eyes. "Anyone who tired of rejection, of a fugitive's life, of persecution for being different, could step through that Portal, follow the seraphs, hope for the best."

He stared hungrily at the pulsing alcove. "So many nights I've sat in this place, imagined myself stepping over that threshold, feeling myself caught up by some six-winged angel, just as Khaemwaset must've been, soaring out among the stars. So many nights, so many. And I thought I was ready, I really thought I was ready, until..." His voice trailed off into murmurs.

"Until what?" asked Annie gently.

His face turned to hers.

"Well, until I met you."

"Oh." She took his hand in hers.

Eruptions of barks from the dogs. "What is it, guys?"

Loud scrabblings from the entrance tunnel.

"Well, you're a hard man to find." Ricky Atlas, slapping dirt from his ratty coat. Followed by Harriet Kronsted, and Ignatius Forsythe, and Nadia 'Ateeyah.

"But...but how did you...I mean..." A very bewildered Gaunt the scarecrow, on whose face flashed a mix of fear, confusion, hurt, and joy.

"The credit goes to Iggy here," said Nadia, after introductions and hugs all around. "He's the one who picked up the clues from that dreadful Bellevue video."

"You kept saying something about a castle and Montezuma," explained Iggy, "and then I remembered the Arizona roadmap I used to study, when I wondered where you used to go on your hitchhiking ventures."

"But never mind that," said Ricky eagerly, unslinging his backpack. "Wait till you see what I found."

He offered the shrouded object in both hands to his old friend.

"Is this...?" The pterodactyl-crow swallowed hard.

"Yup. Straight from Yemen. What the locals there refer to as property of King Solomon. More properly known as one half of the wand of Prince Khaemwaset."

Francis Valerian Hammond breathed deeply, ran a hand up and down the staff. "This," he said, "this...To think this was once handled by Khaemwaset himself. This is what he dreamed over, in his Falcon's Perch at Abu Sir, while seraphs danced about him."

"I can't begin to thank you enough." He smiled at Ricky, then turned to the others. "Thank all of you. To touch this even once: the fulfillment of a lifetime."

"And I'm afraid," said a voice from the tunnel entrance, "once is all you'll be allowed."

The group pivoted. There, gun in hand, stood Mustafa Hamdi. Flanked by two men they didn't know, and one they knew all too very well: Professor Robert Thwarter.

chapter 60

Inside the Cliff-Face Grotto
Montezuma Castle
Verde Valley, Arizona

"INTRODUCTIONS, FIRST OF all." Mustafa Hamdi spoke with the assurance of a man who knew he controlled all possible outcomes. "Professor Thwarter is known to most of you already. But you may not have met Mister Joshua Lundgren yet."

He nodded to one of the two men at his side, a squat thick-necked individual in a sharply tailored business suit. "Mister Lundgren works in the extractive-energy sector and is also employed as a consultant for Firthland Oil Ventures. He's here to assess the potential profitability of this site—and also the profitability of what you're holding right now, Mister Hammond."

"Profitability? Extraction?" cried Nadia 'Ateeyah hotly. "What gives you the right..."

"And I'd expected a bit more loyalty from you," continued Hamdi smoothly, "considering the thousand-dollar-bonus I paid you."

"I made good use of it," she retorted with a proud toss of her head, "for good people."

"So I gather." A dry chuckle. "Nonetheless, we had little trouble tracking all of you from Bellevue to Arizona. Which led us to the man and the place we wanted: Francis Hammond and his Portal."

He turned his gun on the knot of friends. "And of course I'm delighted to see, one last time, another former employee of mine: Richard Greyling Atlas."

This elicited a hiss from the second man standing beside Hamdi. "Atlasss."

"I beg your pardon: one more introduction to make." Hamdi turned to a young man—slight in build, but clad in an oversized bulky army fatigue jacket that he wore buttoned up to the chin. "This is Mister Hasan Zubayr, an adherent of a Yemeni association called *Ansar al-Din*."

"You," exclaimed Zubayr in Arabic, jabbing a finger at Ricky Atlas, "killed my sheikh, my mentor. You butchered 'Adnan al-Harithi."

"I don't suppose it matters at this point," replied Ricky defiantly, "but I don't even know who you are."

"Ah, but Hasan Zubayr knows you." Amusement on Mustafa Hamdi's face. "And what's more important, he *remembers* you—courtesy of a Hellfire missile from a Predator drone that wiped out his colleagues."

"Hellfire missile?" Harriet Kronsted stepped protectively between Ricky and the gun that pointed at him.

"Don't worry, Miss Kronsted. I'm not going to be the one to shoot your friend." Hamdi bobbed his head at Hasan Zubayr. "I've promised my assistant he can have Richard Atlas all to himself."

"Atlasss." Zubayr took a step forward, unbuttoned the top of his coat.

Hamdi laid a firm hand on his shoulder, pulled him back. A few words of command in Arabic: *Istanna shwayya, ya sadeeqi. Istanna. Al-sabar gameel.*

"What's he saying?" asked Annie Martinez worriedly. The dogs—sensing the fear in the chamber—shrank against her side.

"*Wait just a bit, my friend,*" translated Frank Hammond grimly. "*Wait a bit. Patience is a beautiful thing.*"

"Mister Zubayr can have Atlas once we're all outside," said Hamdi. "But first I'm going to turn my attention to something more urgent. Mister Lundgren, may I have the object you've been so kind as to carry for me?"

The Firthland Oil consultant reached into an attaché case and drew forth an artifact Ricky Atlas recognized at once. "That's the finial I heisted from the Egyptian Museum!"

"Yes, it is," agreed Hamdi. "One half of the treasure known to Arab legend as *'asaayat Suleiman*: King Solomon's wand. But *we* know that this was the tool used by Akhenaten and Khaemwaset to summon the seraphs."

"Not a tool," rasped Francis Hammond. "Never a thing of coercion!"

"No?" Mustafa Hamdi waved the gun in his hand. "It was a means of control, just like what I'm holding now. Great Ramses was the only man to understand that, to show he could use that tool to extract the seraphs' life energies and redirect them to his own purposes. Just as I intend to do now."

He handed the pistol to Robert Thwarter, took the finial in one hand. "And now, Mister Hammond, I'll have the other half of the wand."

No one moved.

In the tense silence, no one noticed that Hasan Zubayr had furtively undone another button on his bulky coat.

Thwarter barked an impatient order. "Budge. Take the thing from Hammond. Bring it over here."

Ignatius Forsythe shook his head no.

"Take the thing from Hammond," repeated Thwarter, "or I'll blow a hole in that big belly of yours."

Again a defiant shake of the head.

"Mister Forsythe seems to have some fondness for Miss 'Ateeyah," observed Hamdi. "He wouldn't want me to tell my colleague to shoot her, would he?"

Misery plain to see on his face, Iggy stepped to where Frank Hammond stood. "Sorry. Sorry."

Francis Hammond stared down at the artifact.

Saying goodbye, thought Iggy, *to Khaemwaset.*

Then Pharaoh Frank surrendered his half of the wand.

"At last." Triumph glittered in Mustafa Hamdi's eyes as he fitted the finial-crest atop its staff. "The power once wielded by Ramses, now mine."

He held the wand high in the air, beneath the lofty dome of the cave. "His power to extract life-forces, now mine."

A long moment he held it high.

Then exultation changed to puzzlement. "I feel nothing."

He brought the object close to his nose, studied it. "Nothing's happening! No energy surge. No power."

"Perhaps that's because," said Frank Hammond from across the chamber, "there are other powers in the world besides authoritarian coercion, or intimidation, or hatred."

"But what else is there?" blurted Thwarter in genuine wonder.

"A different kind of power," Crazy Frank said simply. "Love."

And as Francis Hammond spoke—or at least this was how his friends remembered it later—it seemed as if a corona of light, an aureole of flittering Presences, briefly flickered around him.

Then the flicker was gone.

But Mustafa Hamdi had paid no attention. "Ramses found a way with this thing to bend the Powers to his will." He shook the wand in annoyance. "If he could do it thirty-two centuries ago, then we'll find a way to do it again today."

Hasan Zubayr had finished unbuttoning his jacket.

"Dear God," cried Nadia, pointing to the vest that the young man had kept concealed under the coat. "He's wearing a bomb!"

"What are you doing, you fool?" Mustafa Hamdi turned in horror to the Yemeni.

"*Al-intiqam wa'l-shahadah,*" shouted Hasan Zubayr. "*Wa'l-an sa-adkhul al-jannah!*"

Vengeance and martyrdom: and now I'll enter the garden of Paradise!

Hasan fumbled in his pocket—*looking for his detonator switch,* came the thought to Annie.

Any chance of a distraction? Just one:

She whispered a command to her dogs: "Go ahead, guys! Show him how friendly you are!"

And so Gabby and Micky—named in honor of two guardian angels—bounded across the cave and jumped up and bestowed on Hasan Zubayr's face big slobbering wet-tongue dog-saliva kisses.

He fell hard to the ground, tried to cover his face. "No! No! Get them off! I must remain pure!"

The confusion sufficed for Ricky to slap the gun from Thwarter's hand, for Iggy to push Hamdi aside, and for Nadia and Hattie to wrest the vest from a very demoralized Hasan.

"Got it," gasped Hattie. "We're okay."

"Wait!" Nadia pointed in alarm to the vest.

A timing device of some kind on its front; a digital display blinked a countdown: *00.23, 00.22, 00.21...*

"My reserve device," said Zubayr grimly, still wiping dog-licks from his face, "an automatic timer. It can't be turned off. All you *kafirs* will be dead in seconds, and I'll still have a chance to enter the garden."

Not everyone could understand his Arabic, but everyone understood the meaning.

...00.18, 00.17, 00.16...

"Get out of here, everybody!" Annie had never heard this tone from Francis Valerian Hammond: imperious and forceful.

Hamdi, Thwarter, and Lundgren had already fled.

Ricky and Iggy hauled Hasan Zubayr to his feet, pushed and shoved him before them.

Hattie and Nadia, with backward glances at Frank, followed them from the chamber.

...00.13, 00.12, 00.11...

Only Annie Martinez and her dogs remained with Francis and the ticking vest.

"Time for you to go, dear friend." He nodded to the tunnel.

"I'm staying."

...00.08, 00.07, 00.06...

He nodded, looked about the chamber with real regret—the suffulgent radiance pulsing from the walls, the mounded treasures by the Portal: Egyptian, Sinagua, Aztec—then flung the vest to the back of the cave.

Dogs and humans hurried through the tunnel, through the entrance grotto, then out into the night.

A roar and a belch of dust and rocks from within the cave.

As the dust slowly settled, Annie and Frank saw that the outside world had yet more surprises in store.

Seated glumly on the ground, surrounded by a cordon of deputy sheriffs, were Hamdi, Thwarter, Lundgren, and Hasan Zubayr.

The Yemeni rocked mournfully back and forth, head in hands. "I was absolutely ready to go to Paradise," he shrilled. "Absolutely ready."

"So was I," said Frank softly. "So was I." He patted the young man's shoulder, not without sympathy.

But Yavapai County deputy sheriffs were not the only officials present. A dozen burly men in black t-shirts stood clustered under the pines. White lettering on the shirts identified them: *FBI*.

Apart from them stood a trim square-shouldered man in the uniform of the United States Air Force.

"Colonel Gordon!" exclaimed Ricky Atlas. "Last time I talked with you, you were sending me a little help from Djibouti."

"Good to see you again." Gordon introduced Ricky to a white-haired man with a pleasant grandfatherly smile. "I'd like you to meet a colleague. Alastair Wilcox."

Wilcox was in the process of tucking *'asaayat Suleiman*—the wand that had once been handled by Akhenaten, and Khaemwaset, and Ramses, and Francis Hammond—away in a briefcase.

"Very pleased to meet you, Mister Atlas." A friendly shake of the hand. "My congratulations on helping secure this apparatus." Ricky watched as Alastair Wilcox nestled the wand amidst a sheaf of papers.

"Are you in the Air Force, too, Mister Wilcox?"

"Oh, no." Big smile. "A different branch of the government."

"Let me guess. Central Intelligence."

A shrug and an airy wave of the hand.

"What are you going to do with the wand?"

"This apparatus?" The briefcase closed with a tight snap. "Tests. For potential capacities. For national security purposes, in consultation with our armed forces."

"And these clowns?" Ricky nodded at the prisoners.

"Them? Hamdi's claiming diplomatic immunity of some kind, affiliation with Egypt's new revolutionary government. Mister Explosives over there, the would-be suicide bomber: he's on our High-Value Target list. The FBI will be trucking him southeast for some Guantanamo sunshine." A throaty chuckle.

"As for Lundgren and Thwarter: Hamdi's already talking big about his political pull and how he'll have them released in no time. Professor Thwarter will probably be out and back in Chicago in time to teach classes next week." Wilcox shrugged. "The way of the world."

"You haven't heard the last of us," snarled Lundgren from where he sat on the ground. "Firthland Oil always finds a way to extract what it wants. We'll do whatever it takes."

"I'm sure you will," murmured Alastair Wilcox resignedly, then turned to Ricky Atlas and shook his hand once more.

"Must be going."

Wilcox and Colonel Gordon left in a black car with US government plates.

Soon the prisoners and the deputy sheriffs and the FBI agents were gone, too, leaving only the small cluster of friends.

Slowly they walked to the visitors' lot where Annie had left her Olds. The dogs, relieved now to see their humans safe, wagged their tails and dashed back and forth along the trail.

"Blood sugar must be low. Tired." A long weary sigh from Frank Hammond, from Gaunt the pterodactyl-crow. "Could really go for a Dairy Queen Banana Boat."

"I could fix you up a reasonable facsimile thereof," offered Annie, "over at the Sonic Drive-In."

"Sounds good," said Frank, and he smiled.

"Sounds good to me, too," agreed Iggy, as he walked arm-in-arm with Nadia.

"Hey," suggested Ricky, with a wink at Hattie, "if we all grab a spoon and pitch in, is there room in that Banana Boat of Frank's for all of us?"

"I think so," said Annie, as she and Frank exchanged smiles. "I think so."

"In that case, Cap'n"—and at that everyone laughed—"let's all sail away."

END

Want to follow the trail of the Seraphs?
Read David Pinault's new novel
Crater of Thoth: An Interstellar Egyptology Quest
Coming soon!

Coming in 2014:

Crater of Thoth: An Interstellar Egyptology Quest
By David Pinault

The back-story. Planet Earth, present-day: Horrified by the Taliban-style destruction of ancient Egyptian monuments, a group of neo-pagans known as Old Faith Adherents smuggles pharaonic artifacts to a secret haven. The haven proves to be extraterrestrial. Guided by interstellar wanderers known only as the Seraphs, Earth's Old Faith pagans establish a pharaonic Egyptian outpost on a desert-wilderness planet they call Nilotica Nova.

21st century, near-future. Earth's recent Terror-Nuke Wars have devastated our globe's oil reserves. Gasoline is now 98 dollars a gallon. But a mysteriously-discovered form of space transport—jump-world technology—permits Terrestrials to prospect for resources in other star-systems. Earth's Interplanetary Ventures Corporation locates a new source of energy that can be pipelined back to our world. But this new energy source is found only on Nilotica Nova, and it is linked to the Egyptian artifacts that were once smuggled from Earth under the guardianship of the Seraphs.

The action begins in the near-future Egypt of the 21st century. Free-lance archaeological extractor Nicky Winter and his olfactory-enhanced K-9 digger-dog Teddy make a living Earthside plundering pharaonic tombs. Nicky prides himself on his cash-minded survival skills. But near-future Egypt is a tough place to work. Its anarchic deserts have been vitrified by suitcase-bomb blasts. Militant factions shoot extractors on sight. And religious fanatics have vandalized the few monuments from Antiquity left standing.

So when the Interplanetary Ventures Corporation offers Earth's surviving K-9 extraction teams a job hunting for Egyptian artifacts on Nilotica Nova, Nicky and his teammates are glad to accept. But when they arrive, they encounter a series of mysteries, involving the origin and identity of the wanderer-Seraphs, the true nature of the energy resources available on Nilotica, and the significance of the pharaonic artifacts that were smuggled there from Earth.

Nicky and his digger-mates must decide whether to side with the Corporation or with Nilotica's Old Faith Adherents as energy-extraction operations begin on this last planetary refuge for Egypt's ancient treasures.

*Here's a preview of the adventures awaiting you in **Crater of Thoth:***

Chapter 1

On the Hazards of Looting Pharaonic Tombs

MY VERY LAST extraction assignment back home on Earth—the job that ended with me shot and my K-9 snuffed—went like this:

(But let me back up a second and just add that what made things worse was that this was the fourth Oscar-Easy dog I'd lost on the job. I should get used to it, my thicker-skinned colleagues tell me. Goes with the territory, if you want to be an Egyptological tomb-robber—or archaeological extractor, to use the polite term—in the radioactive free-for-all of 21st-century post-Apocalypse Egypt. But four dogs dead in two years: depressing. I keep telling myself: Nicholas Everett Winter, don't get attached to your mutts.)

It was supposed to be a quick in-and-out job. I'd been prospecting for a week in the Valley of the Kings. A good site: canyon walls riddled everywhere with royal tombs that the pharaohs had tunneled straight into the mountains. This was my first time in the Valley with one of the new-model OEC's.

OEC's are Olfactory-Enhanced Canines. Also known as Oscar-Easies. Good critters, these. Pricey, but reliable. Keep one alive for six months, and it'll find you enough choice artifacts to justify the two-hundred-thousand-dollar price tag.

I was working the Valley with Warlock. He was a Malamute husky-wolfhound mix, one hundred and forty pounds of bite-you-dead meanness. Warlock had been through a lot with me.

We crouched in the predawn dark before KV8, the tomb of Pharaoh Merneptah. A dealer in L.A. had contacted me and said he had clients willing to pay plenty for jewelry from the grave of Merneptah's wife Isis-Nofret. Of course this tomb had been plundered and excavated many times. But the new Olfactory-Enhancement technology allows K-9's to sniff out loot that's been overlooked for centuries.

I took out the syringe and got ready to shoot up my mutt with the DNA dope for this job. Warlock was always patient with the needle. I looked across the valley floor and in the dark could just see the outline of the entrance to Tutankhamun's tomb.

That was a sight that always made me sad. My grandfather had been a tour guide here, back in the days when foreigners like us were still welcome. As a kid I'd follow him about on his tours and listen to him tell the tourists about Tut and all the treasures buried with the boy-king.

Of course that was before the Xenophobe Riots and the International Terror-Nuke Reprisals and the Civil War that split Egypt into fourteen feuding provinces. Also before the jump-world technology that enabled folks to find new homes on other planets and get as far away as they could from this burnt-out nuclear-wasted shell we call Earth.

I finished snout-lining Warlock and put away the syringe. He sneezed the way he always did after his shot. I fitted the Kevlar vest over his chest and flanks. Then I stood and slipped his leash and said what I always say: "Let's go make money."

Dead silent in the Valley. Not a sound except the dog's panting and the crunch of gravel underfoot and the wind blowing hard among the cliffs overhead. Funny to remember how this place used to be alive with tourists and souvenir sellers and guides speaking a dozen languages. My grandfather worked on a Nile cruise boat called the *Amenhotep*. He gave good tours. I remember how patient he was, how he'd stand around with his customers and smile and pose for photos in front of the entrance to their favorite pharaonic tombs.

Tombs like this one. I shone my flashlight over the cave-mouth and checked for booby traps. No one would want to pose here for tourist-snaps anymore. The iron gate had long since been torn away by looters. The entrance-way was pocked with bullet holes, its ancient murals defaced. All this would've made my grandfather sad.

But we weren't here to admire murals. The entrance corridor sloped down, burrowing into blackness, over ground piled high with trash and rubble that had fallen from the ceiling.

Before we entered I noticed the graffiti painted by the entrance. Beside the usual assemblage of "So-and-so was here" scrawlings, there was something more striking: the letters NN, faded but still legible, surmounted by a crowned falcon. I'd seen that mark before.

These were the initials of a group called Nilotica Nova. Even though the group had had its glory days here on Earth over twenty years ago, folks still talked about it. Nilotica Nova was supposed to have been made up of neo-pagans, religious visionaries, individuals of that ilk. They'd tried to revive pharaonic worship, something crazy like that, back in the late twentieth century. None of them remaining on Earth any more, I gathered, and just as well. I had my own memories linked to the words 'Nilotica Nova,' and they were not pleasant to recall.

Enough distractions. Useless to waste time with such thoughts. Back to work.

Warlock slipped ahead of me into the tomb, taking point as he always did. A comfort in this solo line of work, seeing my K-9 take the lead.

Plenty dark in here. I switched on the headlamp atop my hardhat to add to the beam from the flashlight. No need to linger in the entrance corridor. We'd explored here the day before and found nothing.

A noise ahead of us. I swung the flashlight and unholstered my pistol. Claim-jumpers, maybe, wanting in on my private dig. Or maybe jihadis wanting to kill more foreigners. Either way, unlikely to be well-wishers. I drew my gun.

My flashlight caught something in its beam.

First: on the wall, a painting of Osiris and Isis and a bunch of other gods in the Hall of Judgment. Pretty ho-hum: I'd seen the stuff a million times, and the gods could do nothing for me.

Second: in the garbage at the foot of the wall, something a bit more lively—a cluster of rats, fighting over fresh trash. I knew it was fresh because I'd tossed it there myself the day before: the remains of a super-sized apple-fritter doughnut I'd bought from the coffee shop at the Ramses Marriott.

The Marriott's the last hotel still open in the neighborhood. I don't know why I bother buying lousy food like this. My colleague Lars says it's a toss-up whether the Marriott's take-out snacks taste more like play-doh or chewy cardboard or simple unadulterated cat-poop.

Be that as it may. Warlock charged the rats and scattered them and snatched the trash as a prize of war. Before gulping, he turned to me for permission and I told him to help himself. His big mouth wolfed the fritter down and he grinned. I felt glad to have all those teeth on my side.

"Back to business," I said.

The entrance corridor narrowed and ended at a doorway choked with broken limestone. This was as far as we'd gone the previous day. Warlock turned and looked at me. "We're not making any money," I said, "just standing here." He climbed over the mess and I followed.

Past the door was a new corridor plunging steeply down to the left. The air was close and stale in here. Strong smell of dust and bat-droppings. Hard to breathe. None of this seemed to bother Warlock. He kept sniffing for the loot he'd been programmed for. A reassuring presence of muscle and fur, testing my path for me in the dark. My idea of a friend.

This new passage leveled off abruptly and opened into a chamber. My headlamp caught the outlines of a big stone sarcophagus, its lid long since forced open.

Pharaonic discards lay scattered on the earth. Broken alabaster canopic jars. Terra cotta unguent potsherds. Shards of coffin lids, their surfaces painted with protective deities.

A real archaeologist would've spent weeks on hands and knees cataloguing all this stuff. But this is the new Egyptology, post-Apocalypse, post Terror-Nuke Wars, and me, I'm just an extractor.

"Find me something good," I told the mutt.

Warlock sniffed about. The DNA polymers I'd snout-lined him with would let him know if there was anything here to match our client's order.

The K-9 ranged up and down the burial chamber and nosed the trash bit by bit. I stood about and waited. It used to be all these things interested me. If my grandfather had been here, he'd have been lecturing me about the meaning of the afterlife scenes painted on these walls.

Easy to imagine his voice, since I'd accompanied him on so many tours when I was a kid. "Nicky, do you recognize that hieroglyph?" Well, once upon a time I did. Once upon a time ancient Egypt held magic for me. But that was before my grandfather got killed in a jihadi attack.

Now everything had changed. Now all this represented no more than a job. Hard to say why I still did this. "Man's got to do something for a living," I said aloud. A job like this gives a guy plenty of chance to talk to himself.

A graffito on the wall. The twin letters NN again, surmounted by a falcon. Nilotica Nova.

My grandfather had told me about this group. They used to do what they called 're-consecration ceremonies' in the old pharaonic ruins. Well over twenty years ago that would have been, in the years before the Xenophobe Riots claimed the lives of so many foreigners and Egyptians.

Or maybe the Nilotica crazies who painted their logo in this tomb had been looking for prize artifacts to take away with them, after they'd been given a license to colonize the newly discovered planet they decided to name after themselves.

I didn't know, and I didn't much care. For me the name Nilotica Nova was bound up with death. Specifically the death of my cousin, Johnnie Sacarro. Or to be more precise: the disappearance and presumed death of my cousin. But considering where he disappeared, instantaneous death might have been better than lingering survival. Better not to think about it.

A woof from the dog. He pawed at a crevice low down in the wall. His whine was excited. He'd found something.

I shone my light in the hole. Definitely something there. I resisted the impulse to thrust my hand in and fish the thing out. Jihadis had planted pressure-sensitive dirty bombs in some of the most popular tombs here in the Valley of the Kings, with the idea of discouraging the most die-hard extractors (like knuckle-headed me) and the occasional adventure-tour groups that still came from overseas.

Amazing that any tourists at all could be persuaded to visit Egypt these days, what with the events of the last twenty years and the competition from the fledgling extraterrestrial tourism industry that's been made possible by the new jump-world technology.

I took out my hand-held clicker and checked for radiation levels. Whatever was in the crevice, at least it didn't seem to be a dirty bomb. I took out a probe and snaked the wire into the hole and told Warlock to get back. He whined and growled but knew enough to stand clear.

Contact. No explosion. Seemed safe enough. I got impatient and reached my hand in and pulled whatever it was from the crevice.

And what I pulled out was a human arm, mummified, carefully wrapped in linen. Warlock took a big sniff and barked so loud the burial chamber echoed. I didn't need to be a K-9 mind-reader to get the message. His olfactory-enhancement polymers were telling him we'd found what we came for.

I wasted no time. I took out a folding knife and filleted the mummified arm. Inside the linen wrappings I found just what I'd hoped for.

Jewelry. Lots of it. A dozen bracelets and bangles and armbands, all soft yellow gold, all stamped with cartouches.

I studied them in the beam from my headlamp. My knowledge of hieroglyphs is limited, but I knew enough to recognize royal names from the Theban kings' list. And this was just the name I wanted: Isis-Nofret, wife of Merneptah.

That's when my light went out. Both lights, in fact. First the headlamp, then the flashlight. Darkness shut in all around me. Blind black hell, as sudden and scary as a knife to the throat.

Warlock whined beside me in the dark. I heard him scratch at his Kevlar armor. It was hot in here.

I felt in my pockets for spare batteries. Must have left them back in the hotel. Damn. It was going to be a long climb up through the dark.

Carefully I pocketed the jewelry. At least we'd found what we came for.

Then I remembered one of my grandfather's stories. Tomb robbers in antiquity—and robbing pharaonic burials, he said, was a job with a long history—used to wrench the arms off mummies and set them on fire to generate light while the thieves did their plundering. The mummy's dried resins and linens, he explained, made ideal kindling.

He was right. I took a match from my pocket and struck it and in no time had myself a pretty good substitute for a flashlight. I held the arm by its mummified bicep and lifted it up over my head while the limb flickered and snapped. Not bad as an ad hoc torch.

I told Warlock it was time to clear out. He needed no urging.

As we hurried up the corridors the flame lit the painted deities on the walls. My granddad loved to take me on these tomb-tours. "You can feel the gods all about us, Nicky," he used to say, "if you know how to listen."

Well, maybe, once upon a time. Maybe before my granddad got killed and Egypt nuked itself and the world I once knew went to pieces.

Back to the entrance corridor. Early dawn light at the tomb-mouth. In the rubble I heard more rats scrabble. Maybe they'd found another doughnut. I flung what was left of the mummy-torch at them and said to Warlock, "I'll race you out to the Valley."

Which was stupid, I have to say in retrospect. But I was feeling good. My olfactory-enhanced K-9 had just found me a nice set of items, enough to buy me three months' worth of vacation off-world somewhere. Somewhere far from the charred leftovers of Post-Terror-Nuke Earth.

Race you, I said to Warlock, and the two of us came bounding out of the tomb into gray morning light.

That's when I tripped the cord. Wired, I guess, to some improvised explosive device.

The IED went boom. The world whirled and fell away and I fell with it.

Want more?

WATCH FOR DAVID Pinault's *Crater of Thoth: An Interstellar Egyptology Quest*
Coming in 2014!